The Year
of Love

Books by
Margaret Lee Runbeck

Our Miss Boo
Time for Each Other
The Great Answer
The Secret
Hope of Earth
Pink Magic
Answer without Ceasing
A Hungry Man Dreams
The Year of Love

The Year of Love

MARGARET LEE RUNBECK

DR. ETHYL WOOD CROUSE
RESEARCH ASSISTANT

HOUGHTON MIFFLIN COMPANY BOSTON

1956

THIS BOOK WAS WRITTEN BECAUSE
Dr. Ethyl Wood Crouse
OPENED HER HEART AND GAVE ME INDIA.

1

FOR CENTURIES TIME STOOD STILL IN INDIA.
Then it stirred in its sleep and slowly rose, and now it is on
the march. On the march, even in villages where no
stranger ever has been. For centuries time was a lake, and
now it has become a stream, not swift and noisy, but slow
and pensive. Like all streams it belongs to earth, but it
holds on its surface the reflection of heaven.

The scene and the events of Soni bai's life could have belonged in any of the past twenty decades. But what went
on within her heart . . . and even more, in her mind, which
stirred in *its* sleep and rose as time itself has done, could
have come about only lately.

Soni's village is called Marvali. It stands on a plateau
near the Bandeh Mountains. A branch of the Parma River
runs nearby, a pleasant neighbor. If you stood a hundred
yards away from the village, you might not see it was there,
for like most villages it is surrounded by clay walls, which
lose themselves in the landscape.

If Marvali could boast of anything it is not of its size, for
there are only two hundred and fifty men in the village.
Marvali, as villages of India have always been, is truly a re-
public, electing its own leaders by ballot. Villages are self-
sealed, so that the customs in some other parts of India are
as different as if they existed in an alien country.

Most of the people in Marvali belong to the Kumbi caste, which follows farming. Whether a man owns land, or hires himself out as a servant to the land belonging to others, he follows the general plan of his caste as his ancestors have done.

The wall encircling Marvali stands ten feet high. Gates on opposite sides open at sunrise and close at sunset. There is a narrow one and a wide gate for the passing of carts and hooded tongas, with their gay and sometimes humorous paintings. The great silvery bullocks, those philosophers on hoofs, set the pace for this stream of traffic. The gate is guarded by a tender, whose father held the place before him.

In the center of Marvali is a park, beautiful to all, especially after the monsoons when the tree called the Flame of the Forest is in bloom, lifting its extravagant huge flowers high into the sky. The park, or bagh, is the central meeting place. Nim trees grow here, and banyan trees, their long air-roots cascading richly from the highest limbs, searching blindly for the earth. Mangoes and jackfruit trees belong to everyone for the enjoying. Jasmine and marigolds, equally beloved for fragrance, sweet or camphorous, grow everywhere, waiting to be made into festive garlands. During the hot season the bagh is the coolest place in the village; the very fragrance cools it as much as the deep tree shadows.

At the left of the bagh, and across the road which encircles it, stands a stone-walled temple, its roof tiered as if in steps for the souls of the village to mount when their time comes. Souls are busy in Marvali, where ritualistic religion gives them much to do.

One well serves the village, and this is between the large gate and the temple. It is surrounded by shade trees, planted at a distance so that no leaves will drop into the well, for it is uncovered. The ground surrounding it is wet and trampled with footprints. Early in the morning the women gather to draw water for their households before they go with their husbands to the fields. They walk in a stately, leisurely way, balancing the great clay and brass cudjahs on their heads.

All living things feel free in the village, the bullocks and buffaloes and the ever present dogs, and here and there sheep and goats (and the monkeys, whose god, Hanuman, gave them to everybody to love and laugh at). All run about looking for stray food; even one blade of unguarded grass, they appreciate. Here is a place where life seems smooth and gracious and benevolent. It moves along at the same graceful gait as the women carrying cudjahs on their heads. Burdens carried high make for grace.

May is the marriage month in central India. May comes between the harvesting and the planting. When the work has slackened, men may think of other things, of games and hunger and eternity . . . and of moneylenders. May is the month of poverty, for the harvest is almost immediately swallowed up by the winter's debts. But since everyone knows that the family must mortgage the whole future for a wedding, the marriage-borrowing covers the shame of the hunger-borrowing.

May was eleven months away now, just time enough for Gopal's family to arrange and prepare for the marriage of their daughter, Soni bai.

The moneylenders rejoice in the marriage month. Almost everyone in the village has some part in some marriage celebration, either as family or guest, and it is all expensive, involving new clothes and ornaments, and boastful food. The moneylenders are fatly enthusiastic about marriages. Debts piled up at one marriage celebration have been known to endure through the lifetime of two generations.

But Gopal's family, thinking tenaciously about marriage this year, does not intend to borrow, for they never have borrowed a pice. Gopal's family is one of the few fortunate ones who have acres enough, and not too many sons and their families who must eat from the acres. Money is not a central terror in Gopal's family, as it is for so many Indians from birth to death. That does not mean Gopal is rich; he is only not wretched.

Gopal has been saving every rupee he could spare during the last four years . . . ever since Soni was thirteen, so that she would have a dowry impressive enough to interest the fine and substantial family to whom he is looking for a husband. Ever since his only girl-child was born, Gopal had loved her with fierce pride. He could love his daughter without apology, for had not the gods first given him two sons?

Two sons, stalwart as trees, and then a little daughter fragrant and lovely as a spray of jasmine. That is how he and his wife Mira bai thought of their family, for they were people of the earth, and the earth gave them their figures of speech . . . their sustenance, their religion, their pride, their hope, and their poetry. The earth gave all to them, and they served the earth obediently as good Kumbi-caste farmers.

Some jealous parents in their village wondered why they had kept Soni bai without a husband so long. That was the old-fashioned belief, when it was thought a girl's chastity was so perishable that she must be married before she herself knew the difference between honor and shame. But Gopal and Mira bai loved their child so deeply, they had kept her with them until her seventeenth birthday was in sight. And besides keeping her at home out of love, Gopal had been working to save up the dowry substantial enough to impress that certain family.

Soni's horoscope had been exchanged with but one house. There would be no need to hawk it about from door to door wherever a marriageable son could be found, as common

families did for daughters who were not desirable. Everyone
knew how honorable was Gopal's family. Never in its remembered history had it been in debt. Never had there been
a breath of gossip. When Soni's horoscope was received by
the chosen family (which was the first step in the approach)
the head of the house would make inquiries, and what he
found out would please him.

Her horoscope had gone to Vardana, which was a much
larger town fourteen miles from Marvali. Gopal's best
friend, Jeveram, who lived in Vardana, had carried it per-
sonally, and had ceremoniously presented it to Rama, the
well-to-do head of a big household. Gopal knew Jeveram
through years of selling farm produce to him in the Vardana
bazaar. Gopal had picked up information about Rama's fine
family, and when he asked Jeveram, it was confirmed.

Rama's astrologer had carefully compared the two horoscopes of the young people, and had sent back a favorable
report. There are thirty-six points in which two horoscopes
may agree . . . and these two agreed in more than thirty. It
was most auspicious. Progress would be at a stately pace,
for both families had dignity.

Gopal was not oppressively old-fashioned, although he
could neither read nor write. He wished with all his heart
that he could read. But he consoled himself by knowing that
all truth is not born on a page. A man's intelligence is not a
private shut-away thing; it is a flowing stream, part of the
great river of living. An idea has its own time; it rises across
the firmament of the world, and those who observe may
perceive it freely. Then it feels as if it has come to birth in
each man's brain. He gradually knows. And he recognizes
in other men's faces the matching knowledge. So one day
they speak of it together, and it becomes new fact. That is
how it seemed to Gopal, who learned without reading.

Soni bai knew that the first steps in the marriage arrangement had been accomplished. Her family purposely allowed her to overhear the report. But they did not speak about it openly, for that would have been immodest. Mira bai talked daily to her daughter about her someday marriage. Indeed everything in her training was pointed toward that object. She had known how to make chapattees, those flat delicious breads, since she was eight years old. She had helped to grind the gram flour as soon as her hands were big enough to encircle the peg in the grinding stones. Her mother had always said that a busy woman is a happy one.

Besides her household skills, she had skills of the spirit, for a woman's spirit must be the home in which her husband can dwell in peace and pleasure. There must be inner sunlight, and invisible moonlight in that spirit, and the view of tall mountains, and secret streams and hidden valleys created in a woman for no one but a husband ever to know.

All her waking hours Soni's mind was engaged with thinking about her coming marriage. Now she felt important as never before in her life. She never left the house unless a sister-in-law was with her, and she wore a pottu on her forehead, a tiny circle of yellow ocher paste. After her marriage she would have at least one gold ornament, which would protect her chastity. She would carefully guard her tongue from ever speaking her husband's name aloud, for that would be inauspicious, and might bring harm to him from some evil spirits. She had learned by heart the instructions from the sacred books which would guarantee a perfect and beautiful marriage:

There is no other god on earth for you, except your husband.
Your sole rule of life should be that your good works please him.
You owe him obedience and submission. Sacredly you must

*ever be watchful of your temper, never covetous, never quarrel-
some, never loud or bold. Your first duty is to accomplish your
domestic work on time. You should never possess anything without your lord's consent, nor spend a pice without his requesting
it.*

*If your husband laughs, you must laugh; if he be sad, you must
be sad. Give attention only to him. You are responsible for his
good disposition.*

*Eat only after he has eaten; fast when he fasts; make his com-
fort and pleasure your consuming desire.*

*You must lavish affection and attention on no one but him.
Not even in your prayers must you hold a god above him. For
through him alone can your soul ever hope to gain mukti [eternal
peace].*

*You must bathe every day, adorning yourself. You must attain
a likeness to the godess Lakshmi.*

*When your husband leaves you behind, you must not leave
the house. If he requests you to accompany him, you must always follow.*

Today the household woke early, for Gopal was going to
Vardana to pay a visit to the great house of Rama. Fourteen
miles along the road would bring him to the edge of the
town, and there he would spend the night, wrapped in his
blanket under a nim tree. He would build a tiny fire with
the dried cow dung his wife had packed for him, and over
this he would cook the handful of wheat, and eat the delicious chutney Mira bai had wrapped in a plantain leaf for
his supper. Soni could picture him every step of the way, and
her heart would follow him up to the very threshold of
Rama's house. But there it would turn back in shyness, for
it dared not picture the unknown son who might someday
be her husband.

Would he find her in any way beautiful? Her mother said

she was beautiful, but mothers see with special eyes. She knew her skin was agreeably light . . . almost the color of a melon skin in moonlight. And her eyes, when she looked into a cudjah of water as she was filling the lothis for the household, were large and bright and had lashes like the black stamens of a poppy. She knew her hair was proudly long, and the color of blue-black night, from combing and oiling as her mother had demanded.

She thought shyly of her body, which she herself seldom saw, because of the modest custom of bathing through a sari, and then letting it fall to the ground only as the fresh sari was draped in its place. Would her lord find her body beautiful? She blushed as she thought of its well-rounded slimness, and the strength of her legs from much walking to the well, and working in the fields of sugar cane and peanuts, and the strength of her arms from much lifting of the cudjahs to her head. Work is like the two stones which grind the gram into finest flour; work smooths the body into lean beauty and grace. But there must be eyes to see the beauty, or it does not exist. Would her husband have such eyes?

Gopal expected to find Rama's house more impressive than his own small one. But he was not prepared for actual luxury. He arrived, escorted by his friend Jeveram, just at twilight. His face, schooled by good manners to show no expression, looked up without surprise. But inside, his mind recoiled at the size of the house and the luxury visible even from without. Why, this was as big as the house of their Patel, the mayor! How dared he approach such a family with a marriage proposal? But he was offering to it something beautiful and good, his Soni. And a respectable dowry besides. He saw now in quick adjustment that he would have to lay his hands on a few more rupees, if the offer were to interest Rama. Well, he would find the money somehow. Soni would fit into such a place as a beautiful word fits into a song. The house, of course, was made of mud as was everyone's house in the village; but it was painted white. A long veranda stretched across the front of the building; centered in the veranda was a large doorframe, with an ornately carved blue door.

The oldest son of the house, with whom Gopal had become pleasantly acquainted in the bazaar, was sitting on the veranda, ready to greet the visitors.

"My father is honored," Govind said. "He has been looking forward to your visit."

He pushed open the blue door, and across a narrow hall was another open door which showed a glimpse of the green courtyard. A lacy jacaranda tree sheltered the courtyard, and the rest of the house was built around the large tree, a wing on each side, and a high mud wall across the back, where Gopal knew the family's animals must be kept. Two young boys, wrestling in the courtyard, stopped respectfully. Rama, easily recognizable by his age and dignity, was sitting on a charpai, a hemp-woven coat. Govind took the guests over to his father and introduced Gopal.

"How pleasant this is," Gopal said, looking into the old man's aristocratic face. The moment he spoke he regretted his words, in case this family was superstitious and would fear some evil spirit had overheard his praise.

"Nothing at all," Rama said. Gopal guessed from his words that this was a correctly worshipful family which had no part in the loose modern talk going around some villages denying there were such things as evil spirits who might make mischief.

"I come often to Vardana," Gopal said. "It is my satisfaction that I look at last into your face."

"These boys are always playing games," their father said, changing the subject politely. "Tonight one is winning. Tomorrow it will be the other."

"I have sons of my own," Gopal said companionably.

"Then I don't need to tell you," Rama said in a friendly way.

Govind was building a little fire in the midst of the courtyard, to Gopal an almost unheard-of extravagance. But he showed no surprise, only delight in the scene. Also he was concealing his eagerness to see Anand, the reason for this visit. He had watched the boy from a distance through several years, but he had never spoken to him.

Jeveram, having paid his respects, now took his leave, for this was Gopal's visit and he must usurp no part of it. Govind took him to the door politely and then returned to the fire.

"Sit beside me," Rama invited Gopal. "Tell me about your village. I know you're good Kumbis over there. Govind says you send to our bazaar the best peanuts anybody can grow."

"They're only peanuts," Gopal said modestly. "My father started growing them when he was a young man. Now all the neighbors join in."

Rama began telling him about his own father. But suddenly he realized Gopal's eyes had left his face, for Anand had come into the courtyard from one of the private entrances. He was quite tall and much fairer even than Gopal remembered him, well formed and somehow distinguished-looking. He had a book under his arm, like a student, although he no longer attended the government school. The book looked as if it were a part of his anatomy, and Gopal said to himself, I will never forget this picture . . . it is what the boy *is*.

Anand came over to the charpai and said, "My mother sends her greeting. She hopes you will be comfortable with us tonight, and she wants you to enjoy some of our fruit."

Gopal looked closely at him so that he could describe him to Mira bai. His hair was parted down the middle and was dressed with some fragrant oil. Above his white dhoti, folded sleekly around his narrow hips, his chest was not broad, and the cage of his ribs showed plainly. This was not a stalwart boy; his strength must be somewhere besides in his tall thin body. For a moment Gopal was troubled by this thought, then something stirred in his mind which had never been there before . . . the knowledge that the strengths of a man which are invisible are the ones which really transform life.

Rama said, "My son has taken on many modern ideas. I am not sure I like some of them." Anand touched his father's shoulder and smiled at him, showing white teeth. His gesture was affectionate, but he respectfully made no rebuttal to his father's remark.

"My son speaks very perfect English," Rama said. "He has an important position in the Mission clinic. He does all errands for the doctor sahib who is in charge."

Anand shook his head, expressing subtle deprecation when his father said the word "important."

"I am not important," he said softly. "But I am learning."

Rama said almost angrily. "My son will take his own place in our family farming sometime. I allow him now to work for the burra-sahib at the clinic. Just for now."

A servant came in to the courtyard from the kitchen section, chanting as he carried above his head a large brass tray. In the center of this was a jackfruit, and around it were guavas, borahs and mangoes . . . the biggest mangoes Gopal ever had seen. Even to his uneducated eyes, it was plain that these mangoes had come from grafted trees. These are pukka people in every way, he said gloomily to himself. Can my humble family fit into their properness?

Govind said, "Share this jackfruit with me, my friend." As Gopal ate the jackfruit, the memory of the sweetness of those he found freely in the wild country came to him. We, too, have riches, he said consolingly to himself. We have our *own* riches.

After the fruit, everyone talked awhile, laughing and relaxed. Then Rama rose and said hospitably, "Tomorrow evening let us continue." Gopal's hope spurted within him, for he knew this meant he had pleased the old man.

Not a word of the important mission had been uttered, but Gopal felt now that he would succeed in it.

Rama suggested that he unroll his blanket and sleep on the charpai. But Gopal had never in his life slept on anything but the soft bosom of the earth. It was Anand who perceived the shyness that suddenly came over Gopal when the charpai was mentioned, so he graciously took charge.

"Come with me. We'll sleep on the veranda, you and I," Anand said. Rama said goodnight and took the two youngest boys into the main entrance of the house. Govind and his next brother, Ghulum, each entered their private quarters through separate doors on the left side of the courtyard.

Gopal's heart was full of confusing emotions. He felt his inadequacies as if they were desperate shames. But somehow he knew these men had forgiven him because he was poorer than they, and more inept. The fragrance of jasmine came to him, and he felt at home. Jasmine belonged to everyone. The noisy chatter and flapping wings of the flying foxes settling for the night . . . these, too, were part of the world of everyone. Some things belong to us all; we meet in our love of them. He lay down to sleep reassured.

The boy began talking to him through the darkness, not timidly or restrained because of the circumstances, but freely as if they were old friends, whose fondness for each other was reflected from the past far into the future. He spoke about his work at the Mission, and Gopal could see that it was an opened door in his life which had given him entrance into a wide world. Then he began talking about his family's land, and especially of one beloved spot which they had inherited through the generations. About eleven acres it was, and only a little way from this house.

"It is like another member of our family," Anand said. "A great silent presence that cares for us as long as we care for it. My father and I used to sit under the mango trees when I was a little boy, and talk about the land. We both have loved it all our lives."

In the darkness Gopal's face was swiftly touched with tears, for of all the evidence that could have been given him that this was the right husband for Soni, this appreciation of the land was the one that assured him most deeply. The bones of the boy were sound; all would be well.

He woke in the morning while Anand was still motionless. He reached for his brass lothi, and slipped quietly over to the cudjah to fill it with water. He would have his bath and his prayers somewhere alone, for he wasn't sure how much this modern young man remembered the old traditions. He found a narrow door where the back wall joined the right wing of the house, and went quietly through that. As he had expected, the animals belonging to this household had their stalls behind this wall. Impressive animals, six bullocks, a horse, a buffalo, two cows and a milk-giving goat. To Gopal's eyes they were riches.

When he came back to the house everyone was stirring about, though of course the women were not visible. Anand came and offered him some pink guavas, and said goodbye, for he was hurrying off to his work at the Mission.

"We shall meet tonight," Anand said genially.

"No, I'm afraid not. I must return to Marvali tonight. Some of my neighbors are in the bazaar, and I can ride back with them in an empty tonga."

Rama came up just in time to hear this. "I am disappointed," he said. "Then you and I shall have to make good use of this day."

"That pleases me," Gopal said, recognizing this as a formal declaration that Rama would entertain the prospect of marriage in a favorable mood.

They settled immediately into discussing their two families. Gopal told what he could about his sons and how they worked together. He tried to keep a safe balance between wanting to make a good impression and not building up too high an expectation about the dowry. He could see that Rama had already investigated his status and knew quite a lot about it.

"I tell you frankly that Soni bai is my favorite child," Gopal said. "You would soon understand why." That was all he could permit himself to say, for it would have been improper to boast about her sweetness and her beauty. Those would have to speak for themselves. And they would speak, when they had their chance.

Then Rama began telling about his own household, in a properly disparaging way. Gopal had seen the males of the house, so he spoke of the women. His only daughter was a widow, who had returned to his household. His wife Shushilla bai had poor health, but a good disposition. He was housing his only living sister, a wretched widow, and a tireless worker. Under his good manners, he couldn't help expanding a bit when he told about his women's quarters. He had always provided them with servants, he said complacently. And he kept a house boy.

He talked for happy hours about his fields and crops, and the success he had in multiple farming instead of clinging to the old custom of growing only one crop. He spoke of Anand diffidently, and at last Gopal dared ask, "Have you made any marriage contract for that boy?"

Rama laughed as though the idea of marriage had never occurred to him. He wagged his head playfully. "I'm afraid my learned son is not interested in marriage."

This put Gopal at the disadvantage of having to pretend to introduce the subject as a completely novel idea.

"He has reached the age, that son of yours," he began doggedly. "A man's head may be filled with knowledge, but his body has the needs of any man's body."

Rama cocked his brow as if this thought had never occurred to him. "It is possible," he conceded lightly.

"You cannot imagine that the boy has not thought of marriage. Marriage is natural. He has a winning friendliness about him that tells there is a loving heart within."

Rama stirred uncomfortably, and Gopal suspected this was not a proper conversation. He felt helpless and ignorant. He wanted to talk frankly, for this concerned the most important thing in all the world to him. His Soni bai. She must have the best. Not just physical comfort, but the beauty and blessedness that can come to a woman from nothing except love.

Rama suddenly looked at the country man with sympathy. His eyes, almost hidden in wrinkled lids, glowed with friendliness.

Gopal burst out, "Will you consider my Soni? She is lovely within and without. She has humor in her, but she is also serious. There is not a lazy bone anywhere. . . ."

"I have considered your family," Rama said. "Now we shall call Govind, who will be the leader of my kutumb when

I have laid aside my active work. Govind must sit in on our business talk."

He clapped his hands for a servant, who came running out with some fresh sweet-dripping jellabees especially made for this auspicious moment. Gopal bit into the crisp pastry, twisted like a large pretzel, and as the luscious honey seeped into his mouth, he thought, My Soni would eat such jellabees!

The talk about the dowry was most painful to Gopal, and he had to mop his brow, halfway through it. The figure settled upon seemed impossibly big to him, but he couldn't help seeing that to Rama it represented a generous concession. Besides substantial rupees, the dowry would demand a set of jewelry for Soni, necklace and earrings and one nose ring of gold, with the usual pendant worn by brides. She would have to bring six saris with matching cholis, or blouses, six pairs of slippers, well made, and suitable gifts for her mother-in-law.

When everything was agreed upon Jeveram was summoned to be a witness. To Gopal's surprise, Jeveram was not far off. Apparently he had been brought from the bazaar many hours ago, in anticipation of the agreement. All the time Gopal had been in suspense, to Rama this had been a foregone conclusion! Gopal tried not to let his relief show in his face.

A guru, or priest, also was produced, ready to affix to the document the thumbprints of the two principals, and the witness of each. Govind, however, signed his name in proud Marathi script, for he had learned to write that much at the land office, where for a few pice an old pandit taught those who could learn.

After everything was signed and sealed, they all went to the temple to say their muntrums together. When they came out, Rama made a point of walking with Gopal behind the others.

"There is one more thing, which I did not desire to put into the contract," he said, laying his hand heavily on Gopal's arm.

"Yes? What is that thing?"

"This son Anand is the pearl of my heart," he said earnestly.

"I can see how he might be," Gopal said readily.

"So it seems fitting and good to me that you give me a pearl for myself."

For a moment Gopal floundered between the figurative and the literal, but Rama made his desire explicit. "All my life I have wanted a pearl set in a small earring, which I can wear in my right ear. In my heart I have promised myself that the father-in-law of Anand shall have the honor of giving me that gift."

Gopal was stunned. How could he possibly afford a pearl, when the dowry money and the other gifts were so much more lavish than he had expected?

"We shall speak of it to no one," Rama said. "It shall be a secret pleasure between the two of us . . . a bond of understanding between two fathers."

Suddenly the shrewd countryman stepped to the fore in Gopal. For Soni's sake he would insure her husband's future. The foreign sahib's clinic might be all right, but he wanted *his* child to have the comfort of good land under her . . . land to which her husband held the deed. And what Kumbi, once holding land in his own name, could resist working it? The Kumbi that lay sleeping in Anand would wake now and take possession of his heritage. In a flash he saw his child's future safe.

"I accept that honor," Gopal said valiantly. "And in exchange I ask you to give me a gift."

"What gift?" Rama asked cautiously.

"I ask you to agree that you will put in Anand's own right the eleven acres of land your family inherited. There the best of his education may be put to work, and the useless part will fall away."

"What is the best part?" Rama asked reluctantly. "I call it all useless."

"The boy knows a great deal about the modern methods of farming," Gopal said earnestly. "We talked about it last night before we went to sleep."

Rama looked at him in amazement. Why had not *he* thought of talking to his son as this stranger had talked? He had let his prejudice become a wall between them. But now this simple farmer had shown him what was behind the wall.

Gopal was saying, "Rama, your son showed himself to me last night. He is a true Kumbi. He is very much interested in the kind of cotton we grow at Marvali. I believe he could make a fine crop if he used some of my choice seeds on that favorable land. Give him the land and let him work out his destiny there."

Rama looked at him with even greater respect. He had not confessed to this man the extent of his worry because his own son preferred to work with the sahibs at the clinic, yet this other father had found a good way of drawing the boy to the land where he belonged. Why had *he* not thought of such a thing himself?

Well, it had been thought of in another man's brain, and he was delighted. He tapped Gopal's shoulder gratefully.

"I cannot do less than agree to your side of the bargain," he said. "I can see you are a man of great astuteness. We shall melt down many problems together." Now he beamed without restraint. After all it was good that his family would associate itself with a man who had such perception.

Gopal agreed graciously. But inside himself he said, I hope not, Brother Rama! You ask for an expensive gift, and in exchange I ask you to give *yourself* something even more precious! I am a stupid one! When you give your son the land, you will be giving yourself your son! And I allow you to call *that* an exchange gift for me! I should have asked for some expensive gift for myself. Then I could sell that gift, and buy the pearl. Now, how on earth can I ever afford it?

2

BACK IN MARVALI, GOPAL'S FACE TOLD THE news the moment Mira bai and their sons looked at him. He drew aside the chatia, or straw mat, which gave privacy to their doorway, and called the names of his sons. They came instantly, and Mira bai, too, ran from the rear quarters where she had been making chapattees with her daughters-in-law.

They saw in his face that Rama had been pleased with him. But he kept the pearl from standing naked in his mind, for he did not want them to know about that just yet. That was his private problem until he saw a way of solving it.

Mira bai joined her palms before her face and bowed her head, for even after all these years, her husband's face was too dear to be looked at casually. "Father, you are weary, and your feet are dusty. Let me take the dust from your feet." She bowed down a moment, then rose and ran to the cudjah for fresh water. Gopal seated himself on the rear doorstep, glad to be home.

The sons waited eagerly. "So he approved?" Ghosharam asked.

"We are good friends," his father said, trying not to sound boastful. "We had much pleasant talk. And we signed the agreement. Jeveram was my witness."

He could see that the two boys wanted to ask about the

dowry agreement, but dared not. "I'll tell you all about the arrangements later," he said.

Mira bai, back with the water, reached over and removed his pughri, or turban, and hung it on a wooden peg in the wall. As her hand passed his bared head, it contrived a swift caress which no one saw. Then she washed his feet, and when that was finished she picked up one of his baby grandchildren and handed it to him for comfort and amusement, while she brought his bowl of curry and rice, which had been waiting beside the mud stove.

Soni had been visiting in the next house, but when she heard her father's voice she ran home through the rear door. She came up behind him and placed her hands over his eyes, cupping his cheek affectionately.

"What evil spirit is this that the wind brings in?" he cried, moving her hand down to his mouth for a quick kiss.

"A good journey?" she asked, knowing his answer would tell her more than the mere words.

"The best of everything," he said.

While he was eating, the whole family gathered around. The boys said they had been roving through the dhak jungle yesterday and had found some bushes they had marked so they could gather the fruit later. When Gopal had finished his dinner, he saw in their faces th ir eagerness for the back-sheesh he must have brought them, so he took out his gifts immediately. They were inexpensive trinkets, glass bangles and earrings for all the girls, a dhoti for each of the boys, and for Mira bai a new sari.

"But the best gift I cannot show to your eyes," he said to his sons.

"What is that?"

"The knowledge of the world which I added to myself in even such short hours. Things I have never heard discussed in our village were talked about freely."

"What kind of things?"

"The state of our country in the present world. Much information about the past. Many hopes for the future."

The sons were silent in the presence of what they knew must be the fruits of education.

Gopal went on, "One of Rama's sons can write his name. I saw him do it." As he said these words, it crossed his mind that two of Rama's sons no doubt possessed this ability. But he had not actually seen Anand write. . . . He went on telling about the remarkable incident. "And he has not one, but two names!"

"How is that?"

"His name is Govind. But when he writes that name upon an important document, he adds another, according to the fashion out in the world beyond the villages."

"Where does he find the second name?"

"He could take the name of a god, if he wished. But he chooses to use the name of his caste. So his name is Govind Kumbirum."

The sons looked blank for a moment, then each face brightened. "We could have that name also! We are Kumbis." Then, one laughing and one serious, they tried their own names with Kumbirum.

"So now you are richer by a name!" Gopal said dryly. "If ever you have to go to Delhi, you will be properly named." The thought of any of them ever having to go to Delhi threw them into helpless mirth.

"And yet it is not impossible," Gopal said seriously, for he wanted to push out the horizon of possibility for his children as his own horizon had been extended in the past twenty-four hours. "Last night I heard many interesting facts about our government. People like us are beginning to have ınuch to say about how affairs shall be run."

The boys shook their heads in disbelief, so Gopal went on. "Villages are becoming dissatisfied with the Patwari system of collecting taxes. They are revolting against the Patwaris who keep too much of the taxes for themselves, and bully the people. Maybe a law will be passed, if enough villagers object."

"Who told you all these things?"

Gopal waited an impressive moment, then he said, "Anand discussed it. Anand, who will be your brother-in-law."

They were silenced a moment, and Gopal saw that they were hurt and slightly jealous of this unknown boy who had made such an impression on their father. So he described Anand in as disparaging terms as he could permit himself. But the boys read through the disparagement and knew that something unusual and wonderful was coming into their world. They were not sure whether or not they welcomed this idea, for they didn't want anyone to make them seem ignorant and countrified.

"Now we will go to the rear quarters and talk bundobus," Gopal said at last. The four women got up obediently and departed, for they knew they had no right to overhear talk about business arrangements. When the men were alone, Gopal mysteriously untied some seeds knotted in the corner of his dhoti. He handed them silently to Mahador, and when the younger farmer scrutinized them a moment, he said, "You know what those are, my son?"

"Are they pan seeds?"

"A special variety. Very much in demand in the big towns."

"Some pan is grown in Marvali," Ghosharam said, "but I've never seen any quite like this."

Gopal said, "The pan wallahs in Vardana have promised

a good price for all we can offer them of this. It is not a good habit to chew pan. Everyone knows what it does to ruin teeth. Perhaps we should not grow it."

Mahador said impatiently, "The harm is not in the growing, but in the chewing." They were all quiet a few minutes, each thinking in his own way about the ethical dilemma. But at last Gopal shrugged, so they decided the matter was settled.

"I saw many fine men chewing in Vardana," Gopal said. "They have fancy little boxes that they carry with them, holding the condiments. They fold the pan leaf into a triangle and put on a bit of white lime, a piece of betel nut and perhaps some clove or cardamon seeds. They say it makes the digestion happy. But when you see how it destroys the teeth . . . I wonder."

"I would be willing to grow it," Mahador said. "You get me these big seeds and I'll start my crop."

Ghosharam said, penetrating to what lay behind the pan seeds, "So we shall need more money for the dowry? More than we planned?"

Gopal took a deep breath and began to tell the alarming news. He did not answer the question directly, but told instead about the fine house of Rama, about his sons and their dignity. He tried not to arouse envy again, but instead stressed the advantages to his own sons of such a connection, not only in Vardana but also with their own clan here in Marvali.

"We could not expect to make such a connection without putting forth all the effort we have hidden in us," he said. The sons nodded reluctantly.

Suddenly then, Gopal knew that he could not keep the frightening matter of the pearl a secret from his sons. He could not possibly manage it alone . . . he was not sure they could all manage it together. So he plunged in, trying to be as casual as possible.

"Oh, and another thing," he said lightly. "Rama suggested a most noble gift from us. For himself."

Ghosharam cried sullenly, "A gift? Must the bridegroom's father have a gift? I've never heard of such a thing."

"You would understand if you could see him. And his son, whom he calls the pearl of his heart," Gopal said, trying not to sound apologetic. "So it is a pearl he has wanted all his life. Just a small pearl really. When he compared this trifling gift to Anand, I had nothing I could say."

The boys also had nothing they could say, so they frowned their displeasure.

"But the important thing you have completely overlooked," Gopal cried with sudden inspiration.

"What important thing? All I know is that such a gift will cost eighty rupees . . . maybe a hundred!"

"Is that important beside the real fact?" Gopal said indignantly.

"What real fact?" Mahador asked with filial meekness.

"Why, the fact that this Rama, into whose care we shall trust our Soni bai, is a devout man. You must know what it means to have water poured over a pearl in the morning ablutions! It means that the wearer is thrice cleansed . . . in body, in spirit and in mind. Only a noble Hindu would have desired *that* all his lifetime."

The boys looked ashamed of themselves that they had been so base as to think of rupees, where their father saw only devoutness.

"We shall get the pearl somehow," they said contritely.

"Somehow," Gopal said, getting up wearily to go to his own sleeping quarters. It had been the most strenuous day of his life.

"One thing," he said, turning back to speak to them. "We will get all the stipulated items for the dowry . . . the rupees, the jewelry and the pearl. But my shadow shall not darken the door of Rama's house until Soni goes there herself."

"Why not?" the boys asked in surprise. "You enjoyed your visit, Father."

"Yes, I did. But I do not want that crafty devout man thinking of more things that he can ask us for."

The boys burst out laughing. Their father had dragged them helplessly through the emotions he wanted them to feel. But he didn't want them to be deceived, and he was not deceived himself. They all understood each other perfectly. Gopal put his arms around their shoulders in affection and unity.

"Go to bed, you scamps," he said.

Mira bai was already rolled in her sutherungee when Gopal went quietly into their room. But he knew from her quick breathing that she had assumed this innocent position hastily.

"Shall I tell you all the arrangements?" he asked.

"Tomorrow," she said sleepily. So he was sure from that denial of her natural curiosity, that she had been hidden in the shadows behind the rear quarter's wall listening to everything he had told his sons. If he were a pukka husband he would rise and give her a beating with his slipper. But he was not pukka because he loved her too much. And besides, a woman without curiosity was curry without ginger.

He lay quietly until he was sure she was asleep and not only pretending. Then in his blanket he inched himself over to the corner of the room. Silently he scratched along the dirt floor, and at last he uncovered the brass lothi he had kept hidden there for four years. In the lothi was a cloth containing all the savings of his life, which no one on earth knew he possessed. The coins were more precious than ever now. He unwrapped the cloth, carefully deadening the clatter of the money. He counted it cautiously. Yesterday he had thought it was a great sum. Tonight he knew it was a mere nothing.

3

EVEN THOUGH SONI KNEW AS WELL AS HER
mother that the marriage arrangements had been completed,
it was Mira bai's place to make a formal announcement to
her. To keep it from being an emotional or sentimental occasion, she called her two daughters-in-law, Seetha and Sugya,
and Soni herself, and made the announcement to all the
women of her household. She did it in a brusque manner,
as is proper when Indian women talk alone. Men are lords
of the earth, and in a proper household they must be spoiled
with all tenderness and indulgence. But women must be
stern with each other, so they will be prepared for any hard
blows which life gives them. Women must appear lissome
and submissive in body and spirit; but under that softness
there must be the stamina of stone.

So Mira bai spoke quite harshly about the marriage. But
her harshness was translated correctly by her children.

"So now we are to have the expense and the burden of
marrying off Soni bai," she said when the three were seated
cross-legged before her in their modest quarters. "The marriage will be in May, and we must spend the time between
getting this wretched girl taught the things she must know."

They all looked solemn, as if this were an almost impossible task, but each was aware that Soni could have
stepped this very day into a new mother-in-law's household,

and have done credit to her mother's upbringing. Partly they spoke in this belittling fashion about her talents because praise among women is unseemly, and partly because it is never wise to attract evil spirits by pointing out an excellent fact which they may tamper with and destroy.

Soni looked demure and cast down, but her heart was beating so fast that there was a pink color in her cheeks, and her mother could not help thinking in the safety of her silent mind, How lovely is my child! They do not suspect what a treasure we are giving them for their son. Her dear father would not know how to describe her to them. Her face this morning . . . I shall see it behind my eyelids on the day I die. Her eyes so dark, her lashes so silky . . . and her skin, why, it is almost the color of a guava when the pink ripeness is on it. No girl in our village has such skin! But all the time she was thinking this rhapsody, she was frowning fiercely at her girl-child.

"We shall have to have her wretched ears pierced," Mira bai announced. "My husband is seeing the astrologer this morning to make sure of an auspicious day."

They were still discussing their plans, when they heard a commotion at the front door. Sugya ran out to see why a crowd of excited children and women had gathered. She came hurrying back to tell.

"Our father has arranged it all quickly. The guru is here to make purifying prayers, and the sonhar has come from his goldsmith shop, to pierce her ears. The astrologer decided that unless it is done today there will not be an auspicious time until February."

Mira bai threw up her hands. "Once things begin to happen, they come down like hail!" she said. "Soni . . . get into your best sari. You girls make yourselves tidy. Then we must have our muntrums." She was bustling about in motherly excitement, dabbing at her own hair and tightening the drape of her sari. "Good that I got some marigolds yesterday for us to offer at the temple." She went out and bowed to the guru. The chattering group of children and women quieted respectfully. One neighbor said, "From now on we shall see things happening in this house! We shall all join in, shall we not?"

"By all means," Mira bai said, rather absently. "I should have some jellabees ready for you all. But I didn't know." They shrugged their shoulders and shook their heads in polite denial, but the children couldn't help letting their disappointment show.

When they came back from the temple, trailed by the well-wishers, the sonhar was ready with his small pincers, tongs and the little brass shovel containing hot coals. He was sitting in the middle of the rear court with all his equipment spread on the ground around him. The coals glowed red in the shovel, and the gold needle was wrapped in silk, waiting.

A few women were whispering of accidents they had known about. A girl once in an untouchable leatherworkers' village had died of poisoning of the ears. But that might only mean the gods did not approve of untouchable women wearing earrings. It was all right for the men of course; after all, they had no safe place to keep anything they owned, if they *did* own anything valuable. Occasionally one had managed to convert his life's work into an almost invisibly small gold earring, which he could sell when he needed to. But that was different. The whispering went on, until Mira bai silenced it with a stern look.

"If you wish to watch, you may," she said. "But it should be prayerfully."

Soni, her sari covering her head submissively, knelt as

the sonhar directed. He unwrapped the gold needle, and everyone strained to see it. Such a thing! He laid the silk carefully on a little brass plate. Then with his tongs he held the needle in the glowing coals for a moment. He took it out and motioned for Soni to bend her head. He thrust the needle, swift as a dragonfly, through the lobe into a cork which he was holding behind the ear. Soni closed her eyes a moment, then opened them bravely. He removed the needle instantly and threaded the eye of the ear with a tiny fragment of tulasi stick. The other ear was finished even more quickly.

The guru hastily said another prayer, then both men rose to their feet and looked around smilingly.

The sonhar said, "You will please leave the tulasi sticks in the ears for two days. And you must turn the twigs every little while to keep them loose. When the ears are healed you can put cloves in the openings, until the time for earrings."

All the neighbors came and spoke politely to Soni. Her ears were tingling; it was a strange discomfort, half pleasant. It could not be merely a physical pain, because it was connected with her coming marriage. This morning her girl-body had been altered slightly, to welcome the marriage.

The days passed quickly, for every one of them was packed with preparation. Under the busyness, there was always a little quiver of sadness, because Soni loved her home more than most girls, and now in a little while she would be leaving it, for something new and unknown!

By mid-September the men of the household were busier than ever with their own affairs. Everyone knew they were concerned about the dowry, but it would have been improper for it to be discussed openly. Everything possible was being turned into rupees. The major crops had been harvested now, and the smaller vegetable crops were being gathered, each marked for some special part of the fund. Some would have to go for services rendered the family, others to the bazaar wallahs in exchange for goods, utensils, implements and tools. There were two calves, both little bulls, which could be sold.

The pearl would be bought in Mulkapoor, which was about twelve miles away. Mulkapoor was famous for having the best gems in this part of India. Gopal had always known that fact, but it had never occurred to him that the fact would have any personal meaning for him. He could barely believe it now. He did not know anyone in Mulkapoor, so the Patel, the mayor of Marvali, gave him the name of a man who would help him. Keshub was the name, and the Patel said he was a good and honest Kumbi.

No one except the men of Gopal's closest clan knew what was the real purpose of the trip to Mulkapoor. The rest of the neighbors believed he had word that certain produce could be sold to better advantage there, so many brought to him their extra sugar cane and cotton, and some bags of corn and millet. He had a cart piled high with merchandise to sell, with a borrowed bullock to yoke to his own for the trip.

Then the day before he expected to leave he made an unheard-of announcement. "Our family is about to make a connection with a most progressive family. I have decided that Mira bai and Soni should come with Ghosharam and me on this trip."

Mira bai's face could not hold her astonishment. "I have never been away from Marvali since the last time I went to visit my parents just after Ghosharam was born."

"It is time that you made a journey," Gopal said suppressing his own excitement. "When the mother-in-law of Soni will ask if you have traveled you can say, 'I have been to Mulkapoor. And so has my daughter.'"

Their faces were shocked with the proposal of such audacity. Imagine being able to say such a thing!

"Furthermore, you will see the ag-ghari, the fire wagon, for Mulkapoor is a railway center. Your eyes will look upon a locomotive that has stood in Bombay!"

Mira bai managed to stammer in protest, "But we would not know how to behave near such wonders."

"I will be with you," Gopal said. "I shall tell you. You will see things you will never forget. These are new-fashioned times now. People want to see what is happening in the world. You shall go to Mulkapoor, and afterwards you can tell the women at the well."

A chill of excitement ran down Soni's spine. Her lord would not find her completely ignorant. She would listen submissively when he talked, and if he asked *her* to say something . . . ever . . . she could tell him about Mulkapoor.

All the rest of the day, all the women worked in the cooking quarters, so there would be plenty of food for the journey. Soni could barely sleep, waiting for the early morning start. Before sunrise, they were on their way, sent off by the men and boys of their clan. Even some women followed them to the gate of Marvali, for they all had a feeling that if two women they knew were venturing out into the unknown, something new and daring now belonged to all of them. If it could happen to two, it might happen to all!

The trail leading to the government road was seldom used, and led them through almost six miles of densely wooded area. The bullocks stolidly took their own pace, and this felt like a strange country, for there were no familiar sights such as Gopal usually enjoyed along the traveled roadways. Here there was not even one idol, not even the simple stones painted red, with coconut shells to receive the offerings of travelers. Here there was only the chill filtered morning light sifting through the trees. But there were birds, and suddenly in a turn of the trail they came upon two beautiful saras, crane-like birds with pearly gray plumage. The male was standing beside the female, who was resting, as if on a nest. He had a brilliant red cap on his small head, a short pointed beak, and rather large feet on his long legs. Everyone stared in delight, and Gopal said respectfully:

"You know what an omen this is?" He looked at Soni, who shook her head.

"The sara is the Hindu emblem of marriage fidelity. It is great good fortune for us to see the saras on such a trip as ours."

At the sight of their first salei tree, Ghosharam pointed with eagerness. This was the time of the year when the salei tree was giving off its resin. They let the bullocks rest while all of them gathered it. They could sell it at the pharmacy, to be made into one of the favorite incenses. This was such unexpected good fortune that they felt the whole trip was going to be auspicious.

When they reached the edge of Mulkapoor they found a special resting place for Kumbis. Stakes were provided in the compound where they could tie their bullocks. Gopal asked immediately for Keshub, whom the Patel had recommended, and someone ran out into the bazaar and brought him back. He was a small, wrinkled, pleasant man. It flattered him enormously that Gopal had been put into his care. Mira bai unwrapped the chapattees and chutney and Gopal and Ghosharam ate hungrily with their new friend, Keshub. When they had finished, Soni and her mother ate.

With Gopal and Keshub in the lead, and Ghosharam walking properly behind with his mother and sister, they started into the bazaar. Keshub was gesticulating violently, but talking in a crafty whisper, so they could see he was enlightening Gopal about the dangers and pitfalls which would be the lot of a less well guarded man.

Ghosharam said to his mother, "The gods protect our father."

"The gods protect him because he is a good man," Mira bai said reverently.

The central area of the bazaar was crudely canopied by gunny sacks tied between raw posts. Here oils of all kinds were sold: coconut oil plain or scented, for use on the body; rapeseed oil, in smaller quanties because it was not so popular for anointing; nim and croton oils for medicine; mustard oil for cooking and lighting; castor oil, very crude but necessary for the poor; linseed oil for greasing cart wheels. Set apart on a platform stood a few large tins of kerosene brought in by the Europeans for the luxury of foreign lamps which many used now.

To the left of this area were small stalls, covered with palm fronds or branches of leaves. Small clay stoves called chulas were provided here for passers-by who might want to parch some grain or corn. The storekeepers were calling out such things as, "Ten paces to my right you will find a stall providing the very best grain at the cheapest cost." Then in a louder and more alluring tone, "And the special fire which I burn will be the best suited to parch your grain." Then changing the tone to a drawl, "The taste will be greatly improved by the ghee from my friend Ahir on my left."

Often the stallkeepers rhymed their suggestions to attract more attention:

> "Stop your march;
> Here's corn to parch."

or,

> "What's all the hurry?
> Pause and eat curry."

The two women stood speechless before the stalls where bangles were sold. They had not dreamed there were so many in the world, and each one glistening with serpentine color. There were saris hanging from poles, showing off their elaborate borders and material for rich little choli blouses. There were stalls which sold nothing but confections, wrapped in gold and silver leaf, and those which offered bins of monkey-nuts, and cashews and walnuts. There were silversmiths at work, never looking up, but somehow seeing out of the tops of their skulls when a woman stopped to admire. The Mulkapoor bazaar made the bazaar outside Marvali, which had always before been a dazzling spot, seem a miserable muddy lane.

Gopal and Ghosharam kept their two women discreetly between them. They knew this visit to a strange bazaar represented modern and daring behavior, but they were thrilled because Mira bai and Soni would be able to tell what had been seen. Mira bai and Soni kept their saris drawn modestly across their faces, but their eyes, large with excitement, peered out delightedly, memorizing the sights.

One stall boasted the unusual luxury of gunny-sack floor covers under the palm roof. On this floor were neat piles of salt in various stages. One large stack was the crude dirty rock salt with pieces of actual soil still clinging. This was the cheapest. Other piles were increasingly refined, approaching white in color. Gopal had orders for salt in exchange for sugar cane from Marvali. The cane was judged by diameter and length as well as flavor, which had to be tested by the principals in the transaction, as well as bystanders and advice-givers. The salt would be measured by the handful. The quantity held in the cupping of both hands was called a seer. A seer is generally considered two pounds, though obviously the weight must vary enormously with substance.

While Gopal bargained for the best takers of sugar cane, Ghosharam and a young man whom Keshub provided from nowhere took the women over to a group of dancers and jesters who were entertaining in an open space. They were actually eunuchs intended from babyhood to be singers. The oldest one was a tall emaciated man dressed like a woman, and his song was a tragic plaint about never being one thing or the other. This moment of musical sorrow only prepared the crowd for the dancers, who capered and pranced, imitating various village animals, including Hanuman's monkeys. The Marvali family were entranced and could have stayed on for the rest of the day, but Keshub and Gopal came running back to get them.

"If you're to see the locomotive, you must come instantly," Gopal said. "Keshub has marked with his shadow the right time to go to the station."

Keshub said, beaming happily, "When my shadow is as far ahead of me as my own pace . . . that is the time to hurry."

They resisted everything else now, and ran past many imposing buildings. Some were plainly Moslem and some, Keshub said breathlessly, belonged to white sahibs. In fifteen minutes they approached a sight far beyond anything they had ever expected to see. The railway station had a sloping stone platform, and on this there seemed to be more people gathered than actually lived in Marvali. Small groups were squatting, balancing on their toes, or standing very calmly. Some persons were dashing about, running in and out of the station office waving their tickets and protesting. Many were in line to wash their hands for one last time before they got on the expected train. Vendors with large trays on their heads were offering fruit and jellabees, but few buyers availed themselves of refreshment. Mohammedans and vegetarian Hindus had separate dining rooms, and managed to ignore each other pleasantly. The Mohammedans in white tight-fitting pants and long fitted waistcoats were rather handsome and conspicuous. But the wealthy Brahmins, from whom everyone drew aside for fear of defiling their superiors, were equally impressive.

Then suddenly Gopal's family stopped, for they were about to see something their eyes never before had rested upon. A white face! There was a group of sahibs in white suits and large stiff hats. A pink-skinned woman was with them, wearing a flowered hat, and a green dress that reached immodestly just below her knees. She had a small child with her, pale looking. But its hair was beautiful, as if it had been made on a spinning wheel out of the sunshine.

"Look all you please," Gopal whispered. "Anand sees such a sight every day. Anand works with such people!"

They were speechless, as they stared respectfully. Mira bai said to Soni, "If ever your lord asks if you have looked upon a white face. . . ."

"Why do they call them white-skinned?" Soni cried in disappointment. "They are red-skinned, and the men have chapattee-colored faces!"

"Ssh," her mother said, shocked by this bold discovery.

"And the child . . . he has little gold-colored spots all over his face and hands."

"That's from the sun," Gopal said. "White skin gets peppered with those marks out in the sun."

"White!" Soni said disgustedly. "They're a long way from being white!"

Then the train came in, announced by a bleating little whistle and a stirring of the crowd. A hundred parcels of food and merchandise which had been standing quietly were now flung up to heads or hips. The children, who had been wandering about freely, were gathered close by screams and shouts of warning.

Ghosharam, who had wanted to see such a thing since he was a boy, could barely look. Wheels were screeching and steam was billowing from somewhere as the giant steel monster approached. Now the coaches were spread along the tracks, looking like huge many-windowed houses on wheels. The doors of the compartments flew open, and the two tides, the passengers getting off the train and those trying to get on, clashed and mingled in noisy confusion. Keshub knew everything, and gladly told.

"The first-class compartments are rented at great expense. I cannot imagine who rides in those, but someone must."

Gopal wagged his head in amazement, and clicked his tongue against the roof of his mouth.

"The second-class compartments are for people who wish to lie down. They cost half as much as the first class. But they are very expensive. Inter comes next; not quite as expensive. Then there is a third class, for the poor. For us," Keshub said without malice. "We may sit up on benches."

They approached the train timidly, but Keshub urged them to have a good look, which they did.

Ghosharam said almost with shame, "I want sometime to take a train journey. But I suppose I shall die first."

"Well, you have *seen* a train, my son," Gopal said consolingly. "You have put out your hand and touched it. Many, many men in this world have not had that opportunity."

"The gods are good," Ghosharam said with automatic piety. But inside he was saying, I promise myself I will make a journey sometime on a train. I don't care where I go . . . but I shall go someplace.

When the wonderful spectacle was over, and the train was only dust on the brow, Keshub bowed low, his white teeth gleaming with pleasure.

"Now, my friends, I shall offer my poor house for your sleeping place tonight."

Gopal protested with polite warmth, but his host insisted. "I have sent a boy to my wretched wife to say I am bringing friends."

"We cannot accept such an honor. When the sun rose this morning we did not even know the look of your face," Gopal said gently.

"But we are Kumbis, brother," Keshub said.

"We are Kumbis," Gopal agreed. "And tonight I have confidential bundobus to discuss with you."

"You are welcome to everything I know," Keshub said. "It will be my pleasure to serve you any way I can."

In the morning Gopal left his family with their new-found friends and went early to the bazaar. Keshub, too, had been excited all night, for he, like Gopal, had never expected to come this close to a pearl. He said with positive authority, "There is only one man for us to see, for he is honest and experienced. His name is Dadaji, and you can see by the 'ji' how much he is revered and beloved in our town."

"We shall thank the gods for such a man," Gopal said. "Some gem merchants are not honest. Only experienced."

"His shop is near the center of town, on the main street, right behind the police station."

They found the modest shop down a short alley. Not large by any means. A creaking gate opened into a small anteroom. Keshub could not help letting disappointment show on his face.

"I had expected it to be bigger than this," he said regretfully, standing in the bare room and looking around.

"Bigness is no measure of goodness," Gopal said. "Even a country man like me knows that."

A man had appeared in the hall beyond the door of the

small room and was nodding his head in satisfaction at what he had just overheard Gopal say.

"Come with me," the old man said, beckoning. "We shall talk in more privacy." He led them across a little hall into a stone-floored workroom. Old Dadaji had been working over a fireplace, which was only a small pit sunken in the floor. He picked up his bellows and began blowing at the sulky fire. Around the room were tools of many kinds. The tongs and blower, with which the old man was working, were ancient ones.

"My father made this," Dadaji said conversationally.

Around his neck was a cable twisted crudely of fine gold wires, kept here in the safest possible place. Gopal liked his kind old face, and knew immediately that eventually they would do business together. But of course it would not be a hurried transaction.

He helped the old man blow the fire into a flame while they chatted about his village of Marvali. Keshub very slyly brought out the fact that, although Gopal was a most honored man in his village, he was a poor farmer. This led easily into mentioning the present great dilemma of buying a pearl for a rich prospective father-in-law of his only daughter.

Dadaji looked at Gopal shrewdly but kindly. "As you say, 'Bigness is not goodness.' Thousands of those trapped in this world's allurements do not know that. Only a humble and good man could see it as you have."

Gopal bowed his head modestly, for of course it is God who gives wisdom, not man who originates it.

"That hidden truth applies to gems also," Dadaji said softly. "Many monsoons had passed over my poor wretched head before I discovered that truth. So, because you and I are brothers in discovery, I shall find you a pearl which you can afford to buy, and which will have quality and color about it. You are pleased?"

Gopal could not say how pleased he was. Never in his life had a merchant spoken to him this way. Usually merchants made him feel ignorant and inferior. But this man has penetrated to a new depth of measuring. They met in this new depth, and it was well.

"First let me show you my stones," Dadaji said, disappearing through what looked only like a break in the wall. He returned with a brass lothi, containing a piece of white silk tied with a cord and tassel. Here he concealed his diamonds, pure as dew. They were not large, but all were perfect. They had come from the mines of Punnah, located on the northern buttress of the great plateau of the Central Provinces. He had visited the Myra mine with his father when he was just a boy. The shaft down which they went was exceptionally deep, and so precious are the jewels brought up that the common people of the countryside do not even know a mine is present.

"The diamonds are found in red earth mixed in a silex-quartz formation. Washing out the red clay is a tedious process, carried out by hand in marble troughs. My father, God rest his soul, was told these mines have been worked for twenty centuries," Dadaji said while he was carefully putting the diamonds back in their cloth.

He brought out other lothis, each containing several small cloth sacks or bundles. In one were a few rubies from Burma, in another aquamarines and zircons and a plump bag full of opals and garnets from Travancore.

Then he brought out a large cloth, showing the work he was doing right now. A string of beautiful carnelians which were to be a gift for the wife of an American engineer working in Delhi. He admired the stones and fingered them fondly. "These are rare stones I am cutting. They were brought to me by my own son from Broach, near the town of Ratanpore. Do you know how they become so beautiful?"

The speechless admirers shook their heads.

"Let me tell you. The rough stones are evenly spread out in a guarded place, so that each one is exposed to the sun for nearly ten months. Then they are baked in earthen pots over a fire made of sheep's dung. My son declares nothing but sheep's dung will serve. This baking changes their natural black color to a clearness of red that is something only the blessing of the gods could create."

His old eyes were mellowed as he said, "Now we shall look at my pearls."

"Perhaps I can only look," Gopal warned in a shamed voice. "Perhaps I cannot buy."

"I have told you," Dadaji said soothingly.

He came back from his storeroom behind the broken wall with a very small bag of silk.

"But even if I cannot buy," Gopal said stubbornly, "you have made me a richer man by what my eyes have seen."

Dadaji opened the bag on the palm of his hand, and the little pearls were revealed, their silky skins gleaming with pink and yellow and even mauve. None were large but all were beautiful. After a long moment of silence Dadaji picked out a small sphere, a delicate yellow, and held it between his thumb and forefinger. With benevolence in his voice he asked, "You like this, Gopal?"

"It is too beautiful," Gopal said in a whisper. "I think there is not a merchant in Vardana, where our honorable family-in-law lives, who could match it."

"You may have it for one hundred fifteen rupees," Dadaji said in a very matter-of-fact tone. Quick mathematics ran through Gopal's head. He had sold the produce he had brought for twenty-two rupees and six annas. That produce represented much hard labor. Black sadness, thick as smoke, engulfed his brain.

He turned his head away sorrowfully.

"Or perhaps I could let you have my tiny beauty for a little less," Dadaji said.

"I still could not afford it," Gopal said. "I had no right to waste your time. I robbed you."

The price came down a bit, and Dadaji did not humiliate his customer by meeting his eye. "I think I could let you have it for ninety-one rupees," he said.

"It must be less than ninety," Gopal faltered. "And at that I rob my children."

"Whose children shall we rob . . . yours or mine?" Dadaji asked gently. Then he held out the pearl to Gopal. "Take it," he said. "I give it to you for eighty-seven rupees."

Gopal's eyes almost melted into tears. "But . . . but where should I find any goldsmith who could set such a pearl into an earring?"

Dadaji laughed and wagged his head. "You have got around me, my friend. I would not allow any goldsmith to touch this pearl."

"So?" Gopal was hardly breathing.

"I shall set it myself."

"And the cost?"

"The cost will be counted into the eighty-seven rupees. And when the gods think about what I was worth, they will say, 'He gave an earring to a man because he liked him.' "

Gopal still could not meet his eye, so Dadaji reached out and patted him on the shoulder, laughing with pleasure at his own generosity.

"I can leave one fourth of the price with you today," Gopal said. "That is all I have with me. The rest is at home, safely buried. I will bring it to you when the earring is finished."

All the way driving home that afternoon, Gopal was silent. Everyone else chattered excitedly. But he was beyond words. In his mind he was saying to himself, How strange life is. A man dares to entertain a big thought . . . as I dared to think I might give my Soni bai to such a family . . . and now I am a man who has gone to Mulkapoor and has bought a pearl!

The thoughts that a man dares admit to his mind must be watched closely, for they lead to unguessable events.

4

MANY UNGUESSABLE EVENTS UNFOLDED
during that year. Each month brought its own gifts. In
September the jungle was rich with the most beautiful tree
of all, the gol mohur in bloom. When you stood beneath
it the brilliant red velvet flowers spread a canopy almost as
wide as the sky. October was the time for spinning. Soni
had carded the rough goats' hair since she was scarcely more
than a baby. But now she was expected to prepare enough
wool for a new blanket, and after that there was the heavy
weaving to be done so that the sutherungee would be warm
and durable. There were special humming songs which made
weaving go faster, but nowadays Mira bai used the time to
instruct her daughter in little odds and ends of information
she would need for her marriage.

"Your lord will say his pujah an hour before the sun rises
. . . his prayer and his cleansing ceremonies. You must know
his habits and have everything in readiness. He must have a
clean dhoti every morning. If you ever see him place a twig
in safe keeping, never let your shadow fall near it, for it is
the one with which he cleanses his teeth. In Marvali we have
many of the approved bushes which give the twigs for proper
cleansing, the kikar, the uduga or neradu . . . but if these
are not to be had in Vardana, you must find him the twig
of a thorny or a milky bush. But on the eleventh day of the

new moon, the twig of the nim tree is right to use."

Like the good Hindu she was, she taught her child to keep close watch on the waxing and waning of the moon. When the last few days of its dark period came, she must prepare colored rice, and gather the sacred darbha grass for the temple offerings. When the full moon first made its appearance, the Feast of Dasara must be celebrated.

Mira bai said sternly, "If ever you are so poor that you cannot celebrate Dasara, you must sell one of your children in order to do so. And may you by then have ninety-nine children!"

Sometimes the motherly advice had a very worldly and practical tone. "Remember, it is only through his wife that a man enjoys the pleasures of this world. So learn the arts of deep pleasing.

"A woman's body is the alphabet of delight to her lord; it must spell out sweet and varied sentences for as long as he needs them. If a woman has in any way failed to please her master, she must atone. All the next day she must rub her body with scented oils and saffron or rose water. That night when he comes back from his work, he must find her fragrant with ointment and beautiful with ornament. Her eyes must be brightened with kohl, her hair must be oiled and its part must be freshly marked with vermilion. Her very presence must be unspoken apology, but most of all, it must be a promise.

"There is an art to everything, even to eavesdropping. When a wife overhears strange words coming from her lord's lips while he is entertaining a friend, she must find a way to listen carefully, and to understand. Her business is to know everything possible that will help her to comfort her master.

"Everything a woman has comes to her from her husband. Dearest of all, of course, are her sons which he gave her to honor their ancestors. But also her husband provides her with clothes and jewels; he supplies her with her flower garden, and it is he who brings her sandalwood oil, ocher and sweets for her women guests. Everything good she ever can know comes from him."

Although Gopal was nearly beside himself with worry about the money he must find before the wedding, he went about his work looking calm as usual. But under everything his mind was twisting and turning, trying to find some source of earnings which he had overlooked. He knew that almost any other Kumbi in the village would have gone immediately to the moneylender. But Gopal could not bear to think of such shame.

He had planted extra gram and sugar cane around the cotton field that was on the plateau, but he could not hope for very much increase from that. When it was long past dark and nobody could toil longer in the fields, he had come home and worked in Mira bai's garden, which had been enlarged in every possible way. They were growing lentils in market quantity. And he had urged every inch of the kitchen garden to produce more eggplants and more okra which could be sold in their own bazaar.

The trees that grew on the plateau outside Marvali belonged to anyone who had energy enough to harvest their crops. But time was the problem here, for Gopal and his sons were working every possible hour.

"But we can always get up an hour earlier," Gopal said sternly. So that they did, when the sirsa trees were putting forth their gum. The sal trees, also, were giving off a gum that is white and tasty. Something told Gopal that there must be commercial uses for these resins, if he only knew where to sell them in quantity. The large tikur trees grew in this jungle also, and its roots could be made into a sweet

starchy porridge. There were plenty of medicine trees, like
the koukla and the nermali trees . . . but nobody wanted
medicine until they were forced to buy it. And it seemed
to Gopal an ungenerous and even miserly intention, to try
to *sell* medicine instead of giving it freely where it was
needed.

Late in October some neighbors had an errand in Mulkapoor, so Gopal went with them to claim the finished earring.
The yellow pearl was more beautiful even than he had remembered it, and Dadaji had set it cunningly in a twist of
gold. Gopal showed it to no one, except his two sons. Then
he hid it in the lothi which he kept buried in the ground
where he slept. Almost every night, after Mira bai was
asleep, he got it out and gloated over it.

Eventually another man would believe that *he* owned this
gem. He would wear it in his ear, and pour the cleansing
water over it, for the thrice-purifying. But until the day he
died, the pearl would actually belong to Gopal. For he had
the image of it so clearly set in his mind that it was closer
to him than bread or labor or laughter or pain.

In November and December many days were spent with
the whole family in the fields or the jungles gathering wild
roots, berries, nuts and gum. Gopal's sons knew of two hives
of honey which they told no one about. Neighbor children
tried to trail them to the hives, but no one found the place.
Suddenly the young boys of the village announced that the
great mahwah tree was shaking its leaves, and in a few hours
every house was emptied while families rushed out to gather
them. These precious leaves made softer bedding for sheep
and goats, and also for the human to pile under his blanket.

When the leaves were shaken off, flowers began to form.
Then the whole jungle was scented with spicy fragrance.
Each petal shaped like a small berry, is clustered into a heavy

head. These rich flowers are gathered to eat, and it is said that the sustenance from the mahwah tree is so necessary in the hills that when the trees are destroyed, the people perish.

The flowers her household gathered Mira bai spread on a drying screen which she put in the sun. When they were well dried, she ground them to flour which made a most delicious sweet cake. Some households made wine or vinegar, and some preserved the flowers in syrup as a confection.

Even the bark could be used by the poor, during the tree's dormant period. They stripped off the bark and soaked it, weaving its fibers into a rope, nearly as good as the jute rope which they couldn't afford.

Mira bai said to her learning child, "The mahwah tree is like life itself, ever passing from one stage to another . . . and there is a use for each stage."

February brought to Gopal's house the greatest event of all, completely unexpected. For in mid-February, Soni's prospective mother-in-law came to visit. She brought along her widowed daughter, her woman servant, her oldest son Govind and a manservant. Their chaprassi arrived first, announcing that his mistress was on her way. The whole clan of Gopal was thrown into panic.

But though it was a three-day visit of frank inspection, it turned out to be a lovely occasion, for Shushilla bai was a sweet and gentle woman and she took to Soni the moment she saw her.

"The gods have saved their dearest gift for the last part of my life," she said, patting Soni's head. "This is my own daughter, and at last I have found her."

The real purpose of her visit, she explained diffidently, was to ask a favor of Soni's family. Anything, they agreed readily, although Gopal trembled for fear the favor might involve some added expense. Because of her own delicate health, Shushilla bai could enjoy few pleasures. It would be the crowning delight of her life, if Gopal's family would forget tradition, and allow the marriage to take place in Vardana. Rama had many friends he wished to honor with an invitation to the wedding, and it would be an unforgettable occasion for all. Concealing his relief Gopal thought a few moments, then graciously agreed.

"Since you are so kind about this," Shushilla bai said, "would you also allow us to have Soni join our house a few weeks before the wedding? Then she would be familiar with our family customs, and feel at home." They nodded slowly, not too happy to give up their child before it was necessary.

At the end of their visit the cortege departed, laden down with country gifts. Because Shushilla had admired the rich dark honey eaten on chapattees, the family went to the jungle and brought back the whole structure of combs, knowing they were fatally robbing the bees. Ghosharam and his children also gathered a basket of kurrawandah berries to send back to the household they wished to please.

Now that the date for Soni's leaving Marvali was finally settled, Gopal's worry was a constant unseen presence. He was adding to the number of rupees in the buried lothi but there were still not nearly enough. So at last he had to face the dreaded visit to the moneylender, Two-fingered Mohan. Up to now his dealings with Two-fingered Mohan had been official ones when the moneylender had become too greedy and had pressed some debtor beyond his endurance. Then Gopal, as the senior member of the panchayat, the five men who hovered over the welfare of the village, had summoned him and had reprimanded and warned him. This could have been done by no one but Gopal, since everyone else in the village was directly or indirectly in Mohan's debt. But Gopal had always handled him without fear from the past, or apprehension for the future.

Two-fingered Mohan was not the conventionally fat

moneylender; he was a tall cadaverous man with a beaked nose and discolored snaggle teeth. He always wore a soiled Congress Party cap on the back of his head. Behind his back, his debtors said he had two fingers on his right hand, in order to slip into any pocket, no matter how slim it was, and pick it.

Nobody wants to be seen talking to a moneylender, so most men go to his house at night. But Gopal was too proud for that subterfuge. Besides, his canny countryman's mind told him that since he had never been guilty of borrowing money and no one ever had suspected him of such a thing, the best way to deceive would be to continue to behave naturally. So he waylaid Two-fingered Mohan on his way home from the bazaar, and walked along the narrow lane with him, talking frankly as if they were discussing some other man's business.

The moneylender said, "I will come to *your* house, Gopal. That way, no one will suspect. That way it will look as if I am asking a favor of *you*."

"At twenty per cent interest, that is practically the fact," Gopal said fiercely. Two-fingered Mohan agreed, laughing heartily and gouging Gopal in the ribs with his thumb.

"But what is a man to do?" he concluded ingenuously. Gopal could only agree, noticing he had slipped already into the shameful position of being pleasant to a moneylender. His soul was already stained by the thing.

But he had no alternative. Proudly he would carry the money to Rama . . . who did not need it . . . and then he would not sleep a sweet night until he had paid back the moneylender. But it was for Soni, and since he was marrying her into a well-to-do family, it was necessary to send pride with her. There would be other sisters-in-law in the household, and Soni must hold up her head among them.

He thought of how he had been skillful enough to make Rama promise to give the newly married husband eleven acres of his best land. This debt that had shamed him to himself, was the purchase price of that land. Surely God would help him find a way of paying for that wonderful gift he had bestowed upon his girl-child and her husband. The gift would come to them in another man's name . . . but it would really be Gopal who had purchased it for them.

The tenth day of March marks a religious ceremony on which Vishnu is worshipped. Everyone begins the day by washing his mouth twelve times before prayers can be said. There is music and dancing all day, and before the temple and at the base of many nim trees in the bagh there are little images made of rice flour. Adults may not eat all day, but the children have bananas and coconuts. This was to be Soni's last celebration in her home.

The next day, she and her mother and the sisters-in-law gathered the produce from their chili patch, their last piece of unfinished business. They picked up the folds of their saris in the front and drew them up to the back where they fastened them securely in their waistbands. This formed trousers which were easier for field work than the flowing skirts of the saris. The four of them worked with determined cheerfulness, for every heart was trembling on the edge of sadness.

When they stopped at noon to eat what they had brought from their hut, Soni suddenly put her head against her mother's shoulder. "How can I *live* away from everything I know?" she cried in alarm.

Her mother was silent a moment, shocked by this outburst after years of careful discipline. Then, because there were no strangers to see the indulgence, she put her two hands against Soni's temples and looked into her eyes.

"My child, my child . . . what is your family? It is love for you. It is laughter when you do an amusing, pretty thing. It is your brothers' protection, and your father's affection . . . and from me . . . well, I am your worthless mother who thinks you are beautiful in every motion and good in every thought."

"How shall I *live* . . . separated from all that?" Soni cried again, in terrified honesty.

"You will find your family everywhere laughter is. You will find it everywhere protection is . . . and praise for goodness. Once you have known such a family as ours, you never again can be without it. It is in your heart, my child. It will shine out before you so that when you take a step, you will step into welcoming."

Soni looked up into her mother's face. It had been her very sky for as long as she could remember. But above it now there was a new sky. That would be the face of her husband, and in it she must find everything she needed forever. Mira bai was silent, almost knowing what her child was thinking. She pointed to the actual sky above them, broken into dazzling fragments by the trees, and the birds darting joyfully. There were parrots, the purple blossom-headed ones, chattering and flying about. There were mynahs, dark and plain but more clever than any other birds. They were declaring happiness and love to anyone who needed to be reminded.

The two women under the tree heard what they had to say, and it confirmed what was in their hearts. Their faces smiled at each other now. Perhaps in their whole lifetime they might never talk so intimately again. But that would be all right, for they understood each other and they were not afraid of what was to come.

When they came home that night, Gopal said with elaborate casualness, "Tomorrow I must go with the other chow-dris and take some of our produce to Vardana. Soni's belongings must be in order.

"They are in order," Mira bai said.

"I am in order also," Gopal murmured, twisting his lips into a wry smile, because Mira bai had no idea what anguish lay behind his small sentence.

She looked at him carefully. Was something troubling her lord? With all her care for his comfort, had her wifely clair-voyance been blind about something that concerned him?

He saw that she was troubled, and for a swift moment he was almost tempted to tell her about his debt. But it is a weak man who tells troubles to a wife. He knew she had been eavesdropping the night he told his sons about the pearl, but he had never confirmed to her what she had over-heard. Let her curiosity stew in its own juices, he had said angrily to himself. But he knew his anger was not against her, and it was unfair if he let it touch her. So, to make up for some of his irritableness which must have hurt her, he decided suddenly to show her the pearl.

He unwrapped it from its tiny silk covering, which was tied securely in his dhoti.

"It is for Rama," he said with heroic lightness. "I thought it would be a handsome thing if we gave a gift to him."

She did not attempt to touch the jewel lying in his palm, but her whole being seemed to hover over it.

"We give him a pearl! Besides the dowry?"

"He is a rich man. We cannot have him looking down on our offerings."

She looked eagerly into her husband's face. Her wonderful lord, always seeing a handsome thing to do . . . and doing it!

"That you could afford to buy such a thing!" she breathed. "We must be well off."

"We are very well off," he said valiantly.

Early the next morning Soni and her mother left their hut for their last pujah together.

"We cannot be sad," Mira bai said. "Sadness makes old age. Be happy everywhere you are, Soni bai. Find beautiful things to look at, for they will make you beautiful."

The parting gifts and the new cholis and saris had been tied in a huge bundle. The sutherungee that Soni had believed she was weaving for her father turned out to be for herself. Now it was wrapped around the bundle of her possessions. That brought tears to her eyes, so she turned away quickly.

At last Gopal picked up her bundle without a word. The sisters-in-law squeezed her arms in silent affection. The children embraced her, only half understanding. Mahador and Ghosharam tried to be humorous.

"It's worth everything to know we shall be invited to a rich wedding feast," they said. But their eyes were stretched with sadness, because they knew that never again would this really be their sister.

Mira bai ran along beside the cart to the village gate. She had nothing at all to say. At the gate she held Soni's head a moment between her hands, then she turned quickly and walked away, never looking back. Soni, too, looked only ahead.

5

AT LAST THE WEDDING DAY CAME. BUT BEFORE
that day arrived, lonely weeks had to be passed in the household of Soni's prospective father-in-law. During these weeks
she never once saw her lord . . . nor any of the men of the
household. This period had to be spent among the women,
learning the routine of the house.

Once she heard Anand's voice. She was not permitted
to come near when the meals were being served to the men
of the household, but it was her privilege to help prepare
the food, to scour the large brass serving trays and cover them
with freshly washed plantain leaves, to grind on the stone
the twenty spices for the chutney and curry, and to heap the
rice and fruits upon the tray. One day when she had slipped
down the corridor leading to the room where the men ate,
she heard a voice she did not know. It had a singing over-
tone shimmering across it, as if the speaker were pleased
with life . . . as if he knew a secret about it. She stood motionless, listening. Then she realized that Shushilla bai was
standing behind her.

"What are you doing, my child?"

"I have heard a voice."

"Have you the right to listen?"

"No, I have no right," Soni whispered. "But I am helpless."

Shushilla put her hand impulsively on the slim shoulder in a quick caress.

"It is the voice you hope it may be," she said. "If it is good in your ears, that is because God shaped your ears to hold the sound above all others on this earth."

Soni bowed her head in reverent acknowledgment. The two women stood close, savoring the moment; then Shushilla became practical, as the old always feel they must be in the presence of the young.

"So . . . perhaps this will help you learn your work more perfectly?"

"Yes. More perfectly," Soni agreed. But her agreement was automatic, for her whole body was possessed of the sweet ringing of that voice, not too deep, yet manly.

One other glimpse she had of his personality. On the very first morning after she went to the well with Tara bai, the widowed daughter of the house, she discovered something unusual on the veranda where the huge jugs of water were kept. There were two tall tripods of rough logs, with a cross shelf on top and one at the bottom. These were to hold the large cudjahs, one above the other. When she admired the ingenuity of this, Tara said, "That is Anand's work. He brought the idea home from the Mission and built these for us."

Soni would have liked to ask Tara to tell her everything she knew about Anand's work, but she was too shy. So she accepted only what was offered, and that seemed unbearably little.

Tara said, "Anand knows many things he has learned from the Doctor Sahib. Most of them he does not tell us."

"Why?"

"Because he knows my father is not pleased to have him learning such things."

"Even useful things?"

Tara shrugged. Soni could see she did not want to discuss the matter any further, but she persisted. "I have never seen such a clever thing," she said softly. "Nobody in Marvali has thought of it."

"We find it useful," Tara said sullenly.

"Wherever it came from, it is a fine idea."

"My father does not like sahib ideas. He fears they will take Anand away from the old truths."

"Can anything take men away from truth?" Soni asked with all the ardor of ignorance.

"Many things can," Tara said. "At any rate, new ideas and old men don't belong together."

"But what about young men?" Soni asked gently.

Tara looked at her sharply. "You will do well if you make up your mind that Rama knows best what is right for his sons," she said tartly.

The simple remark was like a sharp knife splitting open a melon in one stroke, laying bare the valley of seeds never before seen. The words split open the future in a dazzling vision, showing seeds from which much trouble could grow. But Soni was too young to believe what she saw in that instant.

So she turned back to the cleverly made tripod and touched it with her hand, risking the shamelessness of having the widow see that she was caressing the symbol of Anand.

Through the next weeks, whenever she came near the tripod, her heart swelled, and if it were possible, she touched the wood with a tingling hand, saying to herself, "My lord's hand made this fine thing."

One disquieting event happened close to the wedding time.

A chaprassi came to the house bearing a wedding gift, a fine foreign-made blue blanket with rich fringe. When the parcel arrived Anand was not at home, and his father was delighted with the gift. A card was attached to it, which of course Rama could not read.

"Who could have sent such a handsome wedding gift?" Rama asked. "I think it must be my friend the Mayor of Kalanpur who wishes to honor us."

But when Anand came home and read the card, Soni heard Rama explode in rage.

"Memsahib Mom? What right has a white woman to send you a wedding gift? Could anything be more improper? She is insulting my whole family."

Then Soni heard Anand's voice, trying to placate his father. "No, you do not understand. The gift comes to do us honor, just as any gift honors."

"She is a woman, isn't she? What dealings has she with any man except her husband?"

Anand repeated helplessly, "You do not understand, father. This is a steamer rug she saw me admire once. She has been most thoughtful about giving it, because she knows it will please me."

"Then you are as corrupted as she is," Rama said. "The honorable thing would be to send back the gift and say that you cannot accept anything from a woman."

"That would be inexcusably rude," Anand said. "I must take the gift in the spirit that sent it."

"I am disgusted," Rama said. "I will not have it displayed among the other gifts where my friends can see it. Memsahib Mom indeed!"

In fear Soni repeated the name over to herself. Who was this white woman? Would she be someone who would make trouble for them some day? Naturally her future father-in-law was right to want to reject the gift.

So at last the wedding day arrived. Soni's family all traveled to Vardana to lodge in the house of old Jeveram, Gopal's friend. It was against tradition for the family to be guests in Rama's house.

It seemed like a lifetime to Soni since she had seen her parents, whom she loved so poignantly. But she was grieved that Gopal looked tired and aged. His thick hair had a new stripe of white running through it, and his cheeks were sunken like an old man's. When she spoke of it to Mira bai, her mother said, "No, I have not noticed it. We are both getting old, my child. You see it because you have been away from us." But Soni was not reassured. She *knew* her father looked weary and worried.

On the first morning of the first quarter of the moon, everyone was up early, for a strenuous week was ahead. Rama had arranged for the wedding music, and he had done this to such advantage that he warned Shushilla bai that she must watch the musicians carefully in case they were planning to make up in eating for the concessions in pay they had agreed upon. Such things often happened, so that one came out of a transaction through the wrong door.

The women had been cooking for days, grinding saffron and cleaning quantities of dal, getting heaps of gram flour ready in which to dip spinach leaves, onions and eggplants to fry for the bajjie. The rice had to be colored, and quantities of sweets laid away in readiness. According to custom, all utensils in which the wedding food was cooked, had to be broken afterwards.

Everyone who possibly could claim an invitation expected to appear, dressed either in new clothes, or in freshly washed ones. A wedding measures the honor a family enjoys, and Rama's family was an important one. The last days before

the tamasha began were occupied in personal preparations,
getting in enough saffron paste to adorn both the bride and
the groom, making sure there was plenty of rose water to
spray generously upon the guests. The sisters-in-law spent
two days stringing flowers so that each guest might have a
garland to wear. The guru came every morning to say special
prayers, and every morning he was given an extravagant
backsheesh.

Soni herself lived in a delirium of muttered vows and remembered instructions. She had been preparing so long that
now the time had come she was slightly numb in mind and
body.

In the front courtyard a ceremonial pandal was built of
bamboo posts and mango leaves. It was lined with marigolds
and jasmine, so fragrant the very air seemed to shimmer with
sweetness. Here the bride and groom would sit throughout the ceremonies, veiled from each other but tremblingly
close.

The most intimate women friends of the family had been
chosen to prepare Soni's body, to scent it and oil it and then
to whisper about its beauty. Her long black hair was braided,
then rolled in a knot on the back of her head, with the end
drawn through the center of the braids. On this end was
tied a brilliant string of tassels of red and gold which quivered down her back.

When she bowed her head so that the central part could
be marked with vermilion . . . the sign of a married woman
. . . she felt as if the line were being drawn upon her very
heart. When they put the wide rich petticoat upon her, and
the light red silk choli, her body was trembling.

"Save the trembling until later," one of the women cried
out with lusty merriment. "The groom measures his success
by the trembling."

They draped the red sari around her, admiring the gold border as it fell into place. Her bare feet were cold when they painted the nails and marked bands of color across the instep. Then at the last they gave her Anand's wedding gift, which was a pair of wide silver anklets and the toe ring to match. Now she would have the right to wear a toe ring, for she would be no longer a girl but a married woman.

When she was all adorned for the final ceremony, everyone left her alone for a while. The other women went out to enjoy the festivity, to laugh among themselves and make deliciously improper jokes to each other. A wedding was an occasion for ribaldry. The men enjoyed it among themselves, and the women, usually demure, also made the most of it.

Just before Soni was to appear before the wedding guests, her mother slipped in for a last moment alone with her child.

"Will I be happy?" Soni asked anxiously.

"You have been a happy child . . . so you will be a happy wife," Mira bai said earnestly. "Happiness is a way of doing whatever you must do. You have learned that way."

Soni cried, "Will I find kindness? How can I be sure all will be well in my house?"

"Only the sea knows the depth of the sea; only the sky knows the expanse of the sky. The gods alone know the power of the gods! But this we have been taught . . . 'Truth is our mother, justice our father, pity our husband, respect for others our friend.' Surrounded by such relatives, we have nothing to fear. The gods alone know the future . . . it is given to us piece by piece. Take each piece and make something good of it."

Then they heard the musicians beginning to play, thin merry music dancing through the air like petals or bubbles.

They knew it was time to leave their privacy and go out to the ceremony. Soni looked around in panic, then she put her sari across her face and bowed her head, for a bride must walk in an abject submissiveness. The room was pink through her veil, a bridal pink. Shushilla bai was waiting at the entrance of the women's quarters, and the three women touched hands and then walked out solemnly.

A murmur of delight passed over the guests, then even the children, in their best clothes, were silent. The three veiled figures walked slowly toward the flower-decked pandal where Anand was waiting, his face hidden by a mask of flowers strung like beads on swinging cords.

Soni cried to herself, He is tall . . . my lord is tall and graceful. He will go before me down through eternity, and his shadow will cover me all the way like a garment. His shadow shall be my home. I shall live in the little country of his shadow, and never want to leave it.

She saw his smooth brown hand below the gold embroidery of his purple satin coat. This hand would give her everything; it would punish her when she needed punishment; as reward it would caress her.

Now they two were taken inside the pandal, and seated on the dais, facing the east. Even behind her sari, Soni's eyes were demurely downcast, but she looked beneath her lashes at her lord. Every line of him pleased her. And was she delighting him?

Rama's servant came in with an earthern saucer on which was powdered saffron mixed with quicklime. The two mothers came forward and knelt before their children. Using softened twigs for brushes, they painted the soles of their feet, for now they would walk in new paths. The whole audience began to sing to the pulsing music of drums. Which was louder, drums or hearts? Soni was crying to herself, Is *his* heart beating as mine is?

Then the fathers came in bearing bridal garlands woven richly with white and pink flowers and real silver threads. These they laid around the shoulders of Soni and Anand, and then backed away. Anand rose and was led to the center of the assemblage, where a blanket had been spread on the ground, strewn with flowers and colored rice. Soni came and sat down back to back with him while a long flattering speech was made by the pandit, praising Rama's and Gopal's families and ancestors.

In old-time weddings, this would have ended the first day's ceremony and two more days of praying and parading would follow. But now most weddings are compressed into a long day and night of celebration. The ceremony of the fire was honored by the bride and groom offering nine portions of food, one for each of the planets that govern marriage. Then, tied together by a corner of sari and dhoti, the bride and groom walked around the fire seven times, pelted by rice from the guests. She saw his back, tall and elegant, but not broad, and his slender neck where the dark hair nestled. She kept her head bowed respectfully, but her eyes were tipped up eagerly to watch him.

Gopal's great moment came in the ceremony when he and Rama stood before the assemblage together. Gopal untied from his dhoti the pearl earring and presented it formally. Seeing the admiration and envy in all the eyes around him was almost worth the agony the pearl had cost. Almost, but not quite. The earring would be discussed tonight in every house represented here. The price would be guessed about. It would be said with surprise that Gopal must be a wealthy man. But none of this would lighten the yoke of debt under which Gopal was going to stagger for a long time.

And now at last the bride and groom would see each other

face to face. They knelt opposite each other with a mirror lying on the ground between them. Slowly Anand removed his own mask of flowers. Through her veil, Soni dared not lift her eyes to look at him. Was he handsome? Had he a bold face or a gentle one? She was afraid to know, for all her destiny lay in the expression of that face.

Then he moved aside the veil from her face. His hand touched her cheek accidentally . . . was it an accident? His fingers were cold on her hot flesh. Involuntarily she raised her eyes and in that instant she saw him. Oh, his face was good. The eyes were gazing at her as if already they loved her. The mouth, firm and yet tender, had a lifetime of playfulness written on the lips. It would be a good life ahead.

They gazed so eagerly into each other's face that they almost forgot to drop their eyes to the mirror, where tradition said they must find their first glimpse of each other. A flutter of delight passed across the crowd. Here was a man and woman who would love each other well!

Now the ceremonies were nearly ended. The feasting could begin, and a good thing, too, for the guests were hungry. But first there must be a procession through the streets of the town. Soni and Anand must walk at the head of the parade, with torches and bands and singing. The whole town of Vardana, even the poorest citizens, would come out from their lanes, and enjoy a glimpse of the beauty and fun. At many houses refreshments were offered, which good manners demanded they should sample.

When they returned to Rama's house, the feast was ready. A dazzling quantity of food, first for the men and then for the women, with the bride and groom, now free to be alone, sitting to one side and watching. No food was offered to them because food might only excite them more than they could bear. A couple so young and handsome surely needed no ordinary food on such a night!

While the others feasted, they sat silent. But now they looked at each other freely; they could not help looking. Their flushed faces, only a few feet apart, smiled, one with timidness and one with joyous boldness. At last they talked in dreamy whispers.

"I would love you even if you were not beautiful," Anand said. "But you are lovely. If I were a poet I could tell you how lovely you are."

"I am a poor-looking thing," she said shyly. "It is your goodness that makes you think . . . whatever you think."

"My sister Tara said I would be pleased . . . but I didn't know *how* pleased," he said excitedly. Then he was momentarily shy. "And how about me . . . do you think I'll be bearable to you?"

"You are my lord," she said with dignity. Then she said in a soft little murmur, "But even besides that. . . ." She could not say any more, and drew her sari across her face and he could not tell whether she was shivering or laughing. Quickly he moved away the sari and he saw her little round face broken up into smiles and dimples.

"You're laughing? At me?"

"How could I laugh at my lord?" she asked, sobering immediately. "I'm laughing for happiness."

"You're tired," he said in a whisper. "I could hold you in my arms and let you sleep. I wish it could be tonight."

Now she *did* need her sari to conceal her shyness, but he held it lightly and would not let her face escape and hide itself. Her face was all he could have tonight. But it was enough, for it was loveliness itself.

The moon was growing pale, and thin as a wisp of smoke in the sky, for the dawn was coming.

The next few days passed in a dream. Gopal's family went home; the wedding gifts, still collected in the big family room behind the veranda, were admired over and over. The blue fringed blanket which had come from Memsahib Mom was not on display among the honorable gifts. Soni wondered fearfully what had become of it. Had it been returned to the white woman? Would she ever know what lay behind the unwelcome gift, which her new husband had defended so passionately?

The beggars came to ask for the remains from the wedding feast. Everything about the tamasha was discussed down to the tiniest item and detail. And at last the household looked as a household should, with all the grown sons married, each with a wife to serve her husband.

Now that Soni did not have to be kept separate from the men of the household, the whole family sat together in the courtyard at the end of the day, talking and joking. Govind's wife Gaura bai and Ghulum's young lazy wife Rukma sat close to their husbands, watchful in case one reached for a piece of fruit or a sweet beyond his hand. Soni sat next to her mother-in-law, and Anand, exuberantly pleased with everything, wasn't too far away.

At mealtime now, Soni served Anand with the other wives. She cooked his curry especially for him, and he told his brothers that he could detect the excellent smell of it among all the other cooking fragrances as he came down the lane to their house. The dal she made of lentils and spices was as smooth as syrup, he said, and he advised his brothers to order their wives to ask her what secret she had. With serious faces they encouraged him to boast about his new wife's cooking, and then they teased him unmercifully.

"The boy's in love," they said, "and as yet he's sampled only her cooking! What will it be like later?"

At mealtime the men sat in a ring on the floor of the main room, each with his shining tray before him, each tray set out with little dishes of condiments and pickles, with mounds of rice and curry heaped between dishes and chapattees. They ate with deft fingers, and after the meal each husband was brought a basin, and water was poured on his fingers by a beaming wife. It was not good manners to allow food to creep up past the first joint of each finger, and Rama's sons ate tidily.

Soni and Anand did no more than smile at each other, for husbands and wives . . . unless they are old and finished with love . . . do not speak together in daylight. But as she put his tray down before him, her soft lashes brushing her shy cheek, he couldn't help touching her hand with one brown finger. He couldn't help making her look up at him sometimes, and then they would catch their breath for a spinning moment.

One afternoon shortly after the wedding, Shushilla bai called her away from the household work.

"It is time, my child," she said simply. Soni knew that behind the small sentence lay tradition and the sanction of their two horoscopes. She walked behind her mother-in-law through the large central room, then past Rama's quarters, which he and Sushilla bai shared with the two youngest boys, then along a narrow hallway to a new room that had lately been built on the house. She had never before entered this place. The only furniture was a hemp-strung cot. It was a small room but it was big enough. A window, with a mat to cover it, was high up where the wall joined the ceiling. On a peg driven into the wall hung Anand's white pughri, and in the corner stood a private cudjah for the new couple to use.

With alarm she saw the handsome foreign-made steamer

rug which had caused such an outburst of anger when it arrived. There it hung across the clothes pole, in the place of honor. Memsahib Mom . . . Soni still did not know who she was and why she had sent this handsome wedding gift. She dropped her eyes shyly and did not glance at it again.

But the most important thing in the room . . . the signature that marked it as belonging to Anand . . . was a shelf of books. Soni stood and gazed up at this group, intuitively knowing that it meant the difference between Anand and all the other men of the world in which she lived. Books. Never in her whole life had she held a book in her hand. Would she ever hold a book . . . except to carry it to her lord, except to clasp it to her heart because it belonged to him?

Shushilla bai stood silently beside her, almost sensing what she was thinking. Almost fearing what the books might mean someday to this new wife. Then the older woman stirred, to break the moment's hold on both of them.

"It is a good room," Shushilla bai said softly. "But nobody can build happiness into a place except the people who live in it."

"We will build it," Soni said staunchly.

"My son is a spoiled boy," the mother said affectionately, almost boastfully. "He will expect everything from his woman."

"He has a right to expect everything," Soni said sternly. Then she threw herself into the older woman's arms, and whispered, "But I am scared to death. Suppose I cannot please him? I'll run away and let wild animals eat me."

"You'll be eaten, all right," her mother-in-law said dryly. "But it will not be by wild animals." Then her thin old face broke into ripples of mirth. "I wish I were standing in your sari right now. It is empty work being an old woman."

Soni hugged her silently, but she could not imagine in any slightest way how it must feel to be old and empty.

"Come, we'll bring your possessions into your place," Shushilla said. "You must make the room your own, the way you want it to be."

Soni carried in, first of all, the sutherungee she had woven believing it was for her father. Then she brought in her little wicker basket with her wedding sari and the red silk choli folded within. Her ordinary saris she put in a neat pile on a little rush mat, and on top of them she put her comb and the tulasi twigs with which she brushed her teeth. Their possessions now were housed together intimately. If a stranger looked into the room . . . as, of course, no stranger ever would . . . he would say to himself, "Here lives a man and his worthless servant who loves him more than anything on earth."

After dinner, when the family gathered in the courtyard, everyone had a twinkling of suppressed excitement and mischievousness, and there were quips between the brothers which Soni did not quite understand. But she understood enough to blush. Nobody had told her marriage would be like this, a thing for fun and playing. It had been all solemnity at the wedding . . . or almost all. Would love, when she knew it fully, be woven of solemnity and fun? It would be woven of everything, she answered herself, for it would be everything in her life.

The women began singing, humming first under their breath, which is the right way to begin a song, and then bursting out in full happy tones. They sang the soft songs of the grain fields, the cool songs of the rice paddy, and then, as the men joined in, they sang of the days of toil, of harvest, of thanksgiving. The little group was caught in a net of happiness, as a true family.

The courtyard was quite bright tonight, and every object was standing on its own pedestal of shadow . . . the tripod, which had once been all of Anand she had to love, the charpai where Rama took his rest, the grinding stones sitting outside the cookhouse door looked like bright drawings in chalk against the dark. Everything was strange and beautiful, and Anand's face was sharply carved by the shadows. She kept her own face out of the light, so she could watch him all she pleased.

"My sons will look like their father," she said joyously to herself. "And may the first one be planted in my womb this very night." Would the gods be good enough to her to make that happen? She had asked it in her pujahs every night and every morning since she came to this house.

At last Rama stood up and fondled the heads of his two small sons, Dhuni and Dhuki. "Come," he said. "This happy night is not for such as us, my boys."

The older sons rose, too, and the sisters-in-law scrambled quickly to their feet. Everyone's face was alert and yet diffident, full of knowledge. They went into their own quarters, dragging their blue shadows after them. Only Shushilla bai was left with her two beloved children.

She reached over and took a hand of each. "When I went to my lord for the first time, my mother had taught me a promise. Shall I say it for you?"

They both nodded shyly, without a word.

" 'My heart shall dwell in your heart as a tiny bird lives in a tree. And if the tree ever shakes the bird from its branches, the bird will perish.' "

Soni said in a whisper, "My heart is such a bird." The old woman joined her palms and bowed her head before them, and it was, of course, the only time in her life that she did a namaska to her children. Then, quiet as a shadow, she slipped into the house.

Anand stood up and drew Soni to her feet beside him. "We have a place of our own," he said with dignity.

He strode ahead of her through the big family room and down the narrow passage, and she, on silent bare feet, crept along behind him, wearing his shadow like a garment. Wearing his shadow now for the first time, as she had dreamed of wearing it down through eternity. The new room had a tide of moonlight welling through it. Outside in the sheltering jacaranda tree, a bird stirred sleepily, spilling a few notes from its throat.

At the sound Anand looked up, and then opened his arms wide as the branches of a tree, and Soni, knowing he was half playfully, half seriously pantomiming his mother's sentiment, crept within them.

"I am your tree," he said, "and you must never venture from my branches."

"No, my lord," she said in her dreamy murmur.

He caught her up close to him then, and after a moment their two faces were lying flat like lotus flowers cupping the moonlight.

"Are you afraid of me?" he whispered.

"Yes, I am afraid. But I am delighted with you, also."

His body was trembling, and the look on his face was sheer ecstasy. It was a new face she never had seen, a face that no one else ever *would* see. This is his love-face, she said to herself, and timidly she put up her hand and touched it. Then she brought her own face nearer to his, and touched the corner of his lips with her mouth.

A tide of sweetness, bright as the tide of moonlight, came pouring through her. It was neither light nor music, and yet it was like both. Her whole body seemed to ache and glow, as if a million invisible blossoms were opening.

6

IN MID–JUNE, BEFORE THE MONSOON BROKE, Rama called his family together.

"I saw two crows fighting on our roof this morning," he said. "They were carrying away bundles of straw pulled from the palm leaves. That means we must put on a new roof, if the old palms are rotted so that crows can tear them apart. We must get it on before the rain comes."

These days, everyone's face was beaded with perspiration, and the children were languid and fretful. But hot as it was now, this weather was mild compared to what would be upon them in a few weeks. The ground was parched and brittle, and a white powder shrouded the trees and the weary shrubs.

Govind said, "Some of the walls must be reinforced, too. I've been meaning to speak about it."

"We'll all stay home tomorrow and work together," Rama said.

"All except me," Anand had to remind him. "At the clinic we're getting the same kind of repairs done."

Rama frowned as he always did when Anand's work was mentioned. How long would he have to endure the indignity of having his son go away each day to do the bidding of white sahibs? He would take things into his own hands one of these days, and simply command the boy to give up his nonsense. He would instruct Shushilla to tell Soni what she was expected to do about influencing her husband. From long yet unacknowledged experience, he knew how much a man's woman could change what went on in his head.

The brothers were discussing the monsoon; most of the wise old people in the village said it was going to be a tremendous one.

Rama said, "The omens point to big rains. Any house that hasn't a pukka roof will melt down to mud again."

"The government inspectors are saying the same thing about the monsoon," Anand said.

Again Rama looked annoyed at this. "Naturally," he said shortly. "Who are the government inspectors? Babus . . . Anglo-Indians, most of them. Men who live their weak little lives on paper! What is paper? We work with *earth* . . . the wisdom of earth. So now their papers tell them what the sky is going to do!"

"It is a great and useful science, Father . . . to be able to predict the weather."

"The gods have written their intentions across the heavens . . . and not in the silly writings of men!"

Anand shrugged noncommittally, for he could not disagree openly with his father.

"The astrologers have announced it," Rama said. "The third night of the new moon will bring the monsoon." He pointed to a place in the sky above the peepul tree. "When the moon reaches that spot in five nights, it will have a dark circle around the glow. That brings the monsoon. You'll see." Then he looked fiercely at Anand. "My father and my grandfather taught me that . . . and they did not have to ask what they needed to know from any government inspectors."

Early the next morning everyone went to work, making

the house a bulwark that neither wind nor rain could destroy. The women all went out to the bazaar and brought back huge baskets of dried dung cakes to be stored away for the cooking fires. Enough for two months, since Rama believed the monsoon would be a long one. The men cleared piles of dead wood in the nearby dhak jungle, and Yasin, the servant, made trip after trip, carrying it home on his head in towering bundles. All this was stored in a special shed near the north veranda.

The new roof was put on with the help of village workmen, and the walls were carefully inspected for any weak places or cracks. The breathlessness of a coming weather event lay over all Vardana. This would be more than just a storm; this would be the gods shaking their fists at mankind, to remind them where power lies.

A few nights before the monsoon broke, Anand came home from the clinic with a mysterious bundle. He slipped into the house without being seen, and hid the bulky package down behind the wicker basket where Soni kept her wedding sari. The bundle was wrapped in newspaper . . . the first Soni had ever seen. She was as much interested in the newspaper as she was in what it concealed.

"What are the tiny pictures all over it?" she asked eagerly. "My eye cannot tell what kind of pictures they are."

"It is printing," Anand said. "To the eye they are not pictures. But they make pictures in the mind."

She shook her head in bewilderment. But he said gently, "I will teach you so that your mind also will see the pictures."

"Is that reading? Of course!" Now she was excited about the inscrutable little marks. She looked at each eagerly, as if she would wrench its meaning from it by sheer desire.

"You won't speak of it to the family," he warned.

"Certainly not, my lord."

"You won't mention the bundle either."

"What is in the bundle?"

"It's my preparation against the monsoon. They gave it to me at the clinic."

Just at the time Rama had predicted, the blue circle around the moon appeared, and at the time he anticipated, it vanished.

"As I told you," Rama said complacently. "We shall have such a bad monsoon, that we may even suffer a drought and famine afterwards. The floods bring drought and the drought brings famine."

He looked at Anand, and for once Anand fell into the trap.

"Someday we shall not wait helplessly as we do now," he said. "We'll know what is cause and what is effect, and we shall prevent the bad effects."

"And how shall we do that?" Rama asked haughtily.

"We'll build dams and irrigation systems, to save up the water to be used when we need it. Water need not be a dangerous weapon attacking the land. Rain should be the servant of our fields, doing what we tell it to do."

Rama's face was darkened by anger now. "That I should hear such words from my son!"

"I didn't think them up myself, Father," Anand said humbly. "I've only listened and learned what the engineers are planning.

"There will be nineteen million acres of land irrigated by the great dams our government is building," Anand went on. "The Konya Dam alone will irrigate thousands of acres. The dams save up the water, and then feed it out as it is needed. I've read about it . . . I've read what the great scientists will accomplish for India."

"Reading!" Rama cried furiously. "I curse the day I let you learn to read! My son! . . . forgetting the wisdom of his fathers, and prattling modern nonsense!"

Anand said, "It isn't nonsense, Father. It is what is going to help India. Some day India's tired, parched land will be rich and fruitful all the year. All this is to help India."

"Will it help India to forget her gods? Will the gods stop decreeing their will, because some modern Westerners have brought blasphemous ideas to India? They will not! What the gods send comes to man for a purpose. Those who understand the lessons brought by the elements are the wise ones."

The older brothers sat silent. When Rama was not present, they sometimes asked Anand tentatively about the things he read. But they knew that it was contraband information, and the last thing they wanted was to displease the head of their household.

The whole family was silenced now, shivering in Rama's rage. Anand went over and stood before his father. "I am sorry I spoke too freely," he said contritely.

"If you think freely, you might as well speak freely," Rama said. "I might as well know what kind of rebellion goes on in my house."

"Learning is always rebellion, in a way, Father," Anand said. "Every bit of new truth discovered is revolutionary to what was believed before."

"Truth . . . since when was truth a modern invention?" Rama cried. "Truth is as old as the moon and the rain. No clever sahibs had to bring it to us as a fancy gift. We have had it always!"

There was no more to be said, and Anand hung his head.

"Now my house will retire," Rama said with dignity. "And tomorrow you will not see a dawn. For the monsoon will break in the night." As he made the prediction, it seemed most unlikely that it would come true, for the moon was

bright and the sky clear. Soni wondered how the proud old
man would face the morning. Surely he would have a bad
time finding a way to explain the sunshine. He would have
to consult the astrologers again . . . they would have to explain away the error.

But in the night, she was awakened by a blow of thunder
that seemed to split the very sky in two. And then, as if the
bottoms had fallen out of the wells of heaven, rain came
down in solid sheets. Walls of rain shut around the house
and closed out the rest of the world.

Anand, his chin against her brow, said softly, "I'm glad.
It's just a coincidence that he should have picked the very
night . . . but I'm glad. It would hurt him to be wrong. A
man so proud must not be shamed."

The rain was drumming down so loudly that one could
barely distinguish it from the thunder. Lightning sprouted
across the sky like flashing vines, seen, then gone.

"Thunder is male," Anand said. "And the lightning is
female. The elements are quarreling now, like fierce lovers."

"Not like lovers, surely," Soni protested.

"Like sky-sized lovers," he said, "not like little ones who
fit together as we do."

They fitted together, every surface touched and satisfied,
every nerve pleased and singing. Then they lay quiet, listening to the drums of the rain, growing wilder in tempo.

"We could shout and no one could hear us," Anand said,
suddenly made exuberant by the violence of the night. "I'd
like to shout something outrageous. I'm tired of saying what
I'm supposed to say."

She could feel that desire quivering in him, and she knew
it would not be quenched by any small symbolic defiance.
Because he was helpless to protest against the unanswerable-
ness of his father's old traditions, he was glorying in the

outrageous violence of the rain and the thunder. She felt a primitive delight mounting in him. The monsoon would wreck and ruin; it would carve its way brutally through the little defenses of the village. And yet, because he himself was so gentle and sympathetic, he couldn't help feeling a frantic exhilaration in its wildness. She did not know how to tell him that she understood all this.

"I hate the chains we are dragging around," he said fiercely. "I'm going to break them for us, Soni. For both of us."

"I have no chains," she said gently. "Only the lovely chains which bind me to you."

He shook his head almost angrily. "No. You are shackled in your mind and in your body. You have worn chains so long you don't even feel them. I hate them. And I'll break them. You'll see."

A moment before she had felt close to him, knowing intuitively how he felt. But now they were desolately apart. She was frightened suddenly, as if something more irresistible than tempestuous rain and wind were beating against the house.

Anand was sitting up now; it was so dark that she could not see him, but she knew how his face was looking, tight and angry at his own helplessness. She put out her hand and tried to draw him down beside her.

"My lord. . ." she said.

His face was above hers now, his whole body quivering with what had been dammed up in him for years. Cruelly he imitated her gentle voice. " 'My lord,' " he said. "You cannot even call me by my name! That would be inauspicious. You must never speak my name as long as you live!"

"Oh no, my lord."

He shook her shoulders angrily. "Well, I want to hear you say my name. I want to hear it on your lips. What do you think about that?"

She was trembling so that she could not speak. A tear fell on his hand, and that made him quiet. Quiet and gentle. He held her close to him, as if she were a child.

"I didn't mean to frighten you," he said. "My sweet, stop trembling. Stop crying."

She could not stop, but she patted his face to show him that she was no longer afraid. He sat up again and gathered her into his arms, so that she lay across his knees. He rocked her back and forth while he tried to think of words that would make her understand the necessity that was seething in him.

He began telling her about the government school he had gone to, and how his mind had been opened into a world he hadn't known existed. He told her about the teachers, one a tall very dark Madrasi in rough, homespun, khadi clothes, who knew what India might become, once she was awake.

Then he told her about the clinic where he worked. He wanted to tell her about Memsahib Mom, but somehow there weren't words enough for that yet. He would have to tell her gradually. . . .

A long time passed while he talked and never had they been so close. Their hearts, not excited like lovers but stilled like rhyming friends, were beating in unison. Then suddenly his heart began to race madly. For he wanted something desperately.

"I do want to hear you say my name," he said again. "Let me hear you say it, Soni."

"I cannot," she said. "Something terrible would happen to us."

"I promise you, it would not happen," he said with passion fiercer than the passion of his body. "You cannot know what it would mean to me."

"Why, my lord?"

"You have given me your body. I want you to give me

your mind." As he said the words, he knew that "give" was not the verb he meant. Quite the opposite. He wanted her to give it to him only so he could give it back to her. How could he tell her that? It was too revolutionary to be said . . . for many years. But some day he would say it to her, and she would love the thought as he loved it.

But now, for tonight . . . he must help her take the first step. He must help her speak his name.

"I cannot," she said again. "I am afraid."

He seized her mouth with his masterful one, and she felt his heart thundering under her breast. Then, as in the tumescent sky over them, she felt the swift lightning of her own desire match the maleness of that thundering heart.

He let her lips slip away from him. He put his hand on her trembling breast and waited.

"Listen, my wife. I want you to say my name. I have a safe and secret place where you can say it." Irresistibly he caught her mouth again and imprisoned it gently, forming as he had promised, a symbolic little world, heaven and earth.

"Anand," she said, "Anand. . . ."

7

THE MONSOON CREATED A NEW WORLD, AND a new way the household lived. A holiday spirit reigned, for the storm made all normal activity impossible. In the mornings the men slept as late as they pleased, and after their leisurely breakfast they sat around together chewing pan and talking by the hour. There had not been as much time in a day since the last monsoon. They brought each other up to date on all the little incidents and events they had not had time to tell. The women, too, sat together cozily, and Rukma, the lazy, enjoying one, wished this life could go on forever.

Hera bai, the ancient widow who was Rama's sister, grumbled as usual, but one could listen to her nagging with a clear conscience, for there was no need to scurry around pretending to be working. Tara, the younger widow, knitted. Both widows, naturally, were the hardest working of all the women in the household. They wore their coarse white cotton saris unprotestingly, and when they moved there was no pleasant faint jingling of bangles or anklets. Hera bai's sari covered her hideously shorn head. One did not glance at either widow unless it was absolutely necessary, for they were unpleasant sights. Being widows and hence half-persons, they had no ages. But Hera bai had a wrinkled hawklike face, stamped with misery and discontent, and Tara, though certainly much younger and with an unshaven head, was fast growing to look like her aunt.

Soni had never before known any widow well, and she often thought her heart would break with pity when she saw these women dragging out their wretched days in drudgery, with no faint gleam of hope that their status ever would be changed. In old times, she knew that widows had been burned with their husbands' bodies on the burial pyre; that cruel custom of suttee was less cruel, she thought, than this bitter living that was not alive. What would it be like to be a woman whose master was not present to bring the light of life to her? Now that she had her own tall lord beside her, she could not imagine living a day without him.

When the household awoke on the first morning of the rains, Rama was smugly triumphant. More than his personal authority had been vindicated; the superiority of the old established lore over the shifting new theories had been proved. He waited expectantly for Anand to speak humbly, and of course the young man did.

"I hope you will remember this happening," Rama said, accepting the apology graciously offered. "The wisdom of the earth will never fail us, if we listen to it, and read its language in the planets."

Anand said, "There *is* the wisdom of the earth, Father. But there is also the hunger of the mind. Both are from the gods, I think."

"Then the gods must satisfy both earth and hunger," Rama said, "and neither must go whoring after dazzling new ways that forget the gods."

When it was time for Anand to leave the house to make the hazardous trip to the Mission, everyone had advice to give.

"Carry dry clothes wrapped in banana leaves," Shushilla

bai said. "That is the only way to work comfortably today."

Govind said mischievously, "I suppose the clinic might let you sleep on one of their floors, as you did last year throughout the rains. Why don't you ask them, Anand?"

Anand said with dignity, "We have not as much space as we had last year. A shipment of supplies is standing in the hall now. I shall come home at the usual time."

Then he went boldly to his own quarters, and came back dressed in a strange-looking black garment. It looked more like a small circular building than a piece of wearing apparel; a top piece fitted over the head, and made a sort of sloping roof from the shoulders. It was so stiff that it crackled as Anand moved.

Everyone gazed in amazement, and Govind cried, "I know what it is . . . they call it a raincoat!"

Ghulum said, "It looks like the black armor the Moguls wore when Genghis Khan came swooping down. I've seen pictures."

The two younger boys, Dhuni and Dhuki, crept inside the huge tentlike garment, and this annoyed Anand, who shoved them out with dignity.

"The Doctor Sahib gave it to me the other day. Everyone wears such things out in the world."

"Out in the world!" Rama said disgustedly. "Here it is beneath a man's dignity to wear such a thing."

Shushilla bai said, "It will keep him dry. Our Anand catches bad colds much too easily. I'm glad he has it."

"No matter how absurd he looks!" Rama said.

Anand did look somewhat absurd, especially when he wrapped his blanket tightly around the whole creation, because he couldn't bear to get the new garment wet immediately. He pulled aside the chatia from the front door and ventured out. Everyone ran to the door to watch him.

"The news will spread over the town like ants," Rama said. "By night everyone will be watching to see him come home under the silly foreign gimcrack." He shook his head disgustedly. Anand, a pillar with a watchtower above, was going down the lane, first mincing along, and then striding, not certain which was the better gait.

The sisters-in-law were covering their mouths with their hands, knowing that laughter would offend Soni. Suddenly then, they saw that Soni's mouth, too, was covered. Her eyes were dancing with mirth. "If it were not my lord, I should be laughing," she said.

"You *are* laughing!" Rukma cried accusingly. "We might as well all laugh, because he is very funny."

But Soni scampered out of hearing. She put her head into a dark storage closet until she could compose herself. Suppose an evil spirit should see her, doubled up with laughter at her lord!

The days went on, walled in by the torrents of rain. The thunder piled up like a dark sea, and rolled across the sky in deafening waves. The wind screamed in rage and shook the trees like twigs. When it was necessary to buy food, Govind and Ghulum, with blankets over their heads, went to the bazaar. Most of the bazaar was vacated, with a sea of mud shifting around the stalls. But a few hardy merchants had rigged up crude wooden awnings over their booths to keep out some of the rain.

Sometimes village men would come to Rama's house, bringing their conversation and their beedis to smoke or Madras snuff to enjoy. On other days Rama and his sons would go visiting. But the women did not visit; actually they had plenty of work to do, drying the blankets and clothes on poles put up in the rooms, and trying to keep the household as normal as possible.

Now that the rains were engulfing everything, hot steaminess was everywhere. Mold formed before one's very eyes; the sandals had webs of green woven mysteriously along the angle between soles and sides. Chapattees were festered with the sprawling mold, and even one's hair, usually sweet, was rancid and never quite dry.

But outdoors, everything was brilliant and shining. The trees had sprung to life again after their crackling dustiness. Every leaf was enameled with light and shimmer, and after even a few days, grass and lovely unnamed weeds were springing up in every crevice. The dogs, who never belonged to anybody, ran around looking for something to eat, with their mangy hair painted flat against their bony bodies. Sometimes a family, eager to make some connection with the outdoors after the days of being shut in, would throw them a scrap of food. But usually they shifted for themselves, and the shifting was poor indeed.

Soni throught of Marvali during this onslaught. How were they faring in Gopal's less sturdy house? Had their roof held up? She remembered once that the hut next to theirs had collapsed in a monsoon, walls of mud slithering down upon the neighbors and burying every possession they had. It had been horrible to see the walls melting like chocolate. Gopal and Mira bai had taken the stricken family into their small house. . . .

There was much discussion about when the monsoon would end. The rival astrologers did not agree. It had gone on for nearly a month now, with very few pauses. The skies were battered and bruised looking with heavy bluish-black and sulphur-colored clouds hanging almost in festoons. There was plenty of rain still to come, Rama said. Then after it stopped there would be at least two more weeks lost from work while the fields dried out. Rain could not be considered pure blessing; a farmer must be patient under its punishing lashes. He could not live without it; and he could not live with it, Rama said, grumbling in a whisper. But he never said such things aloud for fear the gods might punish such audacity.

For Soni the days were filled with family, but the nights were filled with Anand. The rain built them a small snug privacy within the larger privacy it built for the whole house.

During the daytime, she filled many little coconut-shell lamps with oil, and hid them in their quarters so that Anand could read to her through the night. As soon as they were alone, he took a book lovingly from the shelf, and sat cross-legged on the charpai. Timidly she would come and sit beside him, and he would encircle her with one arm, while he steadied the opened book with the other hand. Then his voice, melodious and rich, would build a bridge for both their minds to run across into a new and enchanted world. Soni loved the stories from the Upanishads, and especially she adored the story of the creation.

In the beginning, there was the One alone. Seeing nothing but himself when he looked around, he said "This is I," so "I" became his name forever. Consequently to this day a man thinks of himself first as "I," and he must be taught some other name. But to himself he is "I," for that is the name of the One.

Because he was alone, he felt no delight. But he was large enough to be two, so he allowed himself to fall into two, so he never again would be lonely. From that moment rose up husband and wife. They were each half a shell, so they embraced to fill up the emptiness. And from that embrace, men were born.

She thought to escape him, so she became a cow. And immediately, for that reason, he became a bull and embraced her. Thus cows were born. She became a mare and a stallion embraced her, and one-hoofed animals were born. She became a ewe, and he, a ram, embraced her. In this way, the One became everything that exists in pairs, down to the tiniest ants.

At last he had made a complete creation. And all of it had come from the One, and was the One. He said, "Since it is all I, is there anything to fear from it?" And the answer, for everything in creation, was "No." For fear can spring only from a second, and all was One. So all creatures, when they know they are part of the One, have nothing to fear. Can you feel hatred from yourself? No. And all is Thyself.

When Anand finished reading this story to Soni for the third time he said, "I read this story once to Memsahib Mom. She loved it as you do."

Soni held her breath, and then she asked bravely, "Memsahib Mom. Who is she?"

"Don't you know? She gave us this beautiful steamer rug for our wedding gift. She is the wife of the Doctor Sahib. . . I work for them, Soni. She has taught me more good things than anyone else on earth. And in exchange I have taught her a little Marathi."

So now she knew about Memsahib Mom, and the secret worry melted away. "And you read to her? Can't she read?"

"She reads English, of course. But not our Marathi. So sometimes I read to her and translate. So she will understand our people better. I read her this story once. And she told me something the Christians have in their Bible."

"What was it?"

"When Moses asked God who He was, God said 'I am.' And when Moses couldn't understand what that meant God said 'I am *that* I am.' Maybe God even pointed to Moses and to Moses' little donkey. Anyway I think He meant that He is every *I am* on earth, just as *we* know God is."

After the reading, they always talked. Then they would not sit side by side on the charpai, but knee to knee so they could watch each other's face in the flickering light from the coconut lamp. They would talk until the night was old and the day was new. Neither had dreamed that talking could be so sweet. Anand dredged up many lost and forgotten days from the deep wells in his mind, and spread these before Soni so that she could know everything that had brought him to what he was this day.

Very early in this talking, she had said diffidently, "I, too, have seen things that you might like to hear about."

"What things, my little love?" he had asked in surprise.

"I have been to Mulkapoor."

"To Mulkapoor! Why, that is thirty miles from here!"

"I saw a railroad train," she said. "And there was a white woman wearing a big hat. . . . It had flowers on it. I saw her face very clearly. It was *not* white."

"No . . . their faces are pink, or sometimes yellow. Many colors, I've noticed," Anand agreed.

"Then why do they call themselves the white race . . . and say everyone else has colored skin?"

Anand laughed at her vehemence. "Perhaps color, like beauty, is in the eye of the beholder," he said kissing her cheek. But then he grew serious so she would know he respected her observation.

"Their faces are not different from our faces." he said. "I have seen a great many of them. They are fatter than our faces . . . the bones seem buried deeper under the flesh."

"Our moneylenders have fat faces," Soni said playfully. "Nobody else can afford such fat faces."

"So you have been to Mulkapoor? I had no idea you ever had done such a thing." He was not sure he was entirely pleased with this information, which overshadowed his own experience.

"I have not been so far from home," he said wistfully. "How did it happen that you, a mere girl, should have such a trip?"

"The gods gave it to me," she said demurely, "for a special purpose."

"What purpose?" he asked, almost sulkily.

"So that I could tell my lord about it," she said. "We knew you were educated . . . and Gopal thought I should know *something* that would be interesting for you to hear about."

Anand leaned closer in the rain-noisy darkness to look into her eyes and make sure this was the truth she was telling. Then he laughed with pleasure. "You know many things that I find interesting, my small sweet one."

"I am ignorant and stupid," she said. "I know only how to love you."

"I want you to learn everything I know . . . and much more besides," he said excitedly. "I want to teach you to read, Soni bai. I want to teach you English."

He said the words in italics, and now at last he had told her his great secret intention. She was almost stunned at the daring of him.

"How could we manage such a thing?" she whispered as if someone might hear.

"I don't know yet," he said. "I think about it all the time. Listen. I want . . . we both want . . . our son to be born out of your body. I want to give a son to you, so that you give him back to me. And I want another kind of child to born from us both."

"What kind of child?" she asked in bewilderment. Surely he was not saying he wanted a daughter? No man wanted a daughter. The gods gave them, but they were not wanted.

"A child from our minds, whose name will be 'knowledge.' I want to plant it in your mind, as I plant our son in your body. Then I want you to give birth to that mind-child. We will let it grow between us. . . . Can you understand what I am trying to tell you?"

She nodded slowly, but it was more in obedience to his wish than in real understanding.

"I want a soul to be born in you, Soni."

"I don't know how to make a soul be born," she faltered.

"We will make it together," he said ardently. "Our son will be born from your opened body . . . and your soul shall be born from your opened mind."

"Will it be *my* soul?" she asked wonderingly. He took her face between his hands and kissed it. "Yes, it will be you. You freed from the ignorance and bondage of being a woman."

"A woman's worth is only the serving of her lord," she reminded him.

"No. I have learned better. My Memsahib Mom has shown me."

Then she shrank back, knowing that they were on dangerous ground. "Your father would be angry if he knew what we were saying," she said.

"My father will have to be angry when the time comes," he said firmly. "I have found myself, Soni. And now I am going to find you for yourself."

She shook her head in mute contradiction. She was in a very bad dilemma. She did not know how she could be loyal to the family, and also follow her lord wherever he wanted to lead her. The lines Mira bai had taught her rang in her mind:

When your husband leaves you behind, you must not leave the house. And if he requests you to accompany him, you must always follow.

A blaze of new meaning lighted the words. She had thought they applied literally to staying in one's house, or walking out of it. The words meant something infinitely more. Terrible and dangerous. . . .

8

NEARLY SIX WEEKS HAD PASSED AND THE
monsoon was not finished. But it was drawing toward its end,
for the lightning and thunder came at closer intervals now,
and after the thunder the sky always cleared for a while, and
people ran out and capered in the freshness.

Rama and his sons talked by the hour about their plans for
new crops. Govind took his peace in his hands by suggesting
that, through Anand, they might consult the Mission agri-
cultural institute about some of the new methods of cotton
planting. Rama, of course, was outraged by this, but Govind
had his argument prepared.

"We might as well get some advantage out of the boy. We
do all the family work, while he brings us in only a few rupees
a month from his silly job. Surely the job owes something
else to our kutumb. Let them pay, I say."

"What good is payment if it is only in worthless advice?"
Rama asked rhetorically, but his eyes were gleaming with
dark inquisitiveness.

"Let's hear what they have to say for themselves," Govind
said, pushing home the advantage he saw opening around his
father's curiosity. "This kind jumps into deep water and we
must keep them from drowning themselves."

Rama nodded, delighted that a face-saving attitude had
been found. So that night they suggested that Anand discuss

their situation with the agriculturist who had come from some university in the United States, an elderly fat man who had made a joke of himself in one of the neighboring villages by saying to its best farmer, "There are only three things standing between your soil and fine crops."

"What three?"

"The first is nitrate."

"And what is the second?"

"Nitrate."

"And the third?"

"Nitrate."

They called him, inevitably, Sahib Nitrate. But that did not prevent some of the canniest of them from quietly buying what they could afford of the chemicals, and secretly plowing them into their weary soil.

Behind his back they laughed at the sahib's terms. For instance, when he fertilized a field he called that "feeding it"; they knew that all proper farmers spoke of "strengthening the land."

He had distributed dozens of iron plows to take the place of the old wooden plows they had used for centuries. No question that the iron plows did the work faster and better, but some people in the villages said that the iron plow would eventually replace women, so what gain would that be? If plowing went too fast, the extra women in a household might have no work, and then who would feed them? Would the professor's nitrate solve *that* problem?

Another of Sahib Nitrate's vagaries that amused the villagers was his notion about seeds. When the crops were in, he thought a family should winnow out the very fattest and best grains, and lay them aside. Naturally people wanted to enjoy their best as food. But the professor said the best should be kept for planting again. As if anyone knew whether they were the best or worst by the time the planting day finally came! They were simply the *only* by then, so naturally they became the best.

But the point about which nobody could forgive him, was the cow dung. Everyone knows that shane diluted with water makes a cleansing and purifying covering for floors and walls. No family is too poor to take that precaution as often as possible in their homes. But Professor Nitrate said this was a gross waste of good fertilizer. If you listened to him, you'd put every speck you could find on your land. He never realized how much prestige he lost by that jolly insistence of his. If a man were completely blind to the basic importance of the gifts of the cow, how could you believe anything else he said?

But in spite of all the arguments against him, there was no answering the sturdier jowari he grew on his demonstration acre in the middle of the Vardana fields. And there was no answer to the black richness of that soil, compared to the gaunt gray powder of the other fields.

Naturally Rama's men were too proud to attend any of the free lectures he gave under the nim tree in the village. But Anand saw the professor every day at the Mission. So he could ask casually. Rama was glad Govind had thought of it; why hadn't they thought before? When Anand brought home the silly advice, Rama said he would then know how to silence his neighbors who were weak enough to be impressed.

When Anand transmitted Sahib Nitrate's suggestions, everyone in the family was surprised, and the brothers' and their father's eyes met knowingly and then quickly parted. Why, the boy was speaking like a true Kumbi. He was talking about the land as if he loved it, and it was the first time since he was a small boy that they had detected such a thing in him.

When Rama and Shushilla were alone in their quarters, he said, "The gods are hearing my prayers. This boy of mine is feeling his bonds with the earth. His nonsense is melting away. We'll have him back on the land. You wait and see."

Shushilla bai said, "Then what will happen to his education? Will it all be wasted?"

"We will plow it into the land," Rama said. "Then we will watch for what kind of crop springs up from it."

At the very same moment, Anand and Soni were talking about the same thing.

"But it would not be your life," Soni was protesting. "I know how much you love the Doctor Sahib . . . and Memsahib Mom. And they love you."

"Isn't the greatest honor I could pay them *listening* to what they have taught me? Then living it in my life?"

"But how could you live it in the fields?"

"You have missed the best part of their teaching, my little one," he said earnestly. "Memsahib Mom has shown it to me. And sometimes she has spoken of it quite freely."

"What part is that?"

"It is difficult for me to explain. But I'll try. It concerns a way she and her husband think about each other."

Soni looked alarmed at this. Was her lord going to suggest something different and strange to be brought into their marriage . . . their perfect marriage? She could not bear that; she said a wild quick prayer to Lakshmi.

"They are friends and companions," Anand was saying, wrinkling his forehead as he tried to find words.

"You mean . . . as two men are friends?" Soni cried in horror.

"Yes, you could say that."

She covered her face in shame at the implications. What would happen to all the drama of love between them, to all the poetry that sang in their blood sometimes, to the pounding waves that broke upon the shores of their bodies, and then left them still as the Ganges?

He took her hands down from her face, and he could not help laughing at the dismay he saw.

"It does not mean we will have less . . . we shall have more!"

"How could any man and his worthless slave have more?"

"She is not his worthless slave," he said quite sternly.

"I am, my lord."

"I do not want you as a slave. If there is a slave, it shall be I!"

She covered her ears against such dangerous blasphemy. He took down her hands and held them.

"The Doctor and the Memsahib are friends . . . but they are also lovers," he said. "They work together; they read the same books and talk about them; they have jokes between them that nobody else understands. And all of it is made better, because they love each other. They love each other as we do . . . only more, because they know each other better."

Now her eyes were large with wonder, as she tried to picture what all this could mean.

"Even in the daytime?" she asked in a whisper.

"All the time. Marriage is not just a man's body feasting on a woman's loveliness . . . but our minds loving each other. When our sons come they will feel about us what I feel about Memsahib Mom and the Doctor Sahib. It is fine weather for children to feel surrounding them. I know, because it is fine for me."

"How can we begin?" she asked at last, after she had thought awhile.

"We have begun," he said. "I'm teaching you to read."

"That will take years," she said fearfully. "And perhaps I

have not the kind of brain that will ever learn."

"Any brain can learn," he said. "And it will not take years. We are working together, and it will come quickly to us."

She could not help a little shiver of excitement because by the very way he had said "to us" she knew that already he was thinking of their minds as one. Was it true? Had they already begun to be friends?

"We don't have enough time . . . only at night when everyone else is asleep," she faltered.

"I know. It must be more than that. So I want to tell you something very surprising. I want you to help me decide about it."

"Oh no, my lord," she cried instinctively. "*You* must decide, and then you shall tell me."

"No. This is the beginning of our new way, Soni. We will make up our minds together."

She closed her eyes swiftly, and he could not help knowing she was asking the gods not to let any evil spirits hear such words spoken.

"This is what I have been thinking about," he said. "I wonder how you would like it if we had a little hut of our own, where we could live by ourselves?"

"But what would your father think . . . and Govind, and your mother?"

"But what would *you* think?"

She could hardly take in such a glorious idea. "You mean we would be all alone?"

"We would have as much time together as we wanted. We could play games, and make jokes and if we wanted to kiss, we would kiss."

"In the daytime?"

"Any time," he said daringly.

"But . . . but how will you manage such a thing?"

"I am thinking about that," he said eagerly. "Now that I know you really want it as I do, I shall manage it, never fear."

During the next days she was almost afraid to have any of the women look into her face, for fear they would read the secret there. Even if Anand could not bring the wonderful new state into being, it was bliss to know that he wanted such a thing. A little cricket seemed to be singing in her blood, and what he was saying over and over was, *Magee gher* . . . our own house.

Then the rain finally stopped. The last day of the monsoon was the most violent of all. Thunder and lightning chased each other across the sky, ripping it apart with light, and with deafening noise.

Everyone said, "The male and female are having it out. But they will come to peace with each other. They always do, don't they?"

Everyone chuckled mischievously at this, for it was much more than thunder and lightning to them. It was the hostile yet ecstatic tension of their own maleness and femaleness magnified to sky-size, so it could been seen and enjoyed by all.

After six weeks of the monotony of rain, everyone was keyed to excitement, and easily lured into quarreling or into violent love-making. The leisurely holiday spirit of the early part of the monsoon was gone now, and everyone wanted to be free from the hot and humid house.

The first morning without rain, all the men in Rama's family hurried out to inspect their land. To Rama's surprise, Anand said he would run to the clinic and get permission to stay away from his work, so he could go to the fields with the other men.

The plot that they had rented for years, and on which they had to pay a crippling share to the landlord, was about two miles from their house; they had not seen it for six weeks. The steady downpour had done no damage here, and Govind felt sure the seeds he had planted before the rains were now rooted and would immediately spring up in the sunshine.

Ghulum had some scattered acres of land under his care, and there was much rivalry between the brothers. Before each planting season, they drew lots to decide which would farm the farther pieces and the nearer ones. Each had his own small group of hired land-workers, and each worked his plot of land without interference from the other. But together they took charge of the eleven ancestral acres close to the town; Rama, too, dabbled in this land, for it was his favorite, rich with boyhood memories. Everyone shared equally in the profits from all the plots of ground, as a joint family should. Anand's small salary went into the family treasury, and Rama doled out to him whatever he needed, as he did for all the sons. No one thought to balance earnings against expenditures; everyone worked according to his capacity, and used whatever he needed from the common fund.

As the men came to inspect the beloved eleven-acre plot, they found two mango trees uprooted. The river beside which this land lay was swollen over its banks and the little footbridge had been washed away. Govind had a jealous feeling about this land, with little patience for his father's sentimentality concerning it. Govind wanted all the trees taken down and the whole area leveled and planted to more commercial crops, but Rama always shook his head when this was mentioned.

"I could not bear to see the trees cleared away. I played in those branches when I was a little boy . . . ." he said.

The land looked lashed and whipped; torn by the arrows of the rain, it needed its men badly. Their hearts could not help going out to it.

The ground under their feet responded to their steps as if it were as alive as flesh. Each clod seemed swollen and almost pulsing with that mysterious force of life which always desires to increase and multiply. Vitality quivered in every little blade of wayward growth, and over everything shimmered a haze, a kind of earth song which the eyes caught and the ears imagined.

Anand suddenly found himself saying what he had not intended to say until a few weeks later. But this was the moment for saying it, for his heart was touched now.

"Father, I too want to farm as my ancestors did."

Rama, his eyes almost hidden by their wrinkled lids, turned slowly and looked at him. When he was satisfied that Anand was not speaking on mere impulse, he went over and embraced him tenderly.

"I thought I would not hear those words before my soul left this earth," he said, deeply touched.

Anand's honesty made him speak further. "But wait, Father. I want something from you, also."

"Anything!" Rama said. "I shall have my son back again where he belongs! Anything you want shall be yours."

"You never kept any childish wish from coming true. Now I am asking you something as a man. If I resign my place in the clinic . . . may I have the honor of living on this spot where your father gave you a place to live?"

Instinctively Rama reached up and touched the earring Gopal had given him. Daily he had thrice-cleansed his body by pouring the water over this earring. In exchange for the pearl, he had promised Gopal that he would give Anand the deed to this very land. The pearl had brought the boy back to the land . . . and now he *should* have the land for his own. The old man was so deeply moved, he could scarcely speak. But he had no intention of divulging that unwritten agree-

ment between Gopal and himself. That would remain a secret
between them. The pearl had worked the wonder of bringing
back Anand to the earth; that was the important fact. But
there was no need of letting anyone believe that the gift of
the land would not come from Rama himself, prompted by
no one.

Anand could not help seeing how moved his father was; it
seemed to him there must be something here deeper than met
the eye. So he went on speaking gently, "May I build a hut
of my own under the trees? So that my children may play
where you played at a boy?"

Old Rama now frankly mopped his eyes with the end of
his dhoti, for the tenderest spot in all his memories had been
touched.

"We shall build you a hut," he said, "and your little bird
shall sing to you as your mother sang to me, in our fields. The
land shall be yours, and your grandchildren's. It shall be your
own land, Anand, with a deed in your name."

Govind turned away in silent anger. He had coveted this
land for as long as he could remember, and now because his
brother had learned the smooth flattering ways of education,
he was going to be given it. With a deed in his name! It was
all in the way a man asked for what he wanted. Deserving had
nothing to do with it. In sullen fury, he made up his mind
that tomorrow he would make arrangements to send his son
to a pandit to be taught. Perhaps there *should* be a school in
their town . . . everyone said after the British government
school had been closed, that it was a good riddance. At any
rate, Govind made up his mind to have his son get some
education. Then he himself would learn the ways of flattery
and cajolery from the boy.

Rama walked back toward the house, talking delightedly
about Anand's land and house. The hut would be small at

first, and as time went on, and his family grew, it would be enlarged. Some day it would be as big as their present joint-family house. The thought of two magnificent houses sprung from his own loins pleased Rama enormously. Anand could see he was willing that time should pass in a flash, so that he could peer down from immortality and feast his eyes on such earthly achievement doing honor to his name.

Rama was saying, "We cannot go to work before the land dries out. This would be the right time for you and Soni to pay your proper visit to her family in Marvali. That way you would not waste any working time away from the new field."

"That would be a good idea, Father," Anand agreed readily. "I'm glad you have thought of it." He himself had been thinking of the visit, naturally, and had come to the conclusion that this would be the obvious time for them to make it. But he could see how much it pleased Rama to be the one who decided upon it, so he gave him the credit.

Such a visit, not too long after a wedding, was considered good manners, and the proper way of showing respect to the bride's family. Soni would have to stay longer than he, perhaps even a month. He dreaded the time, but it must be endured. He would work on their little house during her absence.

"I shall have to go to the Mission and ask the Doctor Sahib for permission to leave," he said to Rama.

"Permission? I have given you permission," Rama said haughtily. "After all, whose son are you?"

"It is only courteous that I tell him," Anand said in a conciliatory voice. "I will tell him you have decided."

But when he reached the Mission, he found the Doctor Sahib in a conference. There was no time for more than explaining about the marriage visit, for the Doctor was absent-minded and concerned about other matters.

"Is it absolutely necessary?" he asked irritably. "Yes, I can see it is. Well, we'll miss you, my boy. So stay no longer than you have to."

Certainly this was no time to discuss the rest of his plans. Those he would have to tell them when he came back from Marvali. They would understand why he had to leave his work here. Memsahib Mom would be pleased that he had profited from their way of living, and wanted to make it his own. She had said, "A man and a woman grow up together and know each other best when they can live alone in their own house. A stream of understanding flows between them, when no outsider is present to interfere."

On another day when the three of them had been talking together, the Doctor Sahib had said, "A man and a woman are like the left hand and the right hand. Life can be clasped between them . . . but only when they work together in all things."

He would not have difficulty explaining to them that this was the reason he was going to leave the clinic, so that he and Soni could live out those words in actual existence.

Walking back through the town he brought back the whole of that conversation, for it had stayed alive in his mind. He himself had added something to what the Doctor Sahib had said, for he had caught the point delightedly. "One hand alone can scoop up only a small portion of life," he had said shyly, "but two hands together can measure out a seer . . . two of your pounds."

Memsahib Mom had been pleased with his simile, and had enlarged it further. "Two can hold *more* than twice as much as one alone," she had said, turning to the Doctor Sahib. "We find that so, don't we, darling?"

Darling. Anand made up his mind that someday he would call Soni that special name. She would be working in their house, cooking their dinner . . . and he would stop a moment before he came through the door.

"Darling . . . come meet me," he would cry to her, as loudly as he pleased, for there would be no outsider to hear.

"Darling? . . . what is that word?" she would ask.

"It is a short quick way of saying 'I love you.' "

Would she like it? In his mind he could see her face, shy and yet ardent.

He squatted down by the well, waiting for the men of his family to come along after their bazaar errands. They must all enter the house together, for he knew how much Rama would enjoy making his announcements. Exactly as Anand had picture it, as soon as Rama came into the presence of his women, he said importantly, "I have decided that tomorrow is the proper day for Anand and Soni to leave for the visit to her parents."

For a moment Soni thought she would burst into tears of joy, but then she controlled herself before she disgraced both families.

"Will you like that?" her father-in-law asked her fondly.

"If my lord is pleased with the idea," she said, her eyes amplifying the demure understatement.

Shushilla bai said, "We must find suitable gifts to send along. I have a sari for Mira bai, and some small toys for the children."

The grudging old widow said, "I might as well give them each a piece of my knitting, unworthy though it is."

Rama said, exploding his huge firecracker of news as if it were a mere sulphur match, "Gopal offered to give us some choice cotton seeds, if ever Anand decided to plant our family tract with cotton."

"Anand?" Shushilla bai cried in astonishment.

"Oh . . . we have not told you?" Rama said with maddening

deliberateness. "My son and I have decided that he will give up his work at the clinic, and take his rightful place on our acres. So I am giving him that plot for his own. He shall have a deed, and there will begin another branch of our family."

Everyone received the news with violent though concealed emotions, some of anger and jealousy and some of overwhelming joy. During the evening meal and long into the evening, they all talked about the great development, and about the trip on which the young people would start early in the morning. Rama offered to let Anand drive the tonga, but the young man insisted that since the soft roads had not yet dried out, traveling on foot would be better.

"Then you must promise to find someone coming to Vardana from Marvali when you're ready to come home," Rama said affectionately. "I cannot bear to have you away longer than necessary. I want you near me, my son, for you have made me very happy. And besides, we'll begin working on your house."

Anand was not proud that he was deceiving his father into believing he had abandoned all his interest in education and progressive methods which the Mission represented. Actually this step he was taking was just the opposite from what it appeared to be. While Rama was fatuously believing he had given up his Western notions, he was really embarking on the most revolutionary notion of all, the freeing of Soni from the bonds put upon her by her sex, according to old tradition and custom. Though apparently giving in to Rama's determination to have him back on the land, he was actually establishing a spot of freedom, a tiny province of his own where revolution could be carried on. It made him unhappy that it must be done in this deceptive way, but he had not been able to think of a more straightforward method. He must talk to

Memsahib Mom about that aspect of it; perhaps she could reassure him. Didn't the English have some kind of phrase which said "The end justifies the means"?

When he and Soni were alone in their own quarters, she went immediately to the little images she had made of rice flour, and knelt before them. He knew without being told that this was her first step into their new and daring life. For a moment he hesitated, then he went over and slipped to his knees beside her. In an earnest whisper he said the words he had learned as a boy.

"Behold me in thy presence, great God! I prostrate myself at thy feet! Hold out a helping hand to me and remove the obstacles which I encounter at each step. My feeble will is often led astray; thou alone can give it strength to resist temptation and keep it in the path of virtue."

He glanced at the face of Soni, beautiful and meek in the flickering light from her arati lamp. There were tears glittering on her lashes, and he knew they were tears of happiness, and of gratitude because he was saying his pujah with her.

Progressive man though he was, he still had need of the gods. He would always have need of them.

9

BEFORE DAWN THEY STARTED FOR MARVALI. Everyone in the family saw them off, with admonitions and advice, and with all the gifts they could carry to Gopal and Mira bai. Fourteen miles to be covered in one day would be nothing for youngsters, but Rama warned them about loitering along the roads, for traveling after dark would be difficult for those who did not know the way. The roads today would be crowded with people like themselves, released after the long rain.

Vardana was still sleeping as they passed through the town. Only a few hard-working merchants who must prepare their stalls in the bazaar were stirring. Soni and Anand could barely see each other, for this was the middle of the dark of the moon. But as the light grew stronger, they approached the walls of the Mission, and Anand pointed it out eagerly.

Already there were a few patients waiting for the chowkadar to open the gates.

"They have probably come from a long distance," Anand said. "Someone has told them that Memsahib Mom can cure anything."

"Can she?"

"Of course not. But she can always try. And just seeing her trying makes them feel better."

As she looked into his face, she saw what she knew was a

reflection of Memsahib Mom's own tenderness toward all sick persons.

"Let's sit awhile outside, and then when the Doctor Sahib and Memsahib Mom are awake, let me take you inside and show you to them," he said impulsively.

Soni looked horrified. "I cannot do such a thing," she said. "I would disgrace my lord. I have on my oldest green sari for traveling."

"Who knows whether it is old or new?" he asked, laughing.

"Memsahib Mom would know," Soni said, "and she would pity my lord for marrying such a wretched-looking girl."

"You are just afraid," he said. "But I would be with you, and I would tell you how to act."

"They understand Marathi and they would know I was ignorant," she said. "They would see that I am both wretched outside and stupid within."

"Well, perhaps we would have to wait too long a time for them to wake up and see us," he said reluctantly, saving face for her timidity. "We shall come another time, for I want them to see my great treasure. And when they do, they will understand why I want to live in a hut of our own with you, and teach you."

The roads were becoming fuller and fuller of travelers now, walking at a swinging easy pace, some alone and others in groups. When a man and a woman traveled together, the woman was always a few steps behind the man. But Anand insisted that Soni walk only a step behind him, close enough so they could talk, for it seemed to him life would never be long enough to get all the things said that they needed to say between them.

As they went along he told her more and more about Memsahib Mom and she found the story difficult to picture. She could not imagine such a woman . . . coming to a strange country when she was young and unmarried. *Unmarried* . . . and daring to venture out alone!

"How could she do such a thing?"

"I asked her that once, when we first knew each other," Anand said. She said, 'I loved you people on the other side of the world. I felt the suffering as if it were my own.' I reminded her, 'But you had never seen us.' She said, 'I had felt you with the heart. The heart can see farther than the eyes, Anand.' That's what she said. Oh, she is a true woman, Soni."

"Some women cannot even feel the suffering of the people in the lane half a mile away!" Soni cried. "But it is not our fault! Everything teaches us to care only for our families."

"That is true," Anand said, loving this glimpse into the moment when an idea, entirely new, cracked through from darkness into the light in which ideas can grow.

He said, "Everyone who is ill or friendless is Memsahib Mom's business. She doesn't care whether they are sweepers or Brahmins. She wants to make them well and help them be clean. She works harder than anyone I ever saw."

"And the Doctor Sahib?"

"They are alike."

"A woman is like a man?" Soni cried in horror.

He rolled his head in despair, for this was the point she never could understand, and he could never find the right way of explaining it. They *were* alike, and also different. That was the wonderful secret of their fascination for each other.

"Are there many such women outside in the world?" she was asking timidly, as if they were speaking of a strange race.

"Yes . . . Memsahib Mom says more and more girls are growing up to be this kind of woman. Even in India there are many. Women who want to serve the needs of humanity . . .

they bring their motherness out . . . into a wider circle . They find their children everywhere. Can you understand what I am saying, my little one?"

She shook her head in dismay. "Why do they want to get out beyond the shadow of their lords' orders?"

He thought quite a long time and then he said, "Their lords must be men who also have great hearts. They have to be a new kind of men. Before we can have new women in India, we must have bigger men."

For a long time then they walked in silence, each thinking deeply. Talking must be done when people who love each other are together, but it is not always a conversation which requires words. Sometimes Anand would point to a flock of green parrots swooping low and then peppering the distance, or Soni would stoop and pluck a piece of aromatic herb and offer it for chewing.

At noon they had reached a place Govind had said would be right for stopping and resting. There was a sanctuary here where travelers of their caste had worshipped. Several rocks had been heaped together to provide for the safe dwelling of an idol.

"I was told that when we reached this shrine, our feet would have traveled nine miles," Anand said. "That leaves us less than six more miles. I am sorry to see the miles disappearing behind us, Soni."

"I am sorry, too, my lord," she said, dimpling.

After they had done their pujahs before the shrine, they walked a little farther and found a footpath running across a field, to a village they could barely discern. All villages hide themselves in distance, slipping back into the earth from which they have been conjured up. A number of people were leaving the road and walking along this path, so Anand inquired what was the attraction.

"A fair! We must see it," he cried.

First they withdrew to a place of privacy curtained off by some banyan roots, to eat the food sent along by Shushilla bai.

"What did my mother prepare for us?"

"Some brinjal curry and chapattees," she said, and then when his face showed disappointment because there was no fruit, she said, "But other hands besides hers added what your stomach loves . . . dried figs and one small poot melon."

She set the food before him, and then withdrew from his presence, pretending to be very much interested in a bulbul bird singing high in the banyan tree.

Anand thought, someday she will understand me well enough to know that I want her to eat beside me. But it is too soon yet for her to break such a stern tradition.

After she had eaten her hasty meal, he came over and handed her a piece of the poot he had saved for her pleasure.

"The melon was for my lord."

"Your lord can enjoy it better if his darling has shared it," he said, slipping in the English word and knowing that she would be too timid to ask him the meaning. But she would not always be so timid. . . . There would come a day! There would come a day for everything.

After their meal they rested a while, and Anand took out of his sutherungee a thin book of poetry.

"Someday when we travel we shall have to carry two books," he said. "We shall sit beside each other and open our books, and you will take your private journey, and I shall take mine, and we shall look up from the pages and catch each other's eye and smile." She could see that picture was his dearest imagining. She took the book in her hands and opened it, and looked at the pages. They were covered with black seeds. There were tiny curved husks here and there across the page from which the little seeds had fallen into patterns. It was wonderful to think that their crop could grow so quickly in the mind of the reader. . . .

"What does the page say?" Anand asked playfully.

"It says beautiful things, which I shall not tell you," she said. "It says the sky is our father and the earth is our mother, and all things are provided for our joy. It says that when you look at me too suddenly my heart melts like a candle caught in a fire. It says you must not make my candle burn too fast, my lord."

"It says all that, does it?" he said, not playful now. "The page says . . . I will tell you a story the teacher told me when he was teaching me to read."

"Tell me a story," she said, touching him with her finger.

"Well, once there was a man who had a fine mango grove and when his fruit was at its best, he gathered twelve fine pieces and put them in a basket, and covered them with paper and called his servant to carry them to a friend three miles away.

"The servant walked along the road, carrying the basket, and when he sat down to rest, he uncovered the basket and looked at the fruit. 'My master would not know if I ate one of the mangoes,' he said to himself, 'and certainly his friend would never suspect.' So he ate a mango . . . and it was so delicious that he ate another one. Then he covered the fruit with the paper and went on his way.

"When he came to the friend's house, he handed over the basket. The friend took it inside and asked him to wait until he had inspected the gift. In a few minutes he came out where the servant was sitting and said, 'My friend, the paper says there were twelve mangoes in the basket. I find only ten. What happened?' The servant was terrified. 'Oh, please do not tell my master, sir,' he cried. 'I ate the two mangoes. I did not know there was anyone nearby to see me do it. I promise, if you spare me, it will never happen again.'

"The next day, the master again picked twelve mangoes, put them in a basket, and covered them with paper, and sent his servant off in the opposite direction to carry them to another friend.

"Again on the road, the servant was tempted. He went behind a tree where no one could see him. Then he carefully took off the paper and folded it into a small square, and put it under a rock. 'Now you cannot see what is happening, and you cannot tell tales,' he said to the paper, making sure the rock covered it completely, while he ate two mangoes.

"After he had finished eating them, he wiped his hands clean and then buried the mango stones. Then he took the paper from under the rock, and covered the basket with it again, laughing to himself, because he had deceived the paper.

"When he reached the house of his master's friend the same thing happened. The friend took in the basket and in a moment he came out and said, 'Something is wrong here. The paper says my good friend sent me twelve mangoes, but I find only ten.' Then the servant fell at his feet, begging forgiveness. 'I implore you to give me that paper for my own,' he said. 'I will hang it in my hut where it can keep its eye on me always, so that I never again will do a wicked thing.' "

By the time he had finished with the old story, Anand was laughing; Soni had listened with such pleasure that each word was memorized, to have for the rest of her life.

They found the fair enchanting. There was a man with a tame cheetah, its golden eyes gentle in its haughty face; performers wearing tall plumes in their hair danced on long stilts, pretending they were about to fall off, and frightening everyone deliciously. There were all kind of sweets for sale, and men with cages of beautiful birds which could be bought for only a few rupees; there were magicians, their faces painted black and yellow.

But best of all was the young girl of surpassing beauty who did the famous egg dance. She wore a short brocaded skirt and an embroidered choli, and her beauty was enhanced by the saffron oil on her bare abdomen. When she moved, there was a tinkling of heavy silver anklets, bracelets and necklaces, sweet as music. She carried a wicker basket of eggs, which she asked everyone to look at carefully and make certain they were genuine. As soon as she was ready to dance, she placed a wicker wheel on her head, held on securely by silver ornaments. From this wheel, threads were suspended, each heavy thread ending in a slipknot kept open by means of a glass bead.

Behind her sat five musicians, each with a stringed or reed instrument, and one with a gourd flute. At a signal from the girl, they played a slow rhythmic monotone to which she began rotating, to a gradually faster and faster tempo. She reached out and took an egg in each hand, carefully inserting them into the slipknots. With a shiver of her torso, and a click of her heel on the ground, she jerked the strings, so that the eggs were held in the tightened slipknots. Now she was whirling furiously, and the crowd, afraid the eggs might smash together, involuntarily pushed back to give her more room. Two more eggs went into place, almost faster than the eye could see.

The eggs on their strings were standing out almost straight and the crowd was scarcely breathing with excitement. But this was not the end, for somehow she managed to slip two more eggs into the dangerous circle. Now the crowd began to wonder how she could possibly stop whirling without breaking the eggs.

Soni was gripping her two hands in agonizing excitement. Surely all this wild beauty would end in catastrophe! But it did not. Swiftly the dancer removed the eggs just as she had put them in place, without losing a step. She was whirling so fast that you could scarcely make out her beautiful face, but her sure hands were more swift than the whirling. Two by two the eggs were removed without harming each other, and suddenly the dancer collapsed on the ground in a climax of music.

"It must be magic," Soni breathed.

But Anand, his dark face flushed with pleasure, had another explanation. "When the eggs are traveling fast along a curved path they cannot escape. A bucket of water hurled in such a circle will not spill a drop. It is called centrifugal force."

She tried to say the words after him, her face rosy with pride in his knowledge. "Centrifugal force? English? But . . . she does not seem English," she said falteringly. "Could such an English thing happen to an Indian girl?"

He wanted to laugh, but he knew that he must not, so he answered seriously. "It is an English phrase for a law that belongs to the earth . . . to every spot on the earth."

The rest of the way she walked along behind him, subdued now, because, wonderful as she had known he was, she had suddenly found he was even more magnificent. How could he want to spend his time with her? A man who knew such things!

When she saw the blurred lines of the walls of Marvali across a field, her heart leaped within her. She arranged what she was carrying so that her arms could rest demurely at her sides, for she must enter the gate of her old village in a posture of servitude. Anyone who looked at her must know that there was nothing but meekness in her heart, and that she was loyally serving her lord. They two must be a picture of marriage as it is meant to be. As for Anand, he was walking with his head proudly erect. No one could have guessed his heart was pounding with excitement, nor that this was the first time he had been so far from his own village.

Neighbors who had known Soni since she was a baby, joined their palms and bowed demurely to Anand as they passed. Let it not be supposed they were curious about the new marriage. They had their manners, even though Marvali was a small world compared to Vardana. But the children did not restrain themselves, and by the time the new couple reached Gopal's house, a band with beaming little faces was bringing up the rear. Mira bai might be so overjoyed at the unexpected sight of her visiting daughter that she would give them some sweets. Likely not, but still one could always hope.

The last few steps down their own lane Soni ran; she could not help running. She pushed aside the chatia hanging before Gopal's door and cried out her mother's name. The children, crowding around the door, turned away from the naked joy in the two faces, as Mira bai took her child in her arms and silently lifted her own face to heaven. The biggest boys in the crowd broke away then; they would go and find Gopal and tell him the good news.

The evening was the happiest Soni ever had known. All that she most loved on earth was held in this small humble courtyard, and the men in her family listened respectfully to everything her husband said. She did not even have to tell them how clever he was; they could not help seeing it. And when he was here in their midst they did not resent him as they had when Gopal described him. He had a smiling boyish way that made everyone like him; he added something rich and good to every man who stood in his presence. He seemed to suggest to other men new dimensions in themselves, for what we can see in others we possess a little in ourselves.

He told with excitement the news about giving up his job

and coming back to the land, and as he told it, the farmers who had felt inferior before, now felt justified and enlarged. If education led a man back to the earth, then they need not feel benighted, for they were already on the earth! Perhaps that meant that education was only a difficult journey that one need not take.

Ghosharam asked suddenly, "Anand, have you ever ridden on a train?"

"Never."

"I expect to, someday."

"Where do you want to go?"

"Go? I want to ride."

Then in his own answer, Ghosharam understood what education might be . . . not a place at which to arrive, but a wonderful method of traveling. He almost heard a new area opening in his mind, and another helpless yearning ached in that mind.

As they were deciding where the visitors would put their sutherungees for the night, Gopal asked Anand, "What land will you be using for your field, my son?"

"My father has promised to give me the eleven acres his father gave him."

"To let you use it?"

"No. My generous father has decided to give it to me legally."

"Has he not done it yet?" Gopal asked, trying to sound casual. But it was hard to be casual, when he felt that *he* himself had had so important a part in that giving. One might say that it was for that he had gone into the shame of debt. For had not the pearl been given in exchange for Rama's promise?

Anand, seeing there was something concealed here, answered with equal casualness. "My father and I came to the agreement only yesterday. Until then I had no need of the land."

"I see. No doubt he will have the contract all drawn up in your name when you come home."

"He may not have," Anand said, defensively. "My father is never a man to hurry. His word has been given and what else do I need from my fine father?"

"Nothing," Gopal said, his uneasiness not quieted. "Nothing at all. But still it is safe to have agreements written on paper. You are an educated man. You know that sometimes the gods take a man from this earth before he has had time to make his word become the deed. But paper neither forgets nor dies."

Anand looked thoughtfully into the older face. The man had some deep reason for speaking as he was. What could that suspicion be? The face of his brother Govind rose unbidden to his mind. He had not thought before this moment how Govind might feel about his younger brother being given the land. It was an unusual thing for his father to want to do, for in a joint family all the brothers share equally. Or if there *is* any preference given, it is to the oldest son.

Then it seemed to him that his father-in-law had known already about the land. Could that be possible? Gopal had brought up the subject, exactly as if he had some knowledge about it.

"My father is so happy about my coming back to work with the family," he said almost involuntarily. "He believes the pearl earring you gave him has used its sacred power to bring me back."

"He believes that, does he?" Gopal said darkly. Without a word, he helped the young people spread out their blankets on the earth of the small courtyard. He went into his own quarters, still silent, for he had nothing he could say about the unjust circumstance. It was he who had given the gift of land . . . and Rama who would be thanked forever. It was he who had the aching yoke of debt across his shoulders day and night . . . and Rama who had eleven acres of land which he *could* give away.

10

THE FIRST MORNING AFTER HIS RETURN FROM Marvali, Anand went to the Mission. He could not help starting earlier than usual, so eager was he to see his friends and tell them of his decision. As he walked through the lanes of Vardana to the other side of the town he felt such a love for the silent houses and the people in them that the words of a Tagore poem which he had learned long ago, said themselves. The poem was called "In My Village," and it was a simple thing:

> *There I find Him near . . .*
> *Near as Earth, near as her flowers and fruits,*
> *Near as wind and water.*
> *As the bird's song, as the water's tune,*
> *As the light of this dawn,*
> *As this softness, as the forest's greenness,*
> *So do I love Him!*

The great urgency that was bringing him back to his father's land included his love for India as he knew it, its inchoate present and its fermenting future. He knew many of his young friends had no faith in the future. Believers like himself must find a way of imparting their faith, for faith not only sees what is not yet present, but actually creates what is desired.

As he walked along, he thought affectionately of Memsahib Mom and the Doctor Sahib and scraps of conversation ran through his mind. He would show them his reasons for this move he was making. He would say this, and they would say that. They would offer to continue to be his friends. He would ask them if they would come and visit his new house when it was built. Without them the new house would never have been possible. Would he be too shy to tell them that, so that they would have to surmise it? He hoped he could tell them plainly, for it should make them happy.

When he went through the gates of the compound, there was the usual straggling stream of people coming for medical help. Veiled women with their sway-back walk, which came from balancing babies on their hipbones, little girls scarcely bigger than the children they carried, old men with visible illness crumpling them toward the earth . . . and the accompanying dogs running here and there, hopefully. He saw this parade every morning and it always touched him. But he was not depressed by it, for he knew the Doctor Sahib would have something for each one.

He loved everybody at the clinic. He would miss the workers who had taken him in so heartily, never dreaming that their blithe friendship had shaken his whole life like an earthquake. He would miss their meals together. . . . It would have distressed his father almost beyond endurance to know that his son was freely sitting at table with those who were out-of-caste. It had taken Anand many months to get up his courage to step across that boundary, but he had done it. He would miss the bright conversations, and the prestige he always felt when someone in authority asked him about some Marathi word or a custom. They knew some things, and he knew others . . . and they mutually respected each other for individual knowledge.

Surely because he was no longer going to be working here every day, he would not have to lose them completely. Couldn't he come sometimes and talk with them; couldn't they be his guides . . . and Soni's? He was not losing one treasure from his life because he was adding a new wealth to it; he could have both.

Almost unconsciously as he passed through the door, his mind shifted from Marathi to English. Within this portal he was a different man, an English-speaking person.

The first person he met inside the door was the young American medical missionary named Steele, who would some day take the old Doctor Sahib's place (though that was difficult to imagine). He was a tall thin man, always jerky in voice and restless in motion.

"So you're back. What're you looking so pleased about, Anand?" he said as greeting.

"Am I looking pleased?"

"Practically grinning."

"I shouldn't be. For I'm half pleased and half sad today."

"Well, you're still ahead of most of the race, in that case."

"I'm giving up my work here," Anand said, getting it out quickly.

Dr. Steele looked at him in surprise. "You're joking."

"No. I've told my father," Anand said, and realized as he said the words that they would not express to the American the finality of the decision.

"Why, I thought we'd have you around here for the next fifty years," Dr. Steele said rather indifferently. "People are going to miss you, I expect."

He glanced down at some papers he was carrying in his hand, and Anand knew his attention had already wavered. But the doctor went on talking anyway, absent-mindedly.

"What do you plan to do? Got a better job somewhere?"

"I'm going to take my place on our family farm," Anand said, unable to keep dignity from creeping into the sentence.

"You don't say," the young doctor said. "I can't imagine you being a farmer."

"My ancestors were all farmers," Anand said.

"That a fact? Well, of course they didn't have any education, I suppose."

"They had a great deal of education, sir."

The doctor looked up at him and then grinned. "Oh, I see what you mean. I suppose a farmer does have to know a certain kind of stuff. Especially to get a living out of the kind of soil you see around here."

Anand said nothing at all to this. For the first time since he had come to this place, he felt alien. Yesterday he had belonged here; today he had put himself over on the other side of the situation. Yesterday he had belonged to the hunger for helping; now he belonged to the earth. But that separation did not state the situation. He had made his decision to go back to the earth because that was the way he could help most effectively. This was the greatest hunger, and he had chosen to satisfy that.

He had been accepted before by the other Mission workers without comment or question. When his colleagues asked him for information about his country they did so with respect. When they spoke to him, they were addressing in him that mysterious something which had made him step out from his own people so that he could help them. Because now he had stepped back among them, this absent-minded doctor had already demoted him in his estimation. Anand felt all this in a quick flash of intuition, and he was hurt and confused. But he reminded himself that he and Dr. Steele had never known each other intimately. This was a longer conversation than they had ever before held together.

"Well, I hope you're not making a mistake, my boy," the older man was saying. "Seemed to me you had quite a good head on you. I understand you've done a lot of translating for the Mission. . . . "

"I'll still have a lot of translating to do," Anand said proudly, knowing that he was giving the wrong impression, but certainly having no intention of telling this unsympathetic Westerner that what he wanted to translate now was life itself for someone . . . and then for other someones.

He went down the hall toward the Doctor Sahib's office. He discovered his hands were trembling. The doctor was busy, so he sat down a moment on one of the chairs outside the door. He had learned to sit on chairs; they were quite comfortable when you got used to them. But they never would be necessary. A man's body stayed flexible from hanging in balance in a squatting position above his own feet. It seemed to have no weight anywhere, poised in the air with knees just below chin. Western bodies became chunky and coarse from sitting on chairs that crowded the flesh into an unnatural cushion under the buttocks. But he could sit either way, and he reminded himself that he must keep his mind just as adaptable. He could *sit* either Western or Eastern . . . and he must be willing to *think* the same way, and not be angry and outraged as he had been a few minutes before.

The Doctor Sahib's visitor came out past him, and Anand stood up and looked into the office.

"Come in, son," his great friend called. "I'm awfully glad you're back. We sure miss you around here."

"I missed the clinic," Anand said. "But I had a fine visit with my wife's family."

"Glad to hear it," the Doctor Sahib said, grinning up at him with friendliness. "Got something on your mind this morning?"

The Westerners said things like that . . . really rather poetic, the way the phrase created a humorous little picture of a man rolling up a memo and tucking it under his scalp . . . "something on his mind."

"Quite a big bundle of something," Anand said. "I've decided to give up my work here, Doctor Sahib."

A troubled expression settled on the white man's face. "Oh, *now* . . . let's talk about that, son. I'm sure it's something we can fix up."

"Nothing is wrong," Anand said hastily. "You know how much I like being here. I've done my level best to please everybody." He liked using expressions like "level best," for they showed he had listened to a great many Westerners.

"And you've pleased 'em," the Doctor Sahib said. "The Memsahib won't hear of this." He called in a chaprassi who was squatting outside in the shadows, and sent him to get Memsahib Mom.

He went on talking persuasively, shuffling papers around on his desk. "Why, she's getting ready to put out some new health folders! She's expecting you to translate them into good village Marathi. She thinks nobody else could do it the way you can."

"I have something more important to do," Anand said. "You'll agree, when I tell you."

"Oh . . . another job, I suppose? Somebody's offered you more money. Well, I'm not surprised. Some of those State Department people I suppose . . . or one of the Foundations. They all have too much money . . . they can grab anything they want!" He closed up his lips angrily and shook his head. "How much are they offering you, Anand?"

"It's not a new job," Anand said uncomfortably. Indians always said that whatever Americans thought about always boiled down to more money, or less. But he had not found it so. It grieved him that the Doctor Sahib was talking this way. He must try to make him understand quickly, before he went on damaging the admiration built up through the last two years. "It hasn't anything to do with money, Doctor Sahib."

"It hasn't?" He sounded as though he could not believe such a statement. "Then what on earth *does* it have to do with?"

Just then Memsahib Mom came in, and Anand looked at her beseechingly. Her short gray hair was freshly brushed and shining, and her merry eyes, behind the huge glasses she wore, made the whole scene seem less strained.

"Thank heaven you're back, Anand," she said.

"Listen to this, darling," the Doctor Sahib said. "Anand's talking about quitting his job."

"He can't," Memsahib Mom said with a quick grin. "We need him here. Quitting indeed!"

"That's what I'm telling him," her husband said.

She immediately sketched in the little pamphlets she wanted to write. They would have funny little drawings, and Anand would translate them so that any villager who could read at all would understand them. That brought up the old conflict between his national pride and his sense of realism, for he knew that no matter how simply they wrote the pamphlets, there would be only a handful of villagers who could read what they said. Sometimes he had timidly suggested that the Mission people might go out into the villages and teach the illiterates to read. But somehow they never got around to this. It was someone else's job, they felt; theirs was to cut down contagion by getting "pinkie" put into the wells once a month, and to persuade the villagers to build pukka covered drains for their houses.

The Doctor Sahib broke in impatiently, "He says nobody

is offering him more money."

"Oh . . . so *that's* it!" Memsahib Mom cried, assuming that just the opposite was true, since it had been denied. "Well, we'll just have to give him a little more. How much do you need, Anand?"

"It is not money," he said. "I am leaving my work here, to go back to my father's fields."

They looked at each other in stunned amazement. "Why, that's nonsense," the Doctor Sahib said. "How many young men would give their right arms to get off the fields . . . millions of them! And you're talking about going back!"

"But I'm married now," Anand said, helplessly irrelevant.

"Married! All the more reason for you to stay out, once you've *got* out," the Doctor Sahib said. "What can the land give you? You're way past that, my son. Nothing but hard work and trouble. A salary is the thing for you."

"Whatever put such an idea in your head?" Memsahib Mom asked almost crossly.

He looked into her face; it was a worried Western face this morning, full of the troubles of the hundreds of people she carried so thanklessly, their stubborn resistance to change, the superstitions of which they sometimes died, their stiff pride, which concealed real reasons and put forth only sham ones. . . .

That was what he himself was doing at this moment, concealing the real reason and letting them think anything they pleased. He wanted to cover his face with his hands and weep because this conversation was representing each one of them so badly. It was like a duel between blindfolded men. Their three long swords were flashing through the air, and all striking in different directions crazily. He wanted to answer her question by saying, "Memsahib Mom, *darling*, you put the idea in my head . . . you and Doctor Sahib . . . I am doing what you showed me how to do . . . I'm going to live what you taught me."

Instead he only stood there in stubborn silence.

"There's something here that doesn't meet the eye," Memsahib Mom said sadly. "This is the way you Indians are *supposed* to be . . . secretive and difficult. But *you're* never this way, Anand."

"You're never this way, either," he said almost beneath his breath.

"Well, what then?" she cried impatiently. "Here we've taught you and helped you, and loved you almost like a son . . . and now suddenly, you want to throw everything away and go back to being a farmer!"

Doctor Sahib said passionately, "What can you learn on a farm? You'll be digging yourself into a hole. I had such hopes for you, Anand. You seemed like a man who might help his neighbors sometime. Don't those poor ignorant fellows make you want to dig *them* out of the mud . . . instead of jumping in with them?"

Now the quick of pride *had* been cruelly touched.

"I do not find my countrymen poor and ignorant," Anand said stiffly. "I am homesick for my own life, and I am going back to it."

The faces of his two friends were flooded with color now, and he wanted to cry out an apology for what he had said, and a plea for them to forgive and try to understand. But he felt his own face stony and set, and the only words that came to his mind were Marathi ones, too subtle for the simple Marathi which was all they understood.

11

THERE WAS SAD JOY IN BEING IN ONE'S
father's house again; every moment seemed double, for every
little deed and event was happening in the present, but also
it belonged to the past. Soni knew the very dents on the brass
lothis she polished beside the door, but they no longer belonged to her real existence. The birds that woke her in the
morning were the descendants of the birds she had known
when she was a child, but now their songs had different meaning to her. She could not explain the difference to anyone,
but she thought that Anand would understand when she told
him about it.

Three weeks would have to pass before Gopal took her
home in one of the Thursday carts, which carried produce to
the Vardana bazaar . . . three weeks when she would not see
her husband's face nor hear his voice, nor know his touch.
Everyone said to her, "It must be wonderful to be here with
your mother again." And she said, "Wonderful!" smiling
convincingly. Had no one ever been in love before, the way
she was in love, so that every hour was empty that did not
hold her lover's presence, or the promise of his coming?

And how was he enduring the separation? He would eat
the curry cooked by the two widows, good curry but not her
own. He would sleep alone in his and Soni's quarters, and
when he stretched out his hand as he often did while he slept,

it would meet only emptiness. The brothers would tease him if he looked pale or downcast; they were always making fun of him because his love for his young wife couldn't help showing. She made believe she never understood what the jokes meant . . . but she knew all right. Rama disapproved of the jokes . . . and he disapproved of the fact that lay behind the jokes. Rama was an old man; he had forgotten long ago what love feels like. He thought it beneath the sovereignty of a man to love his wife openly; Anand had hinted that his father had spoken sharply to him about it. And now, when Rama had his son alone, would he be able to influence him? Might he persuade him to care less? But even her jealous concern had to admit how impossible that would be. One hour together again. . . .

Gopal's house seemed different to his daughter. She tried to make herself believe that it was only because she was now seeing it with maturer eyes. A child sees only the security and happiness of affection all around. But she was no longer a child, and she read the anxiety in her father's face, and heard the impatience in his voice.

Mira bai said, "When you went away, Soni, it was as if he was living in cold weather. We all missed you . . . but *he* is like a man who has a cold wind whipping at him. Nothing pleases him. Nothing gives him rest."

Soni shook her head, unwilling to hear such things. She knew that he had missed her, for there was a special bond between them; there always had been that bond, since she was his girl-baby who rode astride his shoulder when he went to the bazaar, or visited his friends. He was not like other fathers.

"And he works your brothers cruelly. Nothing they do is enough. There should always be more accomplished. They grumble about it to their wives, and the girls don't know what to do to cheer them up. Sugya especially. You know how jolly she always was . . . well, look at her now."

"Maybe he has a pain somewhere," Soni said. "I will ask him when we are alone."

"The pain he has is in his mind," Mira bai said. "Mind-pain is worse than body-pain. He is not generous as he used to be when you were here. He grumbles about the meals . . . why have I made sweets? We do not need sweets. I am extravagant and gluttonous. Why spend money in the bazaar . . . who looks at an old woman, whether or not she has on a pretty sari or a ragged one? He used to bring home bangles . . . now he brings home only grumbling and com-plaining."

"He needs more love from all of you," Soni said. "I am glad I am here to tell you so."

"You cannot give love to a man who is displeased with the world," Mira bai said. "You can give it, all right . . . but it is not received. Giving love to a man with an inner anger is like trying to sing to a deaf man."

"My father is not deaf to love," Soni said sternly. "You should know that. You have lived with him for I don't know how many years."

Mira bai was quiet a moment, making up her mind to offer this next proof. "And now he has beat me twice with his slipper." She said it half in shame and half in boastfulness. "He has not beat me since we were bride and groom, and I used to burn the rice, dreaming about him." A little smile played around her mouth as she thought of those departed days. Shyly she asked Soni, "Does your husband beat you, my child?"

Soni started to say, No . . . I cannot imagine such a thing. This is the gentlest man on earth. And I would die rather than make him angry. Then she saw her mother's face, cher-ishing the old perverted sign of affection, so she said, "Of course he beats me. When I am stupid or silly or lazy." She hugged herself with silent mirth at the absurdity of what she was saying; when she went home she would tell Anand and they would laugh together. But Mira bai was satisfied.

"I am glad to know he is such a man," she said. "A woman will love such a man all her life, because he knows what is good for her."

"My man knows," Soni said, "and I will love him forever."

"Ucha," her mother said complacently. "I am glad he doesn't listen to the modern talk that goes around. Even a good woman needs to be beaten sometimes. Such beating usually ends in love-making. Good beating comes from lust which doesn't recognize itself. But the kind of beating your father has given me lately . . . *that* is only to satisfy some anger in him . . . some anger that has nothing to do with me. It is insulting."

After a moment Mira bai said, "Then there is the matter of the pan crop."

"What about that?"

"Your father knows that pan chewing destroys the teeth. He knows it becomes a bad habit. And the people in our village have been proud that they never learned the habit . . . except a few wretched men like Two-fingered Mohan and the brothers who rent tongas, and such as that."

"So what has my father to do with this?"

"Your father is raising a big pan crop. He says, 'Why should I worry about their teeth? Am I responsible for what they put into their mouths?' But he *is* responsible. For he has always been a man whom other men copy. What he says, they believe. And now he offers them pan and betel, and he tells them that all the smart people in Vardana chew it. So they want to be smart. And all *he* wants is to sell his crop in the bazaar."

"You are hard on him."

"I am hard on him because he is not the man he used to be. Something evil possesses him now . . . *that* is what I am hard on."

"Love him more," Soni said. "All a wife can do is love her husband more. You have always told me that."

"But it is not easy to love this hard man, who has taken the place of my kind lord."

Anand had been gone from Marvali only a few days when Soni knew. She was grinding spices for the dal, when suddenly everything was whirling blackly around her, and in a moment she had crumpled to the floor. Mira bai ran to her, and lifted her in her arms, and then with Seetha bringing a mat, laid her gently on the ground.

"Praise the gods," Mira bai said. "The soul of her lord's son has touched her soul, and has entered into her womb."

Soni opened her eyes then, and saw her mother's face radiantly bent above her, so that she knew.

"I thought the sweet I ate this morning had made me ill," Soni said.

"It was a sweet, my child. But of another variety."

That day and the next two Soni was kept from the eyes of all, while she meditated and prayed about what was now happening to her.

Mira bai had instructions all ready, for she had lived toward this day. "It is written in the Padma-purana that when a woman is with child she must observe certain rites faithfully. Also she must avoid speaking to any woman of doubtful virtue, or to anyone who has lost a child."

"How can I avoid speaking to a mother who has lost a child?" Soni asked. "All mothers have lost a child. Hardly a family that has not lost several."

"No. This decree applies to unborn children," Mira bai said. "This is part of a larger decree that a woman with child must drive from her mind all sadness, and all frightening memories. Such things shall not be written upon the child."

"We shall go and visit Ayie Devi in her temple," Soni said. "I must have her blessing or no happiness can come to my new family."

"That must be done," Mira bai agreed. "But it is better to wait until nearer the birth. Time will pass quickly and the weather will not be hot during your waiting for the month of Vaisaka."

"It will be a lovely time," Soni said. "We shall have our own little house under the trees, and when the morning's work is done I can sit in the shade and be happy."

She knew she could pass that time quickly, but the time that crawled unbearably slow were the two weeks before Gopal was to take her home. She did not speak of this to her mother, for Mira bai was holding on to the hours, wanting them to linger while she kept her child close.

And then suddenly everything changed.

Back in Vardana, the men were working on the hut. The cotton seed Gopal had given Anand was safely stored in a dry place, waiting for the new land to be made ready for its planting.

Rama consulted the astrologer to be sure the horoscopes were auspicious for starting work on the hut. Then he and Anand went out to the ancestral land and marked with stones the place where the hut was to stand. They chose the extreme northeast corner, a lovely knoll studded with trees. The house was to be eight paces long and six paces deep, gently curved like a wide horseshoe. When the time came for it to grow larger, there would be room for expanding. The entire household came to inspect the site, the women bringing on their heads big baskets of cow dung to be made into paste, for of course the ground must be purified before the building could begin. When the thick coating of shane paste had been spread, every one withdrew to a shady spot for prayers and songs while the sacred covering dried.

Then they marked off lines along the four sides with white lime, and painted proper red and white squares for the dwelling places of the household gods, who must be made welcome before human habitation can be safe. The guru came at last and performed his ceremonies, and now that all the important part had been cared for, the work of building could begin.

Hired laborers had dug holes the previous day, and into these were fitted stout poles, one pace apart. The mestri and the laborers he had brought, mostly stood around and gave orders, while Anand and his brothers did the actual work. But somehow that did not displease Anand, for he liked the house to come into being under their own hands. Even the younger brothers were helping enthusiastically, and at last the walls of mud and stone were rising. The town's best mason was in charge of this, and he was proud to have the walls rise up so quickly.

At the end of each day, the family were hungry and weary. But there was a fine feeling among them. Even Govind seemed to have put aside his jealousy because Anand had been given the land and the house of his own. The two widows had a large meal ready for them when they returned home, and after that the whole family sat together and talked about the next day's work. The women and the house servants were to come out as soon as their morning chores were finished. Everyone would carry from the bazaar grasses and twigs and the long palm fronds with which the roof would be thatched.

The central pole of the roof was about eleven feet high, which gave luxurious space to the interior. The walls them-

selves were nine feet high and the roof sloped to the front of
the house. When the thatching was finished the little boys
climbed up and threw buckets of water over the roof to be
sure it was pukka.

When the house reached this point, the older brothers
went to their own fields, leaving the finishing to the women
and Anand and the youngsters. The whole house was once
again covered with shane paste, acrid smelling and clean
seeming. They would build a chula, or cooking place, this
morning, a small clay stove about ten inches high. The south-
west corner of any house is where the fire-god has his quarters,
so the cooking section must be there.

The women looped jute ropes over the rafters, and suspended a pole so that clothes could be kept neat and tidy.
Anand hung Memsahib Mom's gift blanket first, his throat
tight with sorrow. Could he ever make them understand why
he had to build this house, and come back to the soil?

The two younger boys Dhuni and Dhuki scoured the country until they found just the right flat rock to be a doorstep.

At last the family stood off among the trees and admired
the finished hut. They would plant banana trees around it,
for it is a good thing to lie half asleep and hear the wind talking and the banana leaves answering. Anand said he needed
no more help now; he wanted to move all their possessions
into the house with no one else to see the house transformed.

The first things he carried in (after Memsahib Mom's
wedding gift) were his books. If a man is to be truly at home,
his mind must have first place in the house. He stood a long
time looking at his books after he had lined them up across
the shelf he had put up for them. He had collected some of
the ancient, beloved books, such as the Ramayana and the
Mahabharata, and the Bhagavad-Gita, by which a man could
richly live. But he also had some of the works of modern

Marathi writers on this shelf . . . the historical novels of Hari Narayan Apte, and the social and political broadsides of Bhandarkar, Ranade and Keshavant. Some of the books belonged to the Mission; he must carry them back someday, and that would give him an excuse to go and see the friends who thought he had failed them. But for now, it was good to have the borrowed books among his own; they were a visible link with the life he had lost.

Each book was a world. The covers opened like tiny gates; one could step through those gates and live in a secret place. One could step into those worlds, and never again be quite the same man. For those secret worlds he had risked being alienated from his family . . . and from the old contentment.

What kind of man would he be now if he had never opened one of these shut worlds? He would have been like his brothers, content with what could be held in the hands, never missing what the mind had not tasted. He had everything possible to make him happy . . . his mysterious, lovely wife, his doting father, a portion of land that would belong to him and his children forever . . . why did he need the restless urging that was always in him, the hunger, the never sleeping hunger that uncoiled in his mind and would never be stilled?

The Kumbi caste to which he belonged was formed of contented men who knew but two hungers, and these present only to be satisfied. But he knew three hungers, and the third was as sharp as any. Had he a right to open these books to Soni . . . to offer her this never-to-be-silenced need of knowing? A flood of joy was his answer. There was no satisfaction anywhere unless hunger came first. The lethargy of earth and earth-living always sought to lull the mind into deadness. "Sleep and eat and make love . . . and let the mind lie comfortably dead," earth-living urged.

But nothing was really good until the mind had seen it so;

nothing had a voice unless there was an awakened mind to hear. If need be, he would be wretched all his life, but he would stay awake. And Soni would be wakened to live beside him.

It was past dark when he reached his father's lane. Jeveram, Gopal's old friend from the bazaar, was sitting on the veranda of a neighboring house waiting for him. It struck Anand as very odd that the old family friend was not visiting with Rama and the boys.

"I have been to your father's house," Jeveram said hastily. "I've had my visit there. But now I thought I might speak a few minutes with you."

"Fine," Anand said, though he could see in the lined old face that it was not a casual call, and that the old man was troubled. Jeveram got up and came over to look carefully into Anand's face.

"You are a happy boy these days," he said falteringly.

"I have everything with which to be happy," Anand said. "My father has told you about my new house?"

"He has told me," Jeveram said. Then without warning, he put his arm around Anand's shoulders. "Maybe I should not be telling you what I have come to say. Govind says I should not worry you with such news. Nor your old father, either. It may be only rumor, anyway. You know how bazaar talk is . . . "

"What is it?" Anand said quickly. "Whatever it is, tell me."

"Late this afternoon, some traders came through here on their way from Dahagaon. They passed close to Marvali. . . ."

"Yes . . . yes . . . but what did they have to say," Anand cried impatiently.

"There is an epidemic sweeping south from Khumgaon which is not very far from Marvali."

"What kind of epidemic?"

"Cholera. Some magicians passed through that country a few days ago, and one of them was ill. They drank at the well . . . Several people in Khumgaon have died. They're deserting Khumgaon . . . you know how that is . . . The other villages can't keep them out . . . and Marvali is nearby. One cannot measure the fury of the gods when they are aroused. . . ."

Before he had finished the faltering sentences, Anand had broken away. "You were a good friend to come and tell me, Jeveram . . . no doubt my brothers are getting the tonga ready right now for me to leave. . . ."

"Wait . . . one thing more, Anand," Jeveram said, hurrying after him. "I promised Govind I would not tell you. Govind said there was no use to worry you. Govind said it was probably only rumor anyway. . . . So I promised."

"There's no time to bother with that," Anand said anxiously. "If there's the slightest danger. . . ."

"Will you say you heard it as you came into town from your field? I would not want to lose your brother's friendship."

"Yes . . . yes . . . anything. That doesn't matter, does it?" Anand said pulling himself away from the trembling old hand holding him back. If he had not been utterly consumed with fear, he would have had emotion left with which to be amazed at his brother. But the fear was a huge bonfire in the center of his mind, and nothing else had any importance.

He ran through the door of the house, and saw the family seated around the courtyard.

"You're late coming home," Rama called out to him. "We thought you might be sleeping in your new house tonight."

Only the tail of his attention registered the fact that Govind obviously had not told of Jeveram's visit.

"I've heard some terrible news," he said. "Father . . . you've got to let me take the tonga . . . I've got to go to Marvali right now. . . ."

"Marvali? What for, my son?" Rama asked, squinting up into the darkness. "What bad news have you heard? Is Soni bai ill?"

"You've not heard? There's an epidemic raging in the villages around Marvali. The people are running away, and some of them will hide in Marvali. I can't leave Soni there."

"Of course not," Rama said, after a moment. "You must go at once and bring her home. I wish I were younger, so I could go with you."

"I'll go with him," Govind said. "My brother's troubles are my own."

"No one needs to go with me," Anand said. "I've made the journey before . . . there's nothing anyone could do to help me."

12

HORROR WAS IN THE VERY AIR, AND ONE WAS afraid of even the people one loved. The villagers had made the little clay horses, and strung up the tiny chariots of colored thread, and placed them conspicuously at both gates of Marvali so that the goddess Sitala, who brought the illness in her dark garments, would decide to drive away and leave the people to bury their dead. The cholera and the smallpox dead are not burned, as are the ordinary dead, but are buried in the earth. And often those who bury them, bring home the cholera to their families.

Of all the scourges that the gods send, cholera moves most swiftly to the end. A family may look on the illness in the morning, and decide to escape by noon, packing up all they can carry in their cart and hurrying off as fast as bullocks can be made to hurry. But by night, when they have driven innocently into a neighboring village, carefully telling nothing about themselves, one or two of them may be dead, hidden under the blankets with thick black tongues sticking out like pot handles from horrible faces.

Nobody knows how to fight the scourge; sometimes it seems that merely knowing the name of a man who has died with it brings the disease into one's own house. The rottenness of it comes first to the mind as a scavenger, and who knows how to protect the mind? The gates of the village can be shut, and chatias hung over the doors of the houses, and the family huddle quietly together refusing all intercourse. But then the fear comes into the mind and in an hour the child lying on the mother's lap is stricken. When the mother lays the child on the ground and goes to prepare the rice on the chula, the illness goes with her, and when she hands about the rice, she offers death with it.

The carts came streaming from Khumgaon, trying to hide their reason for coming, and the gates of Marvali were shut against them. But the illness crawled invisibly out of the carts, and climbed over the gates and slunk through the lanes and entered whatever houses it pleased, and no one could say how it got in.

Soni was paralyzed with fear. She kept her eyes closed, praying. She kept her two hands gripped over her stomach as if she would make of them shut gates to protect her new child. Her mind muttered the names of the gods continuously, and sometimes it muttered the name of Anand among the gods.

"I must take his child to him," she said over and over. "I cannot let his child stay here where death is looking at us from every corner."

She begged Mira bai to run away with her.

"Two women on the road alone?"

"Then there will be one woman alone on the road," she said bitterly. "I cannot stay."

"You cannot escape, my child. Death is tramping along the roads too. It is blowing in the breeze along the road. Either God must care for you, wherever you are, or you are safe nowhere."

At nightfall across the violet emptiness of the space between Marvali and Khumgaon, they saw the dull blur of pink against the sky and they knew the health officers had decided to burn the village in desperate precaution. Before midnight fell, there was a matching glow in the west, and that meant the sweepers' village was given up. Already people were flee-ing from Marvali, having no idea where they were going, driven only by the fear of being *any* place. Soni would have flung herself into any cart that was leaving but Mari bai held her back.

"Since when have the gods respected those whose bones flow with fear?" she asked sternly. "Hold up your head and pray. And make the child in your womb pray with you, if you do not want him to believe he has chosen a cowardly mother."

"We *are* praying," Soni cried, "and the gods tell us to run."

"The gods tell you no such thing."

"My lord would tell me, if he were here."

"Then we have married you to a cowardly lord."

"Ayie, help me get away. I'm not afraid for myself. It's for the child."

All the next day terror reigned. An old man in the next lane was dead, and a mother and her child over by the river. The illness swam across the river, and flew through the air like a vulture, and nobody knew where it was stalking now, looking this house over and putting its mark on that one for tomor-row. The priests were praying, and men with drums were squatting at the cross-lanes, trying to drive out the evil spirits. But Sitala had set up her ghostly house among them, and she was not going to move on until she wanted to move.

The chowdris and the Patel met in the middle of the bagh and you could see them talking and shaking their heads. Messengers came running from this lane and that to tell of the growing stain of death. Finally the Patel decided that the one hope was to have everyone leave who could leave.

"I will stay," Gopal said. "There will be old people to take care of."

"You are an old man, Gopal," the moneylender, Two-fingered Mohan said to him. "I insist that you leave."

"I helped build Marvali," Gopal said. "I will stay and protect it, so that our people will have something to come back to." Then he saw the look in Two-fingered Mohan's eye, and it almost made him ill to read what was behind the protection in the look.

"We must take care of your health," Two-fingered Mohan said unctuously. "You are a man who is important to all of us."

The Patel said, "You must go with them, Gopal, and keep them from being too frightened. I will stay here in Marvali and make the decisions as they come."

So, near midnight though it was, the whole village was waked . . . if any had been asleep. The chowdris themselves went up and down the lanes, beating on the drums and calling out the warnings.

"Everyone who is well must leave. No sick people can leave. Only the well and strong. We will care for your old people who cannot travel . . . Take what you need . . . Your houses may be burned for safety's sake. . . . "

They took all they could carry, and those families who had lost some member carried along the clothes he had worn as a comforting reminder of him. Soni was the first one to scramble into Gopal's cart, bringing along nothing she owned, but holding to her heart Anand's little book of poetry, which of course she could not read. The sisters-in-law chattered hysterically, remembering this and that item they should have brought with them. But Soni had not a word to say.

The Patel stood at the gate, and spoke to each cart as it drove through. "God be with you. Go out at least two miles from Marvali . . . to the chotta jungle. If anyone falls ill, then you must move on farther . . . after you have buried him."

Almost half the village crossed the river to the chotta

jungle, going as quietly as possible so Sitala would not hear them leaving and follow mischievously.

Morning came, and no one felt like doing anything but praying. Everyone looked suspiciously at everyone else, to make sure the mark of Sitala was not upon him. Somehow the day passed, and a kind of meal was eaten, though a half hour later nobody could remember whether or not food had been swallowed. The sun set, and everyone lay down on the earth.

Gopal stood in the midst of the silent bundles of fear, and spoke to the earth: "You are our mother. For countless generations our ancestors drew their reward from you. They saw your needs and cared for them as we have tried to do, unworthily. Mahadev will never curse you again with a deluge, because we have pleaded. We lie against your breast tonight in our fear, and we beg you to put your hand upon us and keep us from the scourge. We will never desert you, Mandara Pravata, and we beg you never to desert us."

But there was no comfort on the great warm breast of the earth. If your ear could catch the beating of her heart, you heard that it was a troubled beating.

At dawn a cartload of people came squeaking along the riverbank. They had passed through Khumgaon, and had heard the wailing behind the locked gates of Marvali, and they warned that another two miles must be put between the banished ones and their old homes. Then, through the mists that rose from the river, the exiles saw a terrifying sight . . . a few old men and women staggering toward them. Gopal ran out to meet them, so they would not come into the very midst.

"Wait . . . stay where you are," he cried, as if he could see perching on each old shoulder, the silent black bird of Sitala.

"The Patel told us to come," they shouted weakly. "He

said you would take care of us."

"I'll go back and get someone to help me . . . the widows of your families . . . wait just where you are."

But they kept coming, bringing death with them, and it was more than human hearts could do to turn them back or run from them. So they were taken into the groups and fed, and by afternoon when many of them fell into the black sleep, everyone pretended that it was normal sleep. And when they heard the final hiccoughs racking the old weak bodies, they said valiantly, "They are thirsty. Give them my lothi to drink out of."

Then suddenly all hope was lost, for in the sky where Marvali lay, there rose a sudden spreading brilliance. Marvali was being burned. Even from this distance, you could imagine you heard the wailing, and the crackling of the roofs, and the serpents of fire hissing as they ran from house to house, devouring everything they could digest, and jumping angrily over the stone walls which would not burn.

You could see the fire in your own house, leaping from the blazing roofs and hurrying to the sealed-up room where the grain was hidden, so the patwari wouldn't collect taxes for it. You could hear the fire smacking its lips with joy as it ate next season's seed crop. . . . Two-fingered Mohan, who had the only glass windows in town, would not have them any longer, for they would melt or crack or do whatever glass did when it cowered before flame. And the bright saris of the Widow Gupta which she was too wicked to give away when she had to go into her white clothes . . . how those would burn! Like the bright lust she could not hide. And the children's toys . . . and the sacred darbha grass . . . the fire would seize them and run across them as a boy runs across stepping stones in a stream. The fire would run on tiptoe across the sacred darbha grass, and so would reach every part of the house. . . . Every house would have the darbha grass because they had lately celebrated the eighth day of the Moon of Badra.

The glow in the sky died down at last, but the blaze in the minds burned on brightly. All the childhoods, all the young married days had gone up in those flames . . . all memories and all hopes. The women lay on their faces so there would be no shining of tears seen glittering. At last the Patel himself came walking into their midst. His flesh was hanging on his bones like a badly draped dhoti; no doubt he had not eaten these two days; his eyes were carnelians glowing red in his eye sockets.

He wanted to make a comforting speech. He opened his mouth and tried, but his hands only fluttered in the air, and his lips only trembled on the bones of his face. "We will build again," he said. That was his whole speech. But everyone nodded, and the men said, "Yes, we will build again." It was enough of a speech; a man might have talked for an hour, but what more could he have said?

Soni, her hands still clasped around her thin stomach, lay still, half listening and half praying. Now she believed she would never see Anand again. Time had gone mad for her; she did not know whether it was one day or two, two nights or three, since they had left Marvali. The whole world had gone mad, and nothing would ever be as it had been. And she would never find the soul of her lord to tell him that he was to have had a son. He would never know; through all his lives to come, he would never know.

Everything was quiet now, and the wailing that was being done was wailing in the heart, which would not be still for many a year. She slept a little, only a thin veil of sleep not quite covering the consciousness. Throbbing constantly like the measures in the blood awake or asleep, her lord's name was repeating itself. Where are you? Why am I separated from you? My lord, my lord. . . .

Then she was aware of something moving about . . . a shadow, a tall shadow, stopping here and there and bending down, then rising and moving to another bundle. She opened her eyes fully, still not sure whether she was awake or asleep. It was her lord, his smooth hair shining in the darkness, his dark face clouded beyond seeing. But she knew. He had come somehow. He was looking for her.

She sat up quickly, her face lifted to him. He turned and saw her, and ran, half stumbling, and squatted down, crying out half-words. Their hands were cleaving together; there were tears on both faces, and choked senseless laughter in their throats.

"My lord . . . you have come down from heaven?"

"No . . . I came by the road," he said, shivering with relief that could say itself only in mirth. He held her close and covered her face and her hands with kisses.

"I've been half dead with worry, since I found out," he said. "I could not live if anything had happened to you."

"Nothing could happen to me," she said with false bravery, now that she felt his flesh under her hands. "It was only the child I feared about."

"The child?"

"Our son," she said. "The first of ninety-nine, my lord."

13

THE FIRST DAYS IN THE NEW HOUSE WERE enchanted ones, as if heaven had moved so close to earth that one could not tell which was which. Jeveram hurried from the bazaar in the middle of a working day to tell Anand he had word from Gopal. He was safe, and all of his family. Prayers were answered.

"He wants to come and live with me in my wretched house for a while. Since my old wife died, there has been no woman to care for my house," Jeveram said. "Gopal's wife could cook for the three of us."

"But they will be rebuilding Marvali, won't they?" Anand asked.

"So they say. Many families have gone back, and Gopal's sons are making out the best way they can in the open on their own land, so the crops won't be lost. But Gopal wants to try something else," Jeveram said. "He wants to have a stall in the bazaar."

"A Kumbi turned merchant?"

"He has hinted at it before," Jeveram said. "He needs some money, does Gopal. If I did not know what his pride was like about never having his thumbprint fixed to a debt, I'd think our good Gopal had fallen into the hands of a money-lender."

"Other men do," Anand said, "and it is not like crows stealing their peace."

"But you do not understand Gopal," Jeveram said. "Some men are proud of one thing and some are proud of another."

"And will you let him come and work with you in the bazaar?"

"He is my old friend," Jeveram said simply.

When Anand told Soni of this conversation, he softened its import as best he could. "Your fine clever father! Other men will be trying to scratch up the mud with their bare hands to rebuild their houses. But Gopal is going to work and earn some money to hasten the building," he said.

All that it meant to Soni was that she would have her parents living in the same town . . . a circumstance almost too good to be true, when the custom is for daughters to marry and live far away in distant villages.

"The gods are good," she said, "to let my mother be near when my son is born . . . since now they have no home where I could go."

Everyone in Rama's house was gratified that Soni had conceived so soon. It was a good omen, and added one more reason for Rama's delight in his third son. Before his soul left the earth he would see a fine new branch starting from the tree . . . a new line of descendants to honor him. Whatever Anand needed to begin his farming he must have immediately. Even if he wanted to use some of the modern implements, he must have them. If Govind and Ghulum had anything they wanted to say about that, he would silence them immediately. He was still the head of his house, wasn't he?

Rama had intended before this to go to the civic center, and officially register the ancestral land in Anand's name. He had expected to do this immediately after the wedding, but somehow the occasion never seemed to present itself. It must be made a ceremonial event . . . perhaps the right time would be when they celebrated the birth of Anand's son. He smiled happily when he thought of it.

Most of the land Anand was cultivating this first season was to be planted with Gopal's cotton. But a part of it was to be used for vegetables, supplying the family food and providing currency which would pay for various services rendered by shoemakers, carpenters, the dhersi who did the sewing, and the shadowy sweeper who slipped in and out of the back of the house, collecting refuse without giving the offense of being seen.

Soni was to have as much flower garden as she wanted. She began by tucking the seeds of gourds in many places, beside the wall, between naked rocks, and along the path that took her to the well, a quarter of a mile away.

As she planted the big flat seeds, she saw herself soon searching for the prettiest little gourd of them all, which should be a rattle for her son. She closed her eyes and saw him, stout and bright-eyed in his little shirt, running toward her with his arms outstretched, and his legs spread for steadiness, so that his silhouette was a five-pointed star. Squatting with her seeds above the bare ground, she saw a whole life-ful of her son . . . and all her other sons, and her body felt bathed in light as it felt when Anand loved her.

The trees near the hut were already her friends, the familiar peepul and tikur, and between them the beloved tulasi bushes. Her son would love the trees. . . .

The greatest joy of all was that she could step to the door of her hut any time she wished, and shading her eyes against the merciless sun, she could scan the acres and see her husband working. The eyes of most wives were deprived of such a sight, because fields were far from houses. But she and Anand were together, as they had dreamed of being.

Often she ran out and spoke to him for the sheer luxury of knowing no older person was at hand to criticize. Morning and afternoon she took him a cool drink of water and a piece of fruit, and watched him standing beside his plow while he enjoyed it. Could there be a handsomer sight? Nowhere.

After the noonday meal, he rested a few minutes on the charpai which she had pulled out of the house and set in the deep blue shade under the peepul tree. Then he called to her and she came running, her studybook clutched against her heart. After a few weeks she was reading simple books in the Marathi language, and Anand said that surely by next year he would be teaching her English. After the lesson he always read aloud to her. Especially she reveled in the narrative poem called "Kamla," written by the modern Marathi writer who signed himself "Bee." This poem told the sad but heroic story of a young girl, and Soni found it so absorbing that she was guilty of forgetting who it was that read to her. She would not have believed that it would be possible for a book to make a woman forget the man she loved, but it was so. She sat cross-legged beside him on the charpai, and the tree disappeared, and the beloved hut . . . and the birds stopped singing, and the land shimmering with heat . . . all vanished, and a new landscape unrolled in the mind, brighter and clearer than reality.

They carried a rock out beyond the shadow of the tree, and when the shadow covered that rock, it was time for the reading to stop. Otherwise twilight would have fallen and the field would have gone unplowed.

Gradually several young men from Vardana fell into the habit of coming up to Anand's hut in the evenings once or twice a week. They brought their own cottonseed oil lamps with them; for an hour they would sit around the flat stone which Dhuni and Dhuki had set for the doorstep, and Anand would help them with their reading.

Afterwards, as Soni and Anand stood in their doorway

watching their friends go down the hill, their shadows long behind them in the moonlight, Anand would say, "But you are my brightest pupil."

"You say that only to please me."

"I say it because it is the truth. Stone soaks up no water; wood soaks up some; but the Doctor Sahib has sponges which will take all the water offered to them. You are such a sponge."

"A fine name for a wife . . . a sponge!" she cried, so delighted that she had to disguise her pleasure in make-believe offense.

"You'll see . . . next year you will be reading twice as fluently as my men pupils. And you'll be reading a little English besides."

"Next year I'll have my son beside me."

"We'll teach him to read also . . . immediately," he grinned at her.

Surely no woman could have had more cause for happiness . . . a son growing in her body, knowledge growing in her mind, and a heart that was a sponge, taking all the love that was offered to it!

On all days but Thursday she went to the bazaar; Thursday was the burra-bazaar when strangers came from other villages to do business in Vardana. That made everything too noisy and confusing, not suitable for a wife. She had become acquainted with a number of Kumbi women at the bazaar, and while she washed Anand's dhotis and her saris on the banks of the stream. Sometimes in the afternoon they came shyly to visit her, and after a while they looked at the outside of her schoolbooks . . . and then, one day, one of them ventured within. After that, almost every afternoon she had a pupil to teach, often a young mother who absent-mindedly gave her breast to a child, so it would not cry while she studied. Often these grateful students insisted upon bringing some delicacy they had cooked in the morning, or a bit of wool for Soni to knit into a garment for her baby.

"You are a better pupil . . . and a better teacher than I am," Anand said laughingly. "Nobody offers to pay *me* for my lessons! And today we eat a melon from your work, and yesterday we had jellabees!"

"I would give you pay for my lessons, if I had anything more to give you," she said seriously. "But I have promised you everything that I shall know throughout all my lives to come."

Whenever she went to the bazaar, she saw Gopal for a few moments. It was hard to believe the proud old man had come down to haggling about a seer of peanuts with some rude leatherworker, who had the right to speak to him as an equal since he put himself in a bazaar stall. Gopal looked unhappy these days, but, of course, he had little to make him happy since he had lost his home, and his wife was cooking with another woman's utensils. Mira bai was bearing up much better than he, and in fact was enjoying the novelty of living in a strange hut in a strange town. Old Jeveram was grateful for her care, and she found it not a bad life at all, if only her lord could smile again. He had been a chowdri, honored and consulted, in Marvali. But here he was only a dispossessed huckster, eking out a few rupees a week.

He was not popular in the bazaar, and this hurt him and mystified him, for he was used to being loved. It seemed to him now that both gods and men had turned against him. If only he had the blessings of either, to console him for the loss of the others! But he felt utterly alone, and punished for some crime he could not remember committing. The other bazaar merchants, who once had cultivated him because he was a customer, now shunned and abused him because he was a competitor. Old Jeveram could not seem to persuade anyone that his friend needed sympathy and encouragement.

"Let him go back where he came from," they said. "We have all the merchants we need here . . . barely enough trade to go around. And here he is, trying to sell produce from Marvali! Let him bring customers if he wants to bring something!"

Each week when the Thursday cart came from Marvali, Gopal dreaded to meet his old townsmen, for he could not believe they did not detect the disgrace of debt into which he had fallen. And Two-fingered Mohan was not above sending him messages so thinly veiled that it was a mercy of indifference that the messenger didn't see through them.

"Two-fingered Mohan wanted to come with the cart today," the driver innocently reported. "He says he yearns for the sight of his old friend. I didn't know you were friendly with that jackal, Gopal."

"I try to be friendly with all men," Gopal said, flushing uncomfortably. "Tell Mohan I hope he can come next week. There is business in Vardana that I could turn his way."

"I will tell him that," the driver said. "And if he offers me a few pice for carrying the message . . . which I doubt he will . . . I will divide the gift with you." Then, lowering his voice, "But surely there must be less hardhearted moneylenders in Vardana. Why should anyone want to borrow from Mohan?"

"Men have their pride," Gopal said. "And if money can be borrowed from a bania in another village . . . well, the sight of the debt doesn't hang continuously in front of one's eyes. Or at least, that is how I have analyzed it," Gopal said.

"But debt is nothing to be ashamed about," the driver pointed out. "It is as inevitable as losing one's teeth, or not caring whether one sleeps with a wife after a while. Why should a man be ashamed of what is natural to men?"

"Debt is not natural to all men," Gopal said fiercely. "There are proud people who would rather have maggots poisoning the spleen than a debt poisoning the purse."

The driver shrugged his shoulders unbelievingly, "Well, such men are crazy," he said. "I was born with my father's debt on me, and I guess he was born with his father's. I've paid it back at least three times in my life . . . three mountains of interest and one little hill of debt."

He remembered the conversation a month later, when Gopal got into trouble. He asked all kinds of people in Marvali what they made of it. *Had* Gopal stolen the money, or hadn't he? Certainly a man who felt so passionately on the subject *might* have stolen.

It all began with the jowari from Marvali which Gopal had hoped to sell at a good price. Before daylight he had gone out to the other side of town to meet the Thursday cart when it arrived. He crouched beside the road, waiting, his chin on his knees, his eyes filled with the sadness of departed memories. Other carts passed him, but he knew the Marvali one by its creaking wheel. The light from its lantern fell on the swinging heads of the bullocks, and Gopal recognized them as old friends.

He called out to the driver and climbed upon the cart, momentarily happy as if he were now on native ground. The driver told him such news as there was from his village. Some houses were built again, not on the old ground, of course. The government health officers had their reason for prohibiting use of the old ground, but the villagers' reason was that it had been cursed by Sitala. Let the government men prattle their modern talk about rodents and fleas that carried the cholera germs; the villagers knew.

Marvali would rise again, never fear. Gopal's own sons were still living outdoors on the edge of their field, as many families were doing. Water was the difficulty, for the old well had been condemned. Even after all the pinkie the health officers had put in, so that people had to drink dark purple water which tasted of poison . . . still the well was condemned. The driver did nothing but grumble.

"Cheer up," Gopal said. "I'm sending money back with you for the jowari. No waiting, no delay. I have the money ready. How many bags?"

"Thirty bags," the driver said, "and we've never grown better jowari. It is a mystery."

"No mystery. The gods are sorry for us."

Gopal counted the bags. Thirty, as the driver said. He had already made arrangements for their sale. They would deliver them directly to the grain merchant. As they drove he examined the grain. It *was* plump and good. Some of it had come from his sons' own fields. When he put his hand inside a bag and felt it, warm and deliciously clean through his fingers, he felt as if he recognized it for his own. It spoke to him of the hard but just earth which would give a man exactly what he was entitled to, and no more. It made him remember the sky on the thousands of afternoons when he had plowed and sown and harvested. . . . the satiny sky during growing season, which seldom had clouds. It spoke of the weariness that makes a man's ankles feel like stone at the end of the day, and the blinding heat that wrings the sweat from a thin body and takes the strength with it. And it spoke of the nights when the jowari wasn't quite ready to harvest, when he and his sons took turns guarding the crop, for fear some thief would slink into the field and steal their season's labor. (Such things had happened.) All this was in the feel of the grain in the bags, and he let his hand play across the silky smoothness as a lover's hand plays beneath a sari.

He paid a good price for the sacks, and gave the driver the

money right then and there, so that he could take it back to
Marvali instead of promises and delays. The burra-bazaar
was already busy when they arrived, for, of course, they had
had to stop along the way for a morning meal and their
prayers. They drove the cart as close as possible to the stall
of the grain merchant, and carried in the thirty bags. Then
the cart was taken out to the edge of the market so that the
bullocks could drowse away the day, and the driver could rest
and refresh himself as he pleased, before the long drive home.

Gopal had an agreement with the stout merchant named
Chandra, who was purchasing a large quantity of grain to send
to Kalyan, the railway center. Chandra had said he would
give him eight annas profit on each bag, if the grain was as
good as he promised. The profit would be rupees fifteen!

"The jowari is even better than I promised," Gopal said
to Chandra happily. "It has been watered with tears and
trouble and nourished by prayers, and it has grown fat and
rich. Marvali always grows fine jowari, as you know, but this
year with sorrow at every man's throat, the earth has opened
her heart to the Kumbis. You will see."

"I will see," Chandra said unpleasantly, "or I shall not do
business with you."

The grain *was* magnificent; Gopal could see by the quick
flash in Chandra's eyes that it was much better than he had
expected. Kalyan would pay plenty for it.

Chandra said grudgingly, "It is pretty good. But it doesn't
look as if it will be good-keeping grain."

"It is the best," Gopal said, dry-mouthed with fear. "If
you don't want it, I can sell it to someone else."

"I'll take it, my poor friend," Chandra said, smiling in-
solently at him as if he could see into the very pit of his fear.

Before Gopal realized what was happening, the boys who
helped Chandra around his stall had seized the bags and in

a few minutes had dumped the contents on a soiled cloth laid on the ground. The grain heaped up into a golden mountain, sweet-smelling as the earth itself.

Gopal cried, "What are you doing?"

"I must inspect the twenty-seven bags I have purchased," Chandra said in an oily voice. "You would not want me to buy grain without seeing it, would you?"

"Twenty-seven bags?" Gopal gasped. "What are you talking about? I have sold you thirty bags."

"Oh, I am sorry for you, my poor friend," Chandra said in a maddeningly pleasant and sympathetic voice. "Someone must have cheated you. I counted twice while we were talking. Twenty-seven."

"Thirty," Gopal screamed, pouncing on the pile of empty sacks lying in a tangle under the shelf of the stall. He began counting them with shaking hands. Twenty-seven, twenty-eight, twenty-nine, thirty, thirty-one . . . and up to forty-three.

"But surely you aren't going to claim that you had forty-three bags, are you?" Chandra asked, wagging his head with mirth. "Those are some of the other bags I bought this morning."

Gopal was trembling all over now, his tired old face was crushed into a grimace of frustration. From nearby stalls, all sorts of people had surrounded them, drawn by the confusion and by Gopal's hysterically raised voice. Chandra put his arm fondly around his shoulders, trying to calm him.

"But don't be alarmed, my friend," he said soothingly, while the spectators began explaining to each other what was happening. "No need to be worried about anything. We shall measure the jowari. That will be best. Fifty seers to a bag."

"Fifty seers," Gopal agreed, wondering if his brain could have played a trick on him in his chronic anxiety. In the cart he had counted thirty sacks; that was sure.

Chandra's helpers picked up a huge measuring can and began juggling it expertly through the fluid grain.

"Don't waste any, boys," Chandra said sleepily, patting his fat stomach with his smug hands. "We want brother Gopal to have his full due, you know."

The bags, fat and hard, were filled before Gopal's eyes, and the pile of grain left on the soiled cloth was very meagre. Twenty-four bags were filled now, and you couldn't help wondering how they would ever scoop up enough grain to fill the other three. Gopal couldn't believe his eyes. Had Chandra slipped in bags larger than the Marvali bags? Was the measure bigger than is generally used? Something was wrong, for now the twenty-seventh bag was being filled and it was a lean and wrinkled specimen, by no means solid as it should have been.

"Not quite twenty-seven," Chandra said. "But to show you how generous I am . . . because you do not really belong in our town . . . I am going to credit you with twenty-seven bags. Just as I counted."

Gopal looked around helplessly. "I will carry my bags away and offer them somewhere else," he said angrily, "before I will let you cheat an honest man."

Chandra was counting out the money calmly on the shelf, and the silver rupees rang out solidly as he laid them down. The rupees fifteen, which would have been the legitimate profit, were more than wiped out by the chicanery. Gopal would have no way to make up the difference between what he had given to the driver of the Thursday cart and what Chandra proposed paying him.

Suddenly he seemed to lose his senses with indignation and outrage. Before he could stop himself, he had swept the rupees off the counter with an angry reckless hand. They flew in every direction, and the crowd gasped with unbelief that such a thing could happen. Everyone swooped down to pick up the glittering coins, shouting and gesticulating and then holding each other back.

"Don't touch my money," Chandra cried authoritatively. "Call the police. Call the police."

Gopal, his head hanging in shame at the role he could not imagine himself playing, said, "No need for the police. We are all honest people here. I will pick up the coins and apologize. For a moment I didn't know what I was doing."

The boys who worked for Chandra, and the fat merchant himself, were scooping up the money, and laying it back on the counter. At the mention of the police, the bystanders had all stepped back a pace and were arguing and explaining to each other.

"Did you ever see such a thing? He had better count his money. This is a matter for the police, wouldn't you say?"

The policeman, at that moment arrived, his red pughri standing out above the heads of the crowd, his handsome scarlet and purple belt swinging the lathi stick conspicuously, eager for violence. "What's happening here?" he cried, knowing that every eye was on his handsome hatefulness.

Chandra hovering between his bags of grain and the money, both of which seemed now to belong to him, rose and smiled pleasantly.

"I'm sorry, officer," he said. "Nothing is happening. Only a slight argument between my friend and me. He is confused."

Everyone in the crowd was trying to inform the policeman, and he, splendid in his white uniform, was switching his head about so that the purple and gold tassel on his pughri was flashing handsomely.

"We'll have no trouble in this bazaar," he was saying.

"Anyone who wants trouble can find plenty of it with the C.I.D."

"Nobody wants trouble," Chandra said placatingly. "Least of all my poor friend from Marvali, who doesn't know very much about buying and selling."

Now the policeman picked up a few of the rupees and looked at them as if he'd never seen such things before. "I suggest you count your money," he said to Chandra.

"No need to count, I'm sure," Chandra said. "The deal is off now. I'll put the money back in my pocket, and Gopal here can get someone to help him haul away his jowari. He has decided not to sell it."

"Count the money," the policeman said again, still enjoying the sight of the little pile of paper and silver on the counter. "You can't be sure what might have happened in a skirmish like this."

Graciously, Chandra shrugged and nonchalantly counted his money. Everyone knew to a pice how much had been put on the counter. When he reached the end of the counting, his voice nearly failed him, for there were six rupees missing. After a stunned silence, a clamor arose through the crowd, which was thicker than ever now that the policeman had joined the drama.

All looked at Gopal with suspicion in their faces. How had he managed to steal six rupees before their very eyes? He began falteringly to deny it before any words had accused him.

Chandra said, " I cannot believe such a thing! I have tried to help this man ever since he came down here and pushed his way into our bazaar. And now to think. . . . "

The policeman, glad to be doing something important, went over and touched Gopal with his lathi, flipping the old man's hands disrespectfully with the wooden stick.

"Give 'em up," the policeman said. "And come along with me to the police station."

"I haven't the money," Gopal said in a whisper. "I have only three annas tied in my dhoti. You can see for yourself."

Suddenly then there was an uproar from the crowd. The last bag to be filled topped over on its skinny stomach, and out of its wide mouth two silver rupees rolled. Everyone near the bag stepped back as if he might be accused, and every eye in the crowd was fastened on the glittering rupees.

The policeman himself went over and put the bag back on its feet. "What's this?" he cried excitedly. "The money's here in the bag . . . six rupees of it!"

Chandra was standing a long distance from the bag. "Why there must be some mistake," he cried in a loud, incredulous voice. "How could the money get into the bag?"

"How indeed?" the policeman said. "This rascal was going to take the grain away, wasn't he? And six of your rupees with it, I'm afraid."

The indignation then became a tornado that whirled through the whole bazaar. In a few minutes everyone knew what had happened. You remember Gopal, the old man from Marvali that Jeveram is trying to help? He's stolen six rupees from our own Chandra! Who would believe that a man could repay kindness with theft? And he was supposed to be such an honorable man. Well, these days you never can tell.

Jeveram sent his own stall boy running the two miles to Anand's field to summon him. Then he himself hurried over to Chandra's stall and pushed his way through the crowd. The policeman was dragging out the enjoyable encounter as long as possible, for it was a pleasure to enforce his duties. He felt liked here, and that was a novelty to him, for in India, nobody, neither the criminal nor the innocent, really likes a policeman. Village people have their own ways of balancing justice, and they resent the intrusion of legality.

"It's an open and shut case here," the policeman was saying excitedly. "So I'll just take you along to the police station, my man."

Jeveram said loudly, "Who saw him steal the rupees?"

That basic question expressed the whole crux of Indian justice. For evidence is not as convincing as witnessing. Evidence depends on circumstances, and circumstances can be twisted and distorted so that they lie blatantly. Evil spirits can do what they please to circumstances. Only seeing can be relied upon.

The crowd answered nothing, each man knowing that Jeveram had touched the important point.

"The money was found in his bag of jowari," a skinny little man with one eye said. "There's no denying that. We all saw it."

"But who saw Gopal put the money there?"

"We were watching something else."

"The facts speak," someone cried. "We saw the money in the bag."

Jeveram said, "This is an honorable Kumbi. You know him well."

Chandra said mildly, "He's been in the bazaar only a few months."

"But you've seen him coming on Thursdays for many a year," Jeveram said. "His family is the most honorable in Marvali."

"What's that got to do with the rupees in his bag?"

And so it went on, for almost an hour. Every time the policeman grabbed hold of Gopal's arm to drag him off, someone to whom justice was a nagging necessity, reminded them that nobody had *seen* the theft happen. So at last it was agreed that since there was much doubt, they would have an immediate trial by ordeal. The policeman, jealous of his rights, protested in vain, for suddenly this was out of his hands. Justice is older than policemen, and this crowd was now reaching back to the justice its ancestors revered.

"You may watch or you may leave," the policeman was told. "If this man is guilty, we will give him to you. After *we* have punished him. If the ordeal shows he is innocent, your hands will never touch him."

Chandra was protesting angrily at the unexpected development. He and a group of his friends were crying out that they were all modern people now and it was absurd to invoke the old-folk methods.

"Can you say you saw him put the money in his bag?"

"I do not need to see him. I saw the money *there*."

"Then let us ask the gods for their judgment."

Jeveram now had rallied a number of Kumbis to help their caste brother. As he looked around the crowd he saw that someone had brought Mira bai. She had her face covered by her sari, but he could see she was praying. Anand should arrive soon, and he would help. Meantime, they must clear a place in the center of the bazaar and prepare the ordeal ceremony. The ordeal of walking through fire must be endured only in the rainy season; the ordeal of staying under water must be suffered only in the very hot season; the poison ordeal was now against the law. So it seemed that in this case the ordeal by weights and scales would be right and just.

An old crossbeam scale that once had been used for weighing animals was found and set up in the middle of the bazaar. A Brahmin pandit was brought who would take care of the preliminaries. When he understood the nature of the case, he put on a fresh dhoti, and large beads around his neck, and then he decorated his chest and forehead with ashes and white-clay markings, so that the gods might read his plea accurately. He said a long prayer in the presence of Gopal, which ended with the words, "May this day be for thee a day of virtue, on which thy innocence will be proved. But if you are guilty, it cannot be hidden and you shall be punished."

Gopal, his forehead damp with suffering, said his own ritual in a trembling voice. "The gods have ordered a fair and holy decree in trial by ordeal. May they show mercy upon the truth of my word. Honor to the twelve suns and the eight winds. Between them they shall decide my weight. O Godess of Virtue, help me in my dilemma."

Soni and Anand arrived just in time to hear Gopal making his plea. Soni wanted to run to her father and embrace him, but Anand held her back. So she hid her face against his chest and prayed. She had no idea of what Gopal had been accused; but she was positive he was innocent.

All this had taken a great deal of time, and now it was high noon, the most auspicious time to perform the ordeal. The scale was ready, with a white banner above it, and its two huge pans in perfect balance. The priest had knelt down and had written in white chalk on the hard ground symbols of the accusation.

"Who are the accusers of this man?" he asked now in a solemn voice. Gopal stood with his head bowed. Chandra and the boys who helped him in the stall, and a few men who wanted to incur Chandra's good will stepped forward, eight of them. Around Gopal stood the members of his Kumbi caste. If he *had* brought dishonor on their caste, they must devise his punishment. Last year in punishing a man who had stolen a wife, they had accidentally killed him.

The pandit handed each of the accusers a lothi of water. Each passed Gopal in defiant procession, and threw the water into his face, the greatest insult possible.

"Let this sacred water purge you of your wrongdoing," each man said, and Gopal held up his face proudly to receive

the thrown water. If it was an ordeal for him to be disgraced
so publicly, it was a hundred times more terrible for his family
to see it happening. And a few who were not his family also
suffered in their love of dignity.

When the accusers were through with him, his clothes
were wet and he was a bedraggled sight. Some of the crowd
shouted out, "Let him go. He has had enough. We do not
need the scales to tell us about that man."

But once the ritual was started, it couldn't be stopped.
Gopal stepped on the west side of the scales, and the pandit
and his helpers began weighting the other pan with bricks
and sacred darbha grass. Gopal was a thin old man, and not
many bricks were required to lift his end of the scale so that
it hung suspended a foot above the ground. All watched
breathlessly to make sure the balance was perfect. When all
were satisfied, Gopal stepped down from the scale and went
to the little temple, where he performed a holy bath, praying
all the while. The pandit meanwhile asked the sun to dry off
the accused man's clothes, if he were innocent, and the wind
to help in the process. But if he was not innocent, his guilt
would cling to him so that when he stepped upon the scales
again, the crime would weight down his side of the balance.

Gopal and those who had escorted him to make sure he did
not tamper with his wet clothes in any way came back to the
scale in silence. The whole crowd waited breathlessly, and
from Mira bai, her back turned to the horrible sight, one
small sob escaped. The pandit wrote Gopal's crime upon his
forehead in a heavy symbol of white clay.

Then Gopal stepped on the scale again, his head bowed.
Every eye was fastened on the crossbeam, and for a moment
nothing seemed to happen, except that both platforms
trembled. If the scale lifted the bricks and darbha grass,
Gopal would have to be punished, and the punishment would
be severe. The punishment would be more cruel than the

police court would give him; it would be ostracism from his caste and disgrace forever, if the scale testified sufficiently against his innocence.

For a moment nothing seemed to happen, but that was because everyone's heart was beating so hard that eyes couldn't quite focus. Then, ever so slightly the bricks and the darbha grass lowered themselves. Yes, it could be seen quite plainly now. The gods had lifted Gopal a few inches to show his innocence. The sun had dried his garments, and even the clay which the pandit had put on his forehead had not weighed him down. For an innocent man cannot be weighed down; he is upheld by the law of justice.

A cry broke from the crowd now. Shouts and applause were deafening. Everyone said he *knew*. Even the friends of Chandra now said they could see from the first that the poor old man was not guilty. Soni ran to him and threw her arms around him; her face, like the sun which had dried the garments enough, was covered with smiles and tears at the same time.

Only Gopal was quiet. In the center of the cleared place in his own mind, he was still standing in the balance. A man must be right with himself. When he has lost respect for himself, the gods have little regard for him. They are fair, and they would not punish an innocent man . . . but they would devise ways of tormenting a man who has lost face with himself. He understood it very well.

He heard the crowd now turned against Chandra. They were dragging him, squealing like a frightened pig, toward the scales. They were taking the money out of his pocket, shrieking for justice and the right payment. But none of it mattered very much to Gopal, for across his own self-respect had been raised a scarlet welt. It would be a long time before he would not ache because of it.

14

THE TIME WAS DRAWING NEAR. SONI HARDLY recognized her shadow when it walked beside her, a strange squat shadow with the rounded stomach swelling out before it. Sometimes when she sat quietly while Anand read aloud, the child leaped within her, and she said to herself, "He is listening and laughing with joy."

Years ago Rama had built a birth house out beyond the wall of their dwelling, a dark shack, windowless so that no evil spirits could see what was happening within. The unclean process of birth must be carried on in secret, for it must neither pollute its surroundings, nor be menaced by the vindictive spirits of the other worlds.

Because her parents now had no home of their own where she could go to have her child, Soni would creep into this hut when her time was upon her. She would see no one but whatever midwife was there to help her, until the days of her purification were ended. Although they would engage the town midwife, the widowed sister-in-law Tara bai was going to take charge. For ten days after the birth there would be no mention of the event that had taken place. Then the priest would come and perform the Jata-Karma, and the new mother could rejoin the family, and the new son could be presented and honored. The road through the next weeks was laid out inescapably; it had only to be traveled.

Rama had suffered a depleting attack of malaria, and was now convinced that he would never live to see Anand's son. "My bones tell me a sad story," he said to his oldest son Govind. "You will be the head of this house very soon, and I must put it in order before I leave."

Govind knew that his father often before had melancholy convictions warning him about his own death; they must be believed until they passed, then they must never be mentioned again.

Rama was saying, "I had intended to have the ceremony by which I give the land to Anand at the time we take his son into the gotra. But now I am afraid to wait for that, for I may not be present at that time." It would have been atrocious family etiquette for Govind to say anything like "Oh, Father, we're going to have you with us for years to come!" So Govind only bowed his head and was silent.

Then his father said an alarming thing. "I have decided to go to the land office tomorrow and have the land registered in Anand's name. The legal part will then be finished and secure, no matter what happens to me."

Govind said cautiously. "A good idea. But as you know this is the time for us to consult the pandit about the coming year. Wouldn't it be wise for us to attend to that before we honor the business of this world?"

"You are right," Rama said, taking the rebuke. "And may the gods forgive me for reversing the order. It will soon be the first day of the March moon, and the streets will be full of pandits with their calendars on their laps and their styluses in their hands. You will go to our own trusted pandit and he will tell you how the heavens look down on this house for the coming year."

That was all Govind needed. The night before the first morning of the Hindu year, he could barely sleep for thinking of how he would maneuver events. In the morning he neglected his prayers in his eagerness to be the first man at the pandit's little house.

Maddeningly deliberate, the old man gave his seasonal forecasts, naming the most advantageous crops which must be planted next, speaking about feast days which the Kumbis must observe with special care if they wanted good harvests. This was a rather modern forecaster, so he even went into the matter of fertilizers and warnings about irrigation. Govind allowed his fingers to gallop impatiently on his knee as he listened, and at last the pandit could see that he wanted to get on to other matters.

At this point Govind untied from his dhoti corner an unusually generous backsheesh and laid it casually but conspicuously beside the pandit, who discreetly appeared not to notice it.

"I have brought private horoscopes from my family, also," Govind said. "It is a matter of great importance to us. My younger brother will become a father in two months."

The pandit took the papers and scanned them, listening carefully to what was *not* being said, for a good pandit must have his ears tuned to overtones.

Govind went on scrupulously outlining the situation, stressing his father's whim about breaking up the land of the family and deeding a part of it to start another branch. Govind waited a long moment, then he said, "It would not be a good thing, my father believes, to do this under *certain* conditions."

"What conditions?"

Govind caught his eye and held it carefully. "My father would not believe it was wise to break this land from the family holding . . . unless Anand can be certain to have a son."

The pandit bent his head and thoughtfully scrutinized the

charts of both Anand and Soni. He also thought over other matters to which he must give consideration; Govind was the one to be the next head of this gotra; who knew anything about that young Anand, going around with his head stuffed full of Western ideas?

In the beginning of his career, this Brahmin had been a most conscientious adviser and interpreter and guide. Reluctantly he had made inner concessions, always consoling himself with the old Hindu maxim which says, "In order to fill one's belly one must play many parts." Some of the parts he did not like, but he played them zealously.

So now he looked up with great sadness in his face. "I have disappointment for your family," he said, sipping his own words painfully. "I must dash your hopes about a son being born to this family at this time."

Govind looked crushed. "My father will be grieved to hear this."

"But he has been most wise to consult the heavens, before he disposes of his part of the earth in any foolish way."

"Is that the message you wish me to carry to him?"

The pandit clutched at the tail feathers of his own integrity. "It is not my part to advise so wise a man. I tell him only what the stars forecast. I see no son . . . and he must make his decisions in accordance with that."

"I will help him decide," Govind said gratefully. "My father is a man who listens to reason."

The pandit slipped the lavish basksheesh into his coconut shell, and they spoke happily of other things.

Govind hurried through the lanes to Rama's house, his mind eagerly alive with plans. He had worried about this threat for months, ever since Rama had impulsively conceived the notion of giving the land to Anand. And now all that would come to nothing. It showed that a good and pious man who lets the stars help him has little to fear. The heavens are wider than the earth . . . and the wisdom of them is as their width.

He arranged his face into sad folds as he came into his father's presence, so that the old man cried out in fear, "You saw my death!"

"Happily, no," Govind assured him. "The stars had no such blackness in them. No, it is something else."

Rama, in his customary squatting position, was clutching his heart and rocking back and forth on the soles of his feet. "Tell me," he croaked. "All morning I have had a heaviness on me. I am expecting bad omens."

Govind sat down beside him, and put his strong hand on the arm which seemed very feeble this morning. He wanted his father to feel that his family would have a strong man to be at its head.

"The readings show that our family needs strength to carry it through," he said, trying not to paraphrase too widely the meager predictions of the pandit. "A family is only as strong as its head and your family has been accustomed to a powerful and good man."

"Yes, yes . . . but what?" Rama said unwilling to be led through any labyrinthine approach at this moment.

"This is not the time to divide our land," Govind said boldly. "The stars show we shall need my sturdy sons for the future of the family . . . and even Ghulum's boys."

"What do you mean?" Rama asked fearfully.

"There will be no other sons for a while."

"You mean Anand . . . will have no son?"

Govind bowed his head in sadness. "That is the unhappy forecast, father. Anand's child will not be a son. The aspects all agree that it will be a girl-child."

Rama looked stricken at this, and shook his head in disappointment. "It is all this silly learning that weakens a man so that he conceives weak things," he said at last.

"That could well be," Govind agreed, hoping his father would not carry this explanation so far into the realm of reason that it would collapse against the evidence of the educated Western world and its plethora of strong invading men, whom he detested.

"This changes my plans, by necessity," Rama said. "I see it would be madness to put the piece of land into Anand's name. Who knows if he will ever have a son? Suppose I gave him the land and he left no son to serve it as my fathers have served it!"

"I had not thought as far as that," Govind said wrinkling his forehead.

"You must be my sole heir and maintain the head of my household," Rama said slowly.

They sat a while in gloomy silence, and at last Govind suggested, "Wouldn't it be wiser if we did not tell the family about this? Having his firstborn be a girl-child will be a bad blow to our Anand."

"Yes. Perhaps God will warn him Himself, and get his mind ready for knowing when he must know. I have seen such a thing happen."

"And we will not mention the land. It is between ourselves, Father."

Rama nodded his head sagely, but the thought crossed his mind that it was also between himself and that harassed little father of Soni bai, who had extracted from him the promise about this land. His wrinkled old hand went up and fondled the pearl earring, which had been the other half of the bargain. He felt troubled about the whole thing. The pearl and its sacred daily cleansing, he firmly believed, had brought Anand back to serve the land. *Dare* he go back on his part of the bargain, of which this very pearl was the daily reminder? But who knew of it . . . beside that weary-faced little Gopal? And he was always so beset by his own troubles that he had no time to check into other people's concerns.

He said half aloud and half for his own reinforcement, "The heavens direct . . . and we must obey."

"We must obey," Govind agreed piously. "Shall we go to the land office today, you and I, and make sure about all our papers?"

"We shall go," Rama said. "And I thank God for a pious strong son to take my place."

Warmer weather came with the first of May, and the parched earth was even drier to the thousands of bare feet coming home wearily at eventide from the fields.

Mira bai spent as much time as possible with Soni in her hut, as though to shield her from the inevitable event which was both welcomed and dreaded. Neighbors also came visiting, knowing that there would be several weeks after her baby's arrival when they would not be allowed to read with her again.

As was customary, in order to ward off the vindictiveness and envy of the evil spirits, they always said, "Soni bai, you look wretched and weary. The hang of your sari makes me believe you have no child in your belly." Soni demurely agreed, though the evidence shouted contradiction.

One day when Soni thought her back would break in half as she bent over sorting the chilis from the new crop, Mira bai arrived from the bazaar with an unusually heavy basket on her head. To Soni's surprise the basket contained a huge quantity of rough salt.

"What on earth shall we do with so much salt?" Soni cried. "We couldn't eat that much in many years."

"It will be used," Miri bai said. "Your shrewd mother got it at a good bargain. Some of it will be part payment for the worthless midwife, so she can carry it on to her next case."

"It will have to be well cleaned, whatever we use it for. The salt wallah has left in gravel and rocks to add to the weight."

"That I saw, all right," Mira bai said. "But even so, I got it at a good bargain."

They began immediately sorting it over a fine wire tray, putting on a small quantity and then shaking it back and forth until they had screened out most of the pebbles and dirt. Then they put the salt in a piece of old dhoti and carried it down to the stream, where Mira bai doused it up and down in the running water. As the salt became cleaner it had a pinkish color, which in the bazaar brought a forbidding price. Now it was laid on an osier tray and put in a sunny spot to dry.

"I still think you have bought more than all our households will use as long as we live," Soni said, laughing. But Mira bai kept silent, knowing that soon enough her child would experience its painful use.

By bedtime, Mira bai was sure not many hours stretched between this moment and the birth. She lay in her own sutherungee expectantly, waiting to hear Soni's voice in the night. At last she heard a whisper, and then a smothered groan. Over this she heard the frightened voice of Anand.

"My darling, is it now?"

"It is soon."

"I am afraid for you, Soni."

"I'm not afraid. Even if I am torn apart with pain, I love the pain because it is for your sake."

"I wish I had taken you to the clinic. Maybe it isn't too late."

"It is much too late."

"Too many women die. . . ."

"I shall not die."

"Let me take you to the clinic. If I were not a coward I would have done it, no matter what my father says. And then I was a coward in another way, too, Soni. I have lost my Doctor Sahib and Memsahib Mom . . . and I couldn't bear to see them again . . . maybe God will punish me for being such a coward . . . maybe He will take you away from me . . . ."

"No, no, don't be afraid," she said soothingly, as if already she was speaking to her child. The pain was grinding in waves now, and she spoke dreamily. "You must call my ayie . . . we must go down to the birth house now."

As soon as Mira bai heard the word "mother," she was beside Soni, crouching down and speaking softly.

"Now you are in God's hands, my child. God is close to a woman who is doing His work with Him."

For days Mira bai had anticipated this moment, and now she knew exactly what to do. The little boy Dhuki, who had been sleeping on the veranda of the hut, so that he could run any necessary errand, was wakened. Mira bai spoke exaggeratedly to him, so that he would run faster to Rama's dwelling and wake Tara bai and the midwife, already engaged.

"My khunia will die in a few minutes, unless you run faster than you've ever run before," she said. "Wake Tara bai and she will know what to do." The little boy was plunging down the dark footpath to the main house before he fully waked up. The sun was turning the sky to palest silk in the east, and the dew on his feet was delicious. He was helping with an important matter.

Soni and Anand, clinging to each other so that it was difficult to tell which was helping the other, were leaving the hut now, and Mira bai was clucking and admonishing like any excited mother. She had long ago prepared the confinement quarters and she knew everything was ready. Under the trees near the birth house she had laid a fire of sticks to be lighted to heat the necessary water, and she had gathered abundant leaves and heaped them on the mud floor to soften its hardness. Over this she had placed the old coarse blanket which had been used many times before in such an emergency.

They reached the birth house just as the first rim of brightness pierced the horizon, and Anand, faltering unhappily, had to leave his Soni there. He would not see her for many days, and his heart felt as if it were as big as a jackfruit crowding his chest with agony.

In the watery light, the widow Tara bai was waiting, and the old crone who was the town midwife. They had lighted the fire Mira bai had laid and the water was heating, and they were now mumbling their prayers.

Mira bai scooped up a lothi of hot water and gave it to Soni, carefully avoiding meeting her eyes, since that would have been inauspicious.

"Perform your arati, then go into the room that is ready for you," she said gruffly. "You would not want to defile the ground of your good master's family, if the water should come suddenly."

Then she handed Soni a twist of old cotton cloth. "Hold this between your teeth and bite upon it when the pain wants to scream out. No one must hear the pain, for that offends both the gods and men."

The sight of the windowless hut and her mother's face with the eyes not meeting her eyes was swimming and quivering in a daze now, and Soni could barely hear the gruff instructions.

"Sumbala," her mother was saying. "Take off the silver anklets. Give them to me. On my ankles they shall be safe until you can wear them again." When this exchange was made, she gave her child a rough little push toward the doorway, for fear that in another moment she would have disgraced them both by taking her into her motherly arms and carrying her within the room of torture.

"Go . . . go . . ." she said huskily. "You know your ayie is not permitted to enter the room with you."

Soni stumbled into the dark place, glad now to be in seclusion.

Tara bai, who was an experienced midwife, said nothing. This ordeal must be borne in silence; there was no place here for idle talk. Whatever had to be said would be said sternly, for a woman giving birth must be brave and strong, with no touch of sweet weakness to bring relief. She wrapped Soni in her sutherungee with hands that couldn't help caressing, and then lighted the half coconut shell of oil with its wick of rolled rag. This was not for light, for this work could be done in darkness; the coconut lamp was only to be placed on a post to keep away evil spirits always lurking around such an occasion. She left the regular village midwife squatting by the door, and went out and walked a while in the new sunshine, keeping her eye vigilantly on the birth house. She hoped the baby would be born soon; it was always a stronger child born while the sun was young in the day.

Alone in the hut, Soni groveled on the ground, keeping the cloth between her teeth in case the pain caught her off guard. She thought of all the women in the world who had borne children . . . did they all suffer like this, racked and pulled until flesh felt as flimsy as ashes? But if these millions of women had borne such agony, she could bear it. Sometimes, for a few moments she seemed to fall into a black well of comfort, in which she thought nothing and felt nothing. Then a sharp lightning flash would tear through her body, making her teeth clamp down hard on the biting-rag. Time lost all meaning. Sometimes during the eternity Tara bai came in and looked at her, and then went away again. It seemed hours since she had come down the footpath with Anand from their beloved hut . . . maybe it was even yesterday.

She tried to focus her eyes on the doorway, where a chatia kept out the light. Was it night again? No, there was a thread of daylight around the edge of the mat, but it was late light.

Now she must have made some shameful sound, for the chatia was pushed aside, and Tara bai was standing in the door. In a swift miniature picture, she saw her mother standing fifty paces away, beside the burning fire. She was holding a bowl of something, and her attitude was alert and listening. It was a picture that burned itself into Soni's brain, small and detailed and unforgettable.

"Get up on your feet," Tara bai was saying. Soni, writhing with torture, tried to obey, but could not make her muscles unclench themselves.

"Up on your feet, Soni," Tara bai said again, and now she bent over and grasped her shoulders and lifted her to her feet. For a moment Soni reeled and almost fell, then she steadied herself and even tried to smile at the stern face of her sister-in-law. The paid midwife, angrily useless, was muttering critically.

Tara bai said almost kindly, "You must stand in the corner now, facing the wall. When the pains come, bear down. Put your hands on your knees and push down your insides with all your strength." When she was sure Soni understood the best position, Tara bai lay down on the floor herself, raising the soles of her feet and placing them against Soni's quivering buttocks, supporting her and acting as a counter-force for the pushing down. Between the pains, both women relaxed, each panting breathlessly. At last, after seeming hours, the baby's head could be seen. Now was the critical time, and both worked, muttering prayers and sobs and moans. They pushed and bore down in rhythm, until Tara swung to her knees and received the little head in her hands. The contractions now were severe and convulsive, but in a few moments the child was in the world, lying on Tara bai's sloping knees.

She tore a piece of cotton from the old sari she was wearing and tied the cord in two places, then rubbed it apart with two sharp stones which were her only instruments. Still facing the wall, Soni had sagged into a near faint. Her upstretched hands, whitened by the retreat of blood, were clutching at the mud wall; her body appeared to be hanging from her hands.

Somehow Tara bai caught her with one hand and helped the limp form slide to the earth, all the while holding the baby with her other hand.

The mother must take care of herself now. Instinctively Soni covered herself with her stained sari. Every pore felt battered and beaten, but her mind, numbed by the last cruel agony of the long day, was slipping into merciful darkness. The village midwife stooped tenderly and unbent one arm, which was twisted under her body.

Tara bai was rubbing the baby's body with warmed and scented coconut oil. Then she wrapped it in some old cloths and placed it upon the blanket near Soni's head. Now that she had disposed of the baby she shook Soni and forced her to drink some hot water.

Soni's lips moved, but her eyes looked dead. "My lord's son?"

Tara bai said, "You are favored of the gods because you have a good husband."

"Then we have our son."

"Your master might take another wife were he like some men. The bucha is a female!"

15

FOR THREE DAYS SONI LAY JUST AS SHE WAS, half dead in body and numb in mind, grieving and weak. She wanted only to die of shame and disappointment. Sometimes Tara bai thrust a lothi of hot water against her lips and made her drink. On the morning of the fourth day, the widow insisted upon bathing her and combing her long hair, and then dressing her in a clean sari. Nothing mattered one way or the other to Soni, and she did not see how anything ever again could rouse her from her despair.

Even when Tara bai held the baby to her breasts and she could feel the urgent primitive seeking, she turned away her head and would not look at the child. Perhaps it would die, also, as she herself felt dead.

But one afternoon she woke from her lethargy and saw a little frame of sunshine lying on the ground where it had escaped from the edges of the chatia over the door, and she heard Tara bai singing softly. From under her eyelashes she looked toward the old woman rocking back and forth on her skinny buttocks. She was holding a small parcel in her arms. Soni stirred then, and Tara bai looked over at her and smiled.

"Are you ready to see this little girl?" she asked. "She is a beautiful baby, Soni. She asks you not to be angry at her because she is female. She cannot help herself . . . as we could not help ourselves. Have mercy on her."

Soni managed then to lift her arms and stretch them out imploringly toward the infant. "Give her to me," she said weakly.

The widow bent over and put the child beside the still-feverish body. The weakness drained out of it, and a surge of sweet joy came seeping through. The baby was beautiful. She had eyes like Anand's, rimmed with lashes, black yet so shiny they broke the light into rainbow colors as do the legs of a fly. Her tiny mouth, and her exquisite nostrils were so perfect that Soni almost laughed aloud at the sight of them. How could anything so small be so perfect? And her fingers . . . constantly curling and uncurling, were as delicate as the newest fronds of a fern. Even if the whole world were against her because she was a girl-child, her mother would glory secretly in her beauty. She knew now why Mira bai had always loved *her* so much . . . more than the brothers. She saw that her own shriveled heart had grown large again, much larger than it ever had been before, because it was so filled with love for this small creature. Tara bai, who had never had a child of her own, stood silent, knowing exactly what was happening.

"Now you must have some food for your strength," she said at last. "I have some rice and coconut waiting for you."

On the tenth day Tara bai removed the chatia from the upper half of the door, and sunshine and beauty could be seen flooding in from the lovely outer world. The baby now was unbearably precious, and the feeding of her was sheer ecstasy. Every day Mira bai set a plate of food within reach of the widow, though they could not look into each other's faces nor speak until the midwife's time for purification.

Kumbi women are not strict observers of ritual; Brahmin women must remain in seclusion for thirty days when they have given birth to a male, and forty days when a girl-child has been born. Soni's banishment would last about two weeks, and now it was drawing toward its weary end.

By the night Tara bai returned to the house of Rama, Soni's natural happiness and sunniness was almost restored to normal. Somehow, since God had given a girl to the family, He would make it welcome. They would come to love it as she did. Anand, at least, would see how beautiful a little creature she was, and if the others did not think so, then this would have to be one more cherished secret between the two of them.

After dark, when Tara was gone, Mira bai stole into the black hut to see her child and her grandchild.

She pressed Soni's forehead between her two hands, then Soni bent to the ground and kissed her mother's feet.

"It has been so long, Ayie."

"Tonight I have brought you curry and rice. Today these hands made jellabees from the very gram flour we milled together. In a few days you shall go down to the river for a bath. Every day now I shall bring you warm water to wash yourself."

"Come see the baby."

They hung over it idolatrously. "It shall sleep in my arms tonight," Mira bai said. "You would not deny me that."

Timidly Soni asked about her lord. Had Mira bai seen his face? What was the family saying because it was not a son?

Well, Mira bai reported, Govind at least had seemed not too distressed to have a baby girl in the family. Govind said that men must accept what God sent, for there was always a good reason. Soni took what comfort she could from that, but Govind was not the important one. It was Anand that mattered . . . and his father.

"Tomorrow is the day the child may be seen by my master," Soni said breathlessly. "Will you watch his face and tell his servant what he says to Rama? I have been praying that he will not feel too much displeasure."

"I, too, have prayed," Mira baia said. "He is a good man, Soni."

"So good."

The next day as soon as it was daylight, Mira bai washed and oiled the baby with scented sesame; then rolled it carefully in the rug which Memsahib Mom had given for the wedding. She carried the precious bundle and put it in the depression of the roots of the borah tree, where Anand and his father usually sat after their prayers. Then she hid herself behind some nearby bushes so she could hear everything. Soon Rama and his son came up from the river after their morning worship and sacred bathing.

Rama was walking before Anand along the path, and when he saw the bundle he stopped involuntarily, then turned and motioned with his thumb to Anand. Slowly Anand bent over and uncovered the tiny face, gazing at it without a word. To him it was Soni's face in miniature. The eyes were her eyes, as he had seen them bending above her in many moonlights. His heart swelled with compassion for this innocent cause of disappointment.

Unwillingly Rama came over and looked down without a word. He was about to turn away, but Anand stood up and said beseechingly, "Have you nothing to say when you look into the face of my first child?"

"She has a nose, a mouth and two eyes," Rama said ungraciously.

"God has made something beautiful here."

"A female."

Anand's voice was almost angry. "When she is a month old, I shall take her to the bazaar and show her to everyone I know. The friends of our kutumb shall all admire her."

"A female infant."

"Was not my mother once a female infant? And without that female infant, where would we have been? Can you harden your heart when you remember that?"

Rama's face was still stony, and his eyes burned with the emotion he would not express. Because of this infant, he had broken his promise to Gopal about the land; because of this wretched girl-thing he had gone back on his word to his son . . . even though the boy did not yet know about it. He had proudly expected that the child in the womb was to start a long proud line of his family. Could anyone demand that he gurgle insanely with admiration for such a worthless lump of living flesh?

"I shall name her for my mother," Anand said. "She shall be called Shushilla . . . and may she grow to be as fine a woman as Shushilla bai. Tomorrow the pandit shall record the firstborn of the house of Anand by the name of Shushilla."

The two men left, well knowing that some woman of the house was watching the baby from a safe distance. Immediately Mira bai ran out of hiding and gathered the child in her arms, hurrying back to the dark seclusion to tell the good report. Soni listened carefully to every memorized syllable. It did not surprise her that Anand had behaved as he had; she knew she could rely upon her love.

But Rama's unrelenting anger grieved her. She had wanted to bring only honor and delight to his house; she could not help it that she had disappointed him. Tomorrow she would go down and dip herself seven times in the river for her final purification; all today she would pray to God to show her how she might make up to Rama for what she had done to his hopes.

The next morning Mira bai came to help her adorn herself for her return to the family. Together they went to Anand's little hut, and there Soni brushed her teeth with wood ashes, and washed and oiled her long black hair, then braided it and coiled it at the back of her head with the end pulled through the braids as special decoration. The part was marked by the honorable vermilion which a married woman wears proudly. She wove for herself a circle of jasmine flowers, which she fastened around the coiled braids. She smoothed kohl paste on her eyelids, and painted her fingernails and toenails with henna juice, and put on her precious gold nose ring and the wedding earrings.

Mira bai said, "You are wise. The mother of a girl-child must make herself more beautiful than any other woman."

Soni said gaily, "Don't philosophize. Just give me back the silver anklets and bangles which you tore from your child in her hour of weakness! They are turning green on your skin. They have annoyed you too long! Give them to their rightful owner."

Mira bai sat on the floor and let Soni remove the anklets, pretending to protest. While she put them on her own ankles Soni sang a song which said, "Today is my birthday. Today I shall be beautiful. No work can these hands find, so they shall sit in my lap and fondle my good baby. My mother will not let me work today!"

Mira bai sang back, "Today you shall break my back while I do your work. You shall make my eyes fall out of my head with admiration for all your beauty. But I must remind you, my worthless child, that tomorrow is another day."

When the sun was high, all the women of the family came trooping up the footpath to pay a formal visit. Soni was seated on her own doorstep, holding her bucha on her lap, and looking her most elegant. Shushilla and Tara bai arrived first and paid their tribute, then Gaura with her little girl straddled over her hip, and Rukma with her latest boy baby. In a few minutes they were laughing and joking as usual, and giving Soni all the bits of family news. Rama's widowed sister, the champion complainer, had sent word that she could not take time away from her work. "Besides," she had said, "who would waste time looking at the face of another female?"

Govind's wife was the most devout of Rama's household, so she said frankly that she disapproved of Anand's audacity in naming his infant after his own mother. It violated the old custom, and it never could have happened except that Anand's head had become more of a beehive than a head from associating with Westerners. To all this, naturally, Soni made no reply, and the awkward moment passed without doing damage to anyone.

Before the evening meal, all the women escorted Soni back to Rama's house, where tonight she would take her old place serving the food. As they came from the fields, the men of the house had stopped in the bazaar to bring Jeveram and Gopal with them, for this was an occasion for celebration.

But no one mentioned Soni or appeared to notice her as she went about quietly serving the men seated on the floor. Her rosy wedding sari gave extra color to her face as she bent over to offer dal and curry to each big brass tray. When she reached Anand, she was almost afraid to let her eyes meet his, so great was the tension of love between them. Then their eyes did meet, and it was if the male and female of the thunder and lightning in the monsoon sky shook the room. In spite of her girl-child, nothing was changed between them; he loved her as before!

After the leisurely meal of the men was finished, the women hurriedly ate what was left, then shyly they joined their husbands in the courtyard. Now they could talk freely, and laugh and sing bhajans as they always did, under the lacy branches of the jacaranda tree. Gopal thought of his first evening in this courtyard, when he had felt excited and half frightened by the spaciousness of Rama's house. Much had happened to him since then, a lifetime of happenings. The encounter with this family had been good for others, but for him it had brought nothing but suffering and loss. Was that because God saw there was worldliness in his choice of a husband for his Soni? The birth of the girl-child had been his latest disappointment. His head was weary of thinking about it. He wished he had the months back in his hand, still unlived. But how could a man relive time? God ordained its pattern, good or bad, and all that can be done is to bear what comes, humbly.

At last it was time for Anand and Soni to go back to their own house. Properly Anand started up the footpath a few paces before his wife, who was stumbling along behind him carrying the sleeping child and listening to the happy beating of her own heart. Rama shook his head in silent displeasure as he watched the little procession disappear into the darkness. There had been other females born into his family, but the birth of this one had been his greatest disappointment. He was not sure he ever could forgive Soni. It surely must be her fault.

But it could also be the fault of the shameless way Anand loved his wife. Too openly, so that anyone could see it. It was not fitting for a man to display such weakness. That came from his hateful admiration of the Westerners. Naturally, much as it displeased Rama to see such a flouting of old tradition, it must offend the gods even more. He must consult the priest and see what could be done about all this, before worse events thundered about them.

As soon as Soni and Anand were safely out of sight of the family, Anand turned and ran back to her. He put his arms around her and held her close, murmuring her name and telling her how much he had missed her.

"You are not displeased with me?" she whispered.

"How could I ever be displeased with you, my beautiful one?"

He took the child from her arms then, and in the darkness tried to see the little sleeping face. "Let me carry her," he said. "A man must do his part of the carrying."

"That is not what our people think," Soni protested.

"Our new people think that way."

"You do not want to put her under a bush and forget her?" Soni asked, for the joy of hearing his contradiction.

"I want to put her upon a little pedestal and worship her," he said hugging the warm little body to his.

Then he grew serious, "I want my daughter to be educated and free. I want her to grow up to work for the new India. Are you willing?"

She could only nod, but tears of relief were in her eyes. He had found a place for the wretched girl-child in his noble ambitions.

16

THE NEXT MONTHS WERE DIFFICULT ONES. The monsoon held off that year, and many worried Kumbis feared it would not come at all. They would surely have a famine if the sky was going to be punishing the earth. Probably, in that hidden riddle of relationship between earth and sky, a feud was going on, and men would have to suffer because of it. The rains began coming late in August, feverish downpours that lasted a few days, and then blazing sun that sucked up all the healing dampness within a few hours. No one knew how to behave in such weather, and it kept the farmers on edge. Anand caught one of his bad colds, which lingered much too long in the humid weather.

But to Soni, all was delight, for delight was centered in the baby Shushilla, and in the days of studying and reading. She got the household chores finished early, and then sat down with her books with blissful hours stretching before her. Everything a woman could possibly want was in this rain-locked room, her lord, happy and serene, lost in his reading but still present where he could be looked at and loved, the wonderful baby leading its secret uninvadable existence, and the books through which she could travel as she pleased. There were often words which she could not read, and she left those for a later day, knowing that sometime their meaning would be plain to her.

The baby Shushilla seemed the most pleasuresome toy.

Most of the time she was quiet and complacent, and when she did cry, her mother recognized it as perfectly normal behavior. But the ancient aunt, Hera bai, insisted that the baby should not be allowed to cry. During an interlude between rains she brought an opium paste to the hut and instructed Soni about its use. It was to be put under the baby's fingernails when she was restless.

Soni told about this hesitantly to Anand when he came in from his field. "But I have never seen any women in Marvali use opium paste for their babies," she said in a worried tone.

"You are not to use it either," he said firmly. "I must get a book for you that tells you exactly the best way to take care of her."

"But I have watched many mothers taking care of their babies, all my life. Besides, a girl is born knowing about such things."

"There are books written," he said. "I have seen them myself at the clinic. I must find one somewhere."

"Perhaps the clinic would let you borrow a book," Soni said.

His face flushed painfully, as it always did when the clinic was mentioned, and she was sure that this subject hurt him for some reason. As a good wife she must try to find out about this place in his mind which was closed against her, so that she could ease whatever gave him pain.

"They have loaned you other books."

"Yes, of course," he said vaguely.

"You have taken your daughter to show your friends in other parts of town . . . perhaps you might like to show her to the people at the clinic. Then they might offer you the book."

It was one of the few times he became angry with her. "Don't try to manage me!" he cried. "When I want to go to see my old friends I shall go. With no prodding from you."

She bowed her head in meekness; but she knew more than ever that the spot in his mind where the clinic was had been bruised by something, and had not begun to heal.

Nothing more was said about the book for several weeks, then one day he brought in a battered little pamphlet written in Marathi and called *Care of the Baby*.

Her eyes brightened when she saw it. "From the clinic?" she cried, without caution.

"No, it is not from the clinic," he said, immediately disgruntled. "The clinic isn't the only place that owns books. The fact is, a wallah in the bazaar bought a box of trinkets from a trader, and this was in the box."

Soni read the book and studied the clumsy illustrations, and when other mothers came to her house for their reading lesson, this became the textbook. But it made better reading than practicing, for it was filled with strange ideas, such as wrapping a baby in several garments, when everyone knows that it needs but one, a little shirt that doesn't quite cover the navel.

Shushilla was a winsome little creature, and it was impossible to see how Rama could ignore such charm. Yet he did ignore it. No one ever had seen him glance toward the baby, or speak about her. She was invisible and silent as far as he was concerned, and this was the second great sorrow which Soni had in her world.

Rama often came to the little hut and sat on the doorstep, squinting out over the field where Anand and his helpers were working. The vegetable garden was rich now with the bright purple brinjals, the brilliant slashes of color which were the chilis, and the many legumes which would keep the family well fed through the winter. The peace that lay upon the place was also rich, and the old man seemed more contented

in this spot than down in the village. Sometimes he dozed in
the pleasant sunshine, and when he opened his eyes he was
not sure for a moment just who he was, small boy on this land,
lusty young husband, or tired old patriarch.

Soni served him tenderly and well, never forgetting his
strong sweet tea in midmorning and afternoon. He never
could believe that she really knew how to read, secretly sus-
pecting that she had memorized the books she read aloud to
him. He himself knew many stanzas of the old classics by
heart and loved to recite them. Especially he loved the Rig
Veda, and never quoted from it without pointing out that it
is the oldest book the world knows. "And people call reading
modern!" he usually said indignantly. "We Indians wrote
an enduring book when the rest of the world was sitting in
a cave!"

Knowing that his tiny granddaughter did not please him,
Soni kept the child out of his sight as much as possible. One
morning he arrived as she was bathing little Shushilla. Unexpectedly he came up quietly behind her and looked over her
shoulder.

"This morning I must break the little bangles on her arms,
for she has outgrown them," Soni said, without turning around
to invade the privacy of his face. "She has grown so fat and
round since she was born."

He gave a meaningless grunt, and then walked back down
the path, forgetting he had come to visit. Soni got a little
stone and carefully broke the glass bracelets. This should
have been a happy moment, but her heart was sad because
of the indifference of Anand's father. Surely it could not be
good for a baby, even a very young one, to see indifference
and dislike in a face bent over it. Surely the evil spirits would
be attracted to a spot where such an unnatural thing was
occurring. All afternoon she brooded over the danger, and

wondered what she should do.

Then, unexpectedly, Rama came up the footpath again. She called out a welcome to him, and he came over to where she was nursing the baby. He sat down on the ground beside them, and for a long time there was silence, broken only by the satisfied murmurs of the infant, waving its little arms, bare where the bright bangles had been.

Slowly Rama untied the corner of his dhoti. He scooped up five shining bracelets and twirled them on his wrinkled old forefinger, then poked them at the baby's stomach.

"How beautiful!" Soni cried.

"Nothing at all."

"Are they for her?"

"Who else could wear them?"

"Oh Father . . . how good of you!"

He tossed his head from side to side in contradiction of goodness, but his face was pleased. Then he untied another knot in another corner of the dhoti, and produced a collection of larger bangles.

"What are those?"

"When she outgrows the first ones, these will be waiting for her," he said gruffly. "My granddaughter mustn't go bare-armed like an outcaste's bucha."

Soni knew that she must not say anything more to thank him; nothing must be made of his capitulation, or the stubborn old man would be chased back into his old position. So she pointed out a flock of parakeets, blazing across the sky, and he followed her finger and nodded, appreciating her womanly tact.

The Feast of the Harvest customarily was held by Rama's gotra as a three-day celebration, beginning with prayers and climaxed with festivity.

The crops harvested had been divided for storage or for payment of accumulated debts. The customary portion was given to the temple and its priests, each married male carrying his own offering, according to his conscience. Everyone in Vardana had something to celebrate: the Kumbis were grateful for the richness of their crops, the farm laborers for their hiring, the merchants for the trade which came to them when money was briefly in the hand. But most of all the moneylenders rejoiced, for this was the season when they pressed their claims most advantageously.

It was during the preparation for their festival that Anand discovered that the land promised to him had been deeded to Govind.

Customarily all the members of Rama's kutumb came to his house for the feast. But this year, a few days before the celebration, Anand decided to ask his father if he might be host, and spread the feast in his own small hut. After all, he had much to be thankful for this year . . . land of his own, and his firstborn.

It happened that on this night, Gopal and Mira bai, who needed cheering because they had no crop, were invited to the hut for the evening meal. While the two men were eating, Anand said to Gopal, "Would you care to come down to my father's house with me? I am going to invite the family to come and share the feast with me next Friday."

Anand laid his hand on the ground as he spoke, and the older man did not need to be told why he wanted to be the host this year. Land was too much a part of his own inner anatomy, for him not to understand.

"It has been a good year," Anand said.

"A year is always good when the land is good," Gopal said gently, letting his own hand rest lovingly on this soil for which he had a special feeling. Almost he felt like the father of it;

if he had not struck up the bargain with Rama, Anand would not be sitting on his own ground tonight, loving it as a man should and finding new stature in himself because he owned it. Gopal hoped that sometime before he died Rama would be honest enough to tell his son how it came into his possession. Perhaps this very night, when the three of them talked quietly, the wrong might be righted! Then he who had lost so much would have restored to him one great possession, the dignity of having given. Why had Rama withheld this necessary sustenance from him; why could he not understand that a man needs such a thing more than he needs food or clothing?

"You will tell your father why you wish to be the host to the gotra?"

"Of course," Anand said. "It will please him greatly. After all, it was his gift to me."

"His gift," Gopal said, as if he must memorize the words and make sure of them.

"And your gift, too," Anand said surprisingly.

"What do you mean?"

"Why, you gave me the cotton seeds for my crop. I have not forgotten that, Gopal. There has to be a marriage between the seeds and the soil . . . and you gave me the fine seeds."

Gopal, moved deeply by this appreciation, could only shrug, appearing to dispose of the gift lightly. Actually he could not trust himself to speak.

"I have set aside a portion of the profit for you," Anand said. "I meant from the first that you should have your share."

"I expect no share," Gopal said. "I gave it as a gift."

"I know that. But you are to have it . . . for my pleasure."

So now the Feast of the Harvest would include Gopal among the rejoicers, the man who had been divorced from his own beloved land and banished to a bazaar, where he had been insulted and reviled, so that he could somehow pay his debt to a moneylender who never before had dared let his shadow fall across him. Gopal closed his eyes and briefly thanked God . . . not just for the rupees which would represent his share, but for the fact that land which was bone of his very bone, had given life to him again. He felt so deeply about this that he knew he never could mention it to another human being; only to God could he speak about it.

The two men walked along the familiar footpath eagerly; each happy and filled with well-being. The moon was high and nearly full, and each leaf along the way was rimmed with light. Anand thought to himself, I shall never walk down this path at night without remembering the early morning with my little love going to the birth house. How good life is, out-lined with beauty as the leaves are edged with moonlight.

They found the family sitting as usual in the courtyard, Govind and Ghulum smoking their beedies, and Rama lying on the charpai. Two neighbors sitting on the ground sensed that some family conference was going to begin, so in a few minutes they made an excuse and left. The servant came out as usual with the big tray of fruit balanced on his head, and set it down before Govind. Gopal could not help noticing that the tray was no longer placed before Rama, but before his eldest son. Well, that was no doubt proper; the light wanes on one and brightens upon the next head of a family. But no one else took any notice, for they had gradually be-come accustomed to the shift of importance.

"Sit down, Anand," Govind said impatiently, for the tall slim man was still standing a little apart, his shadow long behind him, his handsome face in full moonlight.

"I want to stand, for I have brought an invitation to our gotra," Anand said with obvious enjoyment. "I have come to invite you all to celebrate the Feast of the Harvest on my land."

Nothing but silence filled the next seconds. But Anand, absorbed by the emotion that possessed him, did not notice

the silence . . . he had something more to say. When he
spoke again his voice quivered with feeling. "All the hours
when I have been plowing, and planting the seeds, and working the land around the crop . . . something wonderful has
been growing in me, Father. It was as if I were working two
pieces of earth . . . one under my feet, and an invisible one,
part of myself. Are all Kumbis like that, Father? When they
own their own land is something new given to them inside
themselves? That's how it has been with me."

Still nobody spoke. So after a moment the boy went on.
"Do I sound like a poet? Well, all right. My own land has
given birth to a poet. Perhaps a man is better for being a
poet . . . and loving what is around him, and praising God
for the beauty He has made. You never quite see the beauty
until you give yourself to taking care of it . . . in English the
term for taking care of your own land is 'husbanding it' . . .
it's a good word, isn't it? Well, I have husbanded my land
. . . and it has been wedded to me, and has found good things
in me which weren't there before. The way a good wife finds
new thing in a man."

Rama said, "My son. . . ." and then he couldn't think of
anything more to say. He too, had once loved the land as this
boy loved it; he knew exactly what he meant. And now he
would never be able to tell him. He had lived his life yearning
for a son who could feel about land as he himself felt about
it, and now here the boy stood. But it was too late.

Anand said, "So . . . because all this is true . . . and a hundred more wonderful things are true about the marriage between my land and myself . . . I have come to ask for the
honor of being the host to our gotra. On my own land, in
my little house, with my wife to serve us all. Will you give
me that honor, Father? You have given me so much else . . .
will you give me that also?"

Rama got up painfully from the charpai, and came over

to him. His hands were trembling as he put them on Anand's shoulders and looked into his face. Govind coughed uneasily, and shifted his position. Before anyone spoke, Gopal knew that something was terribly wrong.

"The pandit advised us. . . ." Rama began in a faltering mutter. "We thought it over carefully, Anand." Then he shoved away the temptation to excuse or blame or apologize, and blurted out in a racked voice, "The land does not belong to you, Anand."

"You mean . . . not yet?" Anand stammered. "But it will be mine. You gave it to me. And the formality of the deed . . . that's not the important thing. Your gift was the important thing, Father. When I gave up my work at the clinic . . . you gave it to me, to belong to me and my children forever."

Govind said, "Our father was overcome with emotion that day . . . seeing the trees blown down and the land beaten by the monsoon, and remembering his boyhood on that land. He was carried away; you should have recognized that. We all knew it. He did not mean what he said."

"He gave his word," Anand said dully. "He said he would go to the land office and have it put in writing. I believed him."

"I meant to go," Rama said, and wiped his wrinkled hand over his eyes in bewilderment. "I don't know how it happened that I didn't."

"You didn't, because that would have been wrong, and you are a righteous man," Govind said. "That's why. So don't let's have any weeping and wailing about it. The land of our family should be one land, and should belong to the family." His voice was harsh and impatient.

But not so harsh as the next voice which cut through it, for that was Gopal's voice.

"You have broken your word twice, Rama . . . once to your

son and once to me," Gopal said.

"What are you talking about?" Govind swung toward him. "Keep out of this! This is my family's business . . . and who are you?"

"I am a man who gave a gift which has been stolen before it was received," Gopal said.

Rama lurched toward him, his eyes contracted to pinpoints in the moonlight. "Please! I implore you," he said. "You are a father. You and I should understand each other."

"I am a father . . . to this son also," Gopal said. "I am a father wherever I see a need of justice, and of truth-telling."

Anand came nearer the two men, looking from one to the other, "What is it? What is it between you?"

"Your father will tell you," Gopal said. "Or if he would rather not, it is time I told you."

Rama, involuntarily fingering his earring, was shaking his head in a gesture of fear, as if he could shake himself free from some unwelcome thing that had fastened upon him.

Gopal said, "I gave a handsome marriage gift to your father, as everyone knows. I could not afford such a gift, so with it went my pride and my honor."

"You should not have given what you couldn't afford," Govind said unpleasantly. "But that was your lookout."

"I had no choice," Gopal said. "The request for the gift came after the agreement was signed. But I was willing to throw away my family pride and put myself at the mercy of the moneylender. For the first time in my lifetime . . . and my father's lifetime."

His proud voice broke and for a moment he put his hand up and covered his eyes. None of them had understood the reason for the change that had come over this man since they had known him. Anand thought to himself, My father had no right to do this to a good man . . . he had no need of such a large dowry for Soni bai. We needed *no* dowry at all for such a treasure as she is! And the pearl besides! As if anything that can be held in the hand . . . rupees or a pearl . . . could be worth making a man suffer like this!

Gopal had steadied himself now, and was going on, "But I took on the debt and I am paying it. I shall have it paid before I die. It will not be a yoke upon my sons, as debts sometimes are. I am paying it out of my dishonor and shame, and the agony of being away from my village when it needs me. But I am not talking about that."

"What are you talking about then?" Govind asked cruelly.

"I am talking about the bargain your father and I made when I promised the pearl," Gopal said.

"Bargain? What bargain?"

"He asked me for a gift . . . so I asked him for one in exchange."

"What gift?"

"I could have asked for something for myself. Something I needed or wanted . . . for I too have wanted certain things all my life. But I didn't ask for that. I asked that my gift be given to Anand."

"What gift?" Anand whispered, not quite understanding.

"I asked that the land be deeded to you," Gopal said, turning to the boy. "Rama agreed."

"At the time of the marriage?" Anand asked in amazement.

"A year before the marriage he agreed."

Rama cried out angrily, "I will not have my private affairs discussed before everyone. I am still the head of this family. . . ."

"A year before the marriage? When the agreement was signed?" Anand asked.

"Then."

"He did not tell me. . . ."

"My son had no need of land then," Rama shouted. "My son was held in the grip of his miserable Western friends. What would he have done with land then? When he got back his senses enough to want the land, I promised it to him."

"So it *is* mine, Father?" Anand asked quietly.

Rama swallowed with difficulty, then he said, "No. Circumstances changed. It became a mistake to give you the land deeded in your name."

"What circumstances changed?"

"You . . . you fathered a wretched girl-child," Rama said in a whisper. "Govind thought. . . . "

"Govind!" Anand turned slowly and looked at his oldest brother. "So that was it."

"That was *not* it," Govind said angrily. "The land should not be split up. It belongs to the family, and I shall be the head of the family. Who knows if you ever would have any sons to work the land? It is the Indian way to protect the land, and my father has protected it."

"By going back on his word? By putting it in your name?"

"Yes. In my name," Govind said, defiantly. "And there is nothing you can do about it. So there is no use consulting your fine Western friends about it."

Anand said, painfully, "I have lost my fine Western friends. I traded them for the land . . . and now I have lost both land and friends."

He was quiet a moment, his head hanging in shame. Then he raised his head and looked at Rama. "And I have lost something besides these two. I have lost my father. Of them all, that loss is the one I will grieve about for the rest of my life."

He turned away then, and walked across the courtyard, his long shadow going before him.

Rama called out, "Wait. Let me make you understand it better."

But the boy did not stop. From the doorway of her quarters, his mother ran out to him and put her arms around him. He patted her shoulder, and shook his head at what she was trying to say to him.

"Let him go," Govind called out. "He was always determined to have his own way in everything. Let him go. You don't need him for a son. You have other sons."

Rama turned upon Gopal. "Now I suppose you are happy. You've had your spite satisfied."

"Spite? What would I want with spite?" Gopal asked in honest bewilderment. "I wanted only good for you, Rama. And for all of us."

Govind's wife Gaura ran out of the shadows where the women of the household had been cowering, and spat at Gopal. "Get out of here," she shrieked. "You have caused my lord to suffer anger at you. So get out and don't come back."

Anand had gone back up the footpath, forgetting his father-in-law. So Gopal slipped out the front door and across the veranda into the lane. A knot of neighbors were crowded beside the veranda listening with enjoyment to the raised voices within. Their gentle faces were filled with the glee of malice. Certainly one often had the chance to listen to family quarrels outside lesser houses, but this noisy clamor in Rama's house was a rare and choice treat. By morning it would be a morsel under the tongues in the poorest hovels in Vardana.

Gopal shook his head sadly. It would rob them all; even the poorest outcaste at the edge of the village would have to give up something of the goodness and dignity he thought rested in a man of reputation. Evil spread like a stain when once it started, besmirching everything in its path. A man does not steal from one victim only, but from everyone who comes near to the theft.

17

EVEN BEFORE SHE LOOKED INTO HIS FACE, SONI knew that something terrible had happened to her lord. He came floundering up the footpath like a man who has been drinking toddy, and when he looked at her, it was almost as if he didn't know who she was.

Mira bai said, "Where is my husband, Anand? He went off with you."

"I guess . . . he's probably gone back to Jeveram's house." He made a vague gesture with a heavy arm.

Both women understood that some crushing event had happened; they could see that Anand's trouble was of such magnitude they must not intrude on it.

Mira bai said, "I know my way well, and I'm not afraid. I'll go along to the village."

Anand muttered, "But you need not go alone. I'll walk along with you."

"I cannot be a nuisance to you."

Then his innate good manners roused up and spoke, "Could the mother of my Soni ever be a nuisance? Come, we'll go immediately." He turned and looked down at Soni, sitting on the doorstep with her sleeping baby across her knees. "I may take a walk afterwards. I find myself restless. You go inside and get your sleep. Think nothing of me."

"How could I think nothing of you?" she murmured, but

meekly enough so that he would not believe she was prying into his worry. When he wanted her to know, he would tell her; then her consolation would be ready for him.

Mira bai walked along, six paces behind her son-in-law, admiring his slender shoulders and his proud head whenever a rift in the tree shadows let light fall upon them. She knew this man only by intuition, for naturally, there must always be a vast chasm of unknowing between any man and any woman, except husband and wife. But knowing Soni so well, she knew Anand a little, from the glowing marks which his love and his mind had put upon her child. With all her heart she wanted to offer him some comfort in what she could not help seeing was a suffering moment. But she knew of no proper offering except silence. She remembered an old saying her mother had taught her: "A woman's best gift to a man is quietude. All that she does for him is accomplished by quietude."

They heard someone coming toward them along the path beside the river, and she knew before her sight told her that it was Gopal, coming to fetch her. When the two men met, she stopped demurely, giving them a moment alone. She heard them talking earnestly, and she strained her ears to catch the words. Gopal was comforting him; so Gopal knew about the trouble; Gopal always knew so much . . . often without being told. After all these years of living with him, her heart sometime clenched at the goodness and the wisdom of her man. The two men talked for quite a long time, while she stood six paces away, loving them both, and asking God to help them. Then Anand turned and reached out his hand to her, and she came hurrying to them, but of course the hand she touched was not his, but Gopal's familiar hand.

Anand walked back along the river, noticing now that a big purple cloud had swallowed up the moon. It was very dark suddenly, and it seemed a lifetime ago that the leaves had been rimmed with light. Could that have been tonight? He felt an urgent need to walk upon his own land, and he found himself hurrying, as if the land were suffering as he was himself, and only he could comfort it. And only it could comfort him. They had had so much to say to each other, this wonderful year. The land had talked a kind of Ramayana to him, tender and humorous and wise. Now they would speak in a different mood, the way music shifts into deeper tone. You could not put into words the conversation between a man and his land, but it was as palpable as sound. It became an extra pulse in a man's blood; and throughout the land's dark hidden blood the man, too, became a special pulse beat. The man recognized the feel of his own land under his foot; blindfolded, he would know it. And the land knew the feel of the master's foot, apart from all others.

He had reached his own ground now, and hardly realizing what he was doing, he dropped down upon it and lay prone, his fingers caressing the cool soil. He heard a heart beating and he could not be sure whether it was his own heart, or the heart of the earth speaking to him as a mother-heart speaks to a held child. There was the oldest possible comfort here, and for a few moments he stopped thinking completely and let his primitive body absorb what the earth was saying.

"Do you think you ever can lose me, my son, when once I have entered your heart, and you have entered mine?" That was what the earth was saying, and he let tears of relief fall from his eyes and course down his cheeks.

Since they understood each other so well, how could it matter that this land to which he belonged was written down in his brother's name? It belonged to him, and it would always belong to him, as long as there was breath in his body, and love. Nothing could break the bond between them, no written words on a document, no three-pice stamp proving legality.

The land was not what was lost, unless in puny anger he himself let it be lost, and trampled over by dissent, and torn out of his heart by resentment. His loss was something greater and less tangible than the deed to a property; what he had lost was faith in his father and trust in his brother . . . but most of all, it was favor with himself. *He*, the dreaming student-one, was at fault, for he had been like a child stumbling into a man's world. He knew bitterly what was his weakness; he saw it exposed in all its ignoble shape. It was the apathy of thinking but not thrusting thought across the invisible barrier that separates it from action. He was guilty of non-doing. It was the universal Indian fault, but no less fatal because of that.

He had lost his friends at the clinic because he had not *done* something forceful and positive about wiping away the veil of misunderstanding that fell between them. And he had lost his land because he had not gone affirmatively with his father to the land office and written names and dates upon official blanks. He had assumed all was well, instead of striding in like a man, and *making* all well.

It was a bitter fact to face about oneself . . . that he had a loose and lazy grip from which actualities could slip away. Well, he had faced that fact, and the facing must now take form in doing. What could he do? It was too late for him to recover the land. But it was not too late for him to regain the people he loved at the Mission. He would go tomorrow, and bind up that broken friendship. There was a part of him that belonged forever with them, and he would take that part of himself back to them. It had been hungering and thirsting for the sustenance they gave him, and he had stubbornly starved. He would show them that self of his, and make them know that he belonged with them, in certain ways. Then he would bring Soni to the Mission; they would see in her what he saw.

Memsahib Mom would be pleased at how quickly she had learned to read . . . at how carefully she boiled the water they drank, and cared for the baby in a modern way.

He realized quite suddenly that rain was coming down upon him, big quiet drops strangely warm upon his hands and face. He lay where he was for a long time, feeling an almost voluptuous pleasure in the rain, as if it were an exchange for his own tears. When at last he rose from the ground, he found that his body was heavy with fatigue, as if he had lived a violent love experience. But even the weariness gave him solace, and he knew it was something he never would forget as long as he lived, which could not be told or hinted at to anyone. Not even to Soni.

He went slowly back across his empty field toward the little house. The darkness was so dense with rain that he could not tell in which direction he was walking. He fumbled his way along, letting his feet, which had covered every inch of this land so many times, guide him. His clothes were drenched with the rain now, and his hair was plastered to his scalp. A wind had come up and was whipping at him with cold lashes, and if he had not been so weary he would have run from the cold.

At last he reached the wall separating his little hut from the fields. The stones were chilled as he touched them to vault across. His teeth were chattering, but it was as much with exhausted emotion as with cold.

In the darkness of the hut, he knew Soni was lying awake. He heard her breathing carefully, and stitched across her breath he heard the jerky uneven thread of sound which was little Shushilla.

"Soni?"

"Yes, my darling."

"Tomorrow . . . even if it is still raining, I want to go to the Mission."

So that was it! The old sadness that she had never understood. How could this have come to a climax tonight? Had
he met the Doctor Sahib when he was out walking? That
seemed impossible. Then she heard a strange sound. She
thought at first it must be some little beast that had strayed
into the hut. She struggled to her feet quickly, and groped to
Anand in the darkness. She knew now what it was; his teeth
were chattering with the cold, and his whole body was shaking. But when she touched his damp skin, it was burning hot.

"My lord . . . you're ill. Your cold is worse!" she cried, and
it crossed her mind that his talk about the Mission was delirium.

"I'm not ill," he said impatiently. "But my clothes are
soaking wet, and I'm cold to the bone."

She lighted one of her little coconut lamps, and immediately she saw from his bright-burning eyes how feverish he
was. She put him in the warm place she had left on the
charpai, covered him with her own blanket, and then put his
blanket on top of that. But nothing seemed to warm him.

"Don't bother about the silly teeth," he said. "I want to
tell you something important."

But when he tried to tell her, he found it was too complex
a task. So he only repeated what he had said before. "Tomorrow, first thing, I want to go to the clinic. I want to see my
old friends, Soni. I've been sick with wanting them all these
months . . . but now I'm going to be well."

"Yes," she said soothingly, putting her hand on his flaming
forehead. She found a cloth and tried to dry his hair, but he
shook his head impatiently. "Don't bother about all that," he
said. "It's the rest of me that's all right now . . . my mind,
Soni. I'm whole in my mind again."

"Don't try to talk," she said. "I'll make you some strong
hot tea in a moment." She was running back and forth, starting a fire of dung cakes in the little chula. She could still hear

his teeth helplessly clicking together.

While the water for the tea was heating, she ran out and gathered some round stones and laid them close to the fire. As soon as they were hot, she wrapped them in one of her saris, and laid them against Anand's feet. He had fallen into a noisy sleep, his breath sawing back and forth in a frightening way. When the tea was ready, she tried to lift his head and give it to him, but she could not rouse him enough for him to drink it. His lips muttered words, but they were English words she did not know, and she thought with a pang, He is talking to Memsahib Mom, not to me. He is asking her something, and I cannot help because I can't understand.

She put the useless tea on the coolest part of the chula, and crept into bed beside him, hoping to warm his shivering body with her own healthy warmth. There seemed no way to stop his trembling, and she prayed for help to Lakshmi, who loved her own lord so well.

When dawn came, Anand was wet with perspiration. His mind had cleared now, and the drowsiness was past, but he seemed too weak to move a hand. The Mission was still on his mind, for the first thing he said when he woke up was, "Soni, when it is light, you must take some of the borrowed books back to the Mission. I have been selfish to keep them so long. Take back what you can carry and tell them. . . ." His voice trailed off helplessly.

"Tell them what, my darling?"

"Tell them I am ill. But I am coming to see them. The first day I can."

During the morning he was no better, and his chest seemed to be stuffed with something that kept him from breathing. There was no question of his standing on his feet this morning. Soni wrapped the baby in everything she could find, and put her on the little veranda so her noise would not disturb

Anand. The rain was still pelting down, and since there were no shadows there was no way of telling how much time had passed. Sometimes when he roused up enough to speak she heard him praying aloud, "Ram, Ram, Sita Ram, have mercy on this child. Take the burning from my bones, I implore you, and let me breathe." The praying alarmed her more than his symptoms, for she knew from the praying that Anand realized he was very ill.

All day the house hung suspended between Soni's fear and Anand's illness; it was as if nothing were alive anywhere. No birds were singing; nothing in the trees seemed to be moving; at last even the rain had dried up, and the sky was a gray lid upon the stunned earth. But finally the sun came out and Soni could see it was late afternoon. She wanted to run down to Rama's house and ask one of the women to come up and help her, but she was afraid to leave the sick man alone.

Just before sunset, he called out to her. His voice seemed as weak as an old man's.

As she bent over him, she heard a strange bubbling rattling noise in his chest, as if his lungs were filled with boiling liquid. She cried to herself in fear, It is the lung sickness . . . pneumonia. Our uncle died of it . . . I remember this very sound in his chest. She kept her fear from showing in her face, and put her hand quietly on his brow and smiled confidently into his eyes.

"What do you want? Are you better?"

"I think you should go to the temple, and offer a sacrifice to Ayie Devi."

"Can I leave you alone?"

"I'll be all right. Only hurry, so you can make the sacrifice before the sun sets."

"I'll run," she said.

At his direction she took some money from the lothi buried

beside the wall, and gathered up some unblemished vegetables, and then as her own distinctly feminine sacrifice, she
took her kumkum, the decorative paste which she wore between her eyebrows. She would stop along the way and buy
some marigolds, which the goddess respected. Holding her
sacrifices awkwardly in her arms, she trotted down the path
beside the river, hardly daring to think.

The only other time she had gone to the temple of Ayie
Devi with a prayer, the prayer had not been answered, for her
baby had been born a girl-child. Well, perhaps that was all
the more reason the mother-god would listen now to her plea.

The temple was almost two miles away, and this was the
first time Soni had ever gone along the government road
alone. On either side were large babul trees, and beyond
them were fields which had been planted to jowari and millet.
This was the road that led toward Marvali, so she had traveled
it when she and Anand paid their wedding visit to her family.
She remembered every foot of that journey, and she would
always remember it. She saw now the clump of trees surrounded by a high stone wall, which was the Mission compound. As she came nearer she saw the English bungalows
inside the wall, and through the tall iron gate she saw the path
that led to the little clinic in the distance. Sick people were
coming and going along that path. . . . She remembered what
Anand had told her that other day about Memsahib Mom:
"She feels the sickness of every suffering person as if it were
her own suffering. From the other side of the world, she felt
their suffering, and she had to come to help."

She had asked him, "Can she cure them all?"

"Of course not," he had said. "But she tries, and that makes
them feel better." Did he mean that she did not cure *any* of
them? Or that she did not cure *all*? She had not understood
when he said the words, and now she wondered more urgently.

Perhaps if Memsahib Mom cured *some*, she could help Anand now. The thought shocked her profoundly. Here she was on the way to the temple to ask Ayie Devi . . . and this blasphemous temptation had popped into her mind! How could there be any cure for a good Hindu except the prayers to the gods and the medicine the guru gave? Quickly she covered her traitorous temptation to wish for help from the clinic, so that Ayie Devi would not detect it and punish her. She ran faster, praying anxiously.

At last she saw the two banyan trees standing on either side of the little white temple. The hanging roots made a dense vertical screen, almost hiding the sacred spot. It was a tiny temple, only about four paces square, with steps leading to a small veranda. Seated cross-legged on the plinth was the goddess, carved out of rough stone and painted here and there with crude paint. But there was no question about its being more than stone and paint; it was the goddess herself, beloved and feared and powerful, holy mother of the gods to whom women went in their most dire need . . . illness, and barrenness and the final sorrow of death itself.

At the top of the stone steps she laid down her sacrifices and placed her two palms together at her forehead. She bowed her head three times, then she fell upon her knees and began her supplication.

"Arra, arra, Ayie Devi, you have eyes to see, so can't you see my need? You have ears to hear . . . can't you hear my plea? You have a mouth to speak . . . won't you comfort me? My lord is ill, and I have come to win your favor in his name."

She dared not look up into the face of the goddess then, for she knew that in that sacred instant the stone had turned to flesh and it would be irreverent to presume to witness the transformation with mortal eyes. But she knew it took place. When she was sure the sacred flesh had resumed the appearance of stone, she rose from her knees and offered the gifts she had brought. To her chagrin she realized she had not brought any marigolds. She hoped Ayie Devi would not notice. Backing away, she turned and ran down the steps. She mustn't linger a moment, for it would worry Anand to have her on the road alone after dark.

The way home seemed shorter, because her mind was comforted by the prayer and sacrifice. Surely Ayie Devi had heard her this time, for she had put a ray of confidence in her heart. Anand would be well. She ran the last hundred yards along the river, and up the slope of beloved land to their dooryard. Inside the hut, she waited a moment, panting and eager. Her prayer was answered; he spoke to her through the late dusk in the little room. She ran to him and fell on her knees beside him. To her surprise, he had Shushilla lying beside him.

"The bucha cried, so I brought her here," he said weakly. "We have been talking to each other."

"What did she say to you, my darling?"

"She told me that she must go to school, Soni. She says her mother must start a little school for girls, when she is old enough to attend."

"Would I be able to do such a thing? A poor ignorant creature!"

"Of course you could do it. I have had it in my mind for a long time, Soni. And now the child makes it necessary. She must be educated . . . someday she must go away from us to a college where she can be trained to help our India."

Always that purpose . . . to help India! Tears came to Soni's eyes, and she was glad it was too dark for him to see them. Ill as he was, burning with fever, hardly able to breathe, he was thinking of the future . . . he was giving his girl-child into its hands to help India.

During the restless night, Soni went down to Rama's house and asked for someone to come and be with them. Rama rose from his bed and immediately believed that Anand was going to die.

Shushilla bai said, "What kind of illness is it, Soni?"

"It is lung illness. He can scarcely breathe."

"It does not matter what kind of illness it is," Rama said. "My son is going to die."

"You must not say that," Shushilla cried.

"I will go to my son's guru and ask what we must do," he said. "The guru will get from the vaidya some sacred medicine. But it will not save him. It may ease his discomfort but it will not save him."

"Please don't talk like that, my great lord," Soni begged. "Your son will fill this earth with his presence for many years. You will see."

Even though it was still long before dawn, the old man went down the deserted lanes of the town to the temple where the guru slept. In an hour or so, Rama was up at Anand's hut, with some vile-smelling liquid to be mixed with his tea.

He sat down by his sleeping son and began talking to him as if he could hear. "My son, my dearest son, I have not thought of anything else since we parted. I have begged God to forgive me, and to show me what I can do to make this wrong right to you. A man feels guilty when he loves one son more than the others, and sometimes that makes him too stern. Was I too stern with you when you were a little boy? Then you must forgive me. And now . . . I felt guilty because I wanted to give you the land, and that made it easy for them to persuade me. . . . "

He went on talking and talking, and all the while tears were running down his cheeks, and the boy was lying quiet, not hearing a word.

Then he began to repeat the ritual that is used when a man is going to join his ancestors.

"Please do not use that ceremony," Soni cried. "Don't you

realize that I have made a sacrifice to Ayie Devi? She has promised me my lord will be well."

Rama only looked at her, his wrinkle-masked face heavy with sadness. "You do not know what has happened," he said. "The gods will punish me by taking away my favorite son. I have become unworthy of keeping him in my sight."

When Anand woke he was given the filthy potion which the village vaidya had sent, and in a few moments it broke the fever, but left the sick man too weak to utter a word. A day of nightmare followed, with Rama refusing to eat or be cheered, and through the next terrible night the women began coming to the house, as women do when death has laid an unseen finger across a door. The midwife who had been present when Shushilla was born, and Tara bai and Hera bai, and Soni's mother, and old Shushilla bai, and sundry neighbors, all arrived silently to sit on the veranda and grieve prematurely. Rama's moans could be heard above everything else. At dawn he insisted that his widowed daughter Tara bai go down to the temple and speak to the guru.

Obediently the middle-aged woman covered her head and hastened to the temple, finding the courtyard deserted because of the hour. Under a tall tree the guru was sitting, rocking back and forth in meditation. She approached him with joined palms and fell on her knees before him.

"May the gods have mercy on the needy. Rama has an ill son as you know. He is growing worse. Rama wishes you to implore the great gods for aid."

The guru continued to rock back and forth and then somewhat glibly he said, "There is something to be punished here. Rama's son has allowed Western nonsense to creep into his mind, and plant doubts there so that he believes himself above the station of his ancestors. It is not for man to learn beyond the teachings of the temple."

He got to his feet then, and disappeared through the door of the temple, coming out in a few minutes dressed in his yellow dhoti with an orange mantle over his shoulders. He carried his staff in one hand and a small bowl in the other. Solemnly he walked through the streets of the town, to the river and up to Anand's hut. There he dipped his bowl into the cudjah of water and sprinkled the walls and the floor, saying mantras in a slow tempo. At last he sprinkled the sleeping form of Anand with the water.

"This man has fallen into sinful ways," he chanted. "The gods are angry. My supplications find no relenting. For the sake of the father my efforts shall continue. His house is clean and the greatness of his devotion may avenge the wrong of his failing son who has been a prey to modern godlessness."

Anand tried to raise his head in protest, and Soni ran to help him. She saw the guru's face scowling with displeasure, and falteringly she apologized. Then the guru turned on her and reproached her for also displeasing the gods. The least she could do would be to bring a more important sacrifice to the temple.

"What sacrifice?" she murmured, bowing her head.

"At least a goat," he said sternly. "A goat whose blood shall touch the feet of Ayie Devi."

Soni put her hand quickly across her mouth, and for a moment she thought she would say, "I cannot do it. I could not do such a thing!" But she knew she could do anything . . . anything required to spare the life of her lord.

She looked beseechingly at Anand to see if he was confirming the order of the guru. But he had fallen back into a stupor. How could her sacrifice mean anything, if it had not her lord's blessing? If he did not tell her to go, how could she go? But she must; somehow she must.

Then she remembered he *had* given her an order which she

had not fulfilled. On the first horrible morning of the illness, he had asked her to take some of the borrowed books to the Mission. In her confusion and fear, she had not obeyed his instructions. She would take the books now, on the way to the temple.

She knew there was a hidden motive in her heart, but she could not tear out her irreverent hope. She would give the books to Memsahib Mom, and that wonderful woman would see that Anand needed help. She would come to the hut; she would bring *her* medicines. If the gods had cast off Anand because he loved the Mission people, then *they* must save him. She would not *ask* for their help . . . she would only let them see the terrible need. That way the gods could not accuse and punish.

She snatched up two of the books and a little sickle, and took some more of the buried rupees, and started down toward the bazaar. Alone though she was, she had no fear at all, for the master fear had subdued all the small ones. She bought a young goat from two men who said they would beat tom-toms for her near the temple. The goat was little more than a baby, a frisky happy small thing that would have been a good pet for her own child. Knowing what was going to happen to it, she could not bear to look at its gay, bright-eyed little face, its alert ears and its tidy small hoofs. Resolutely she took the rope with which the goat was tied, and went off boldly, blind to everything around her. The books and the sickle, symbols that contradicted each other, she carried in her right arm, and the rope tied to the goat she held in her left hand.

At the tall iron gate of the Mission compound she turned in without hesitation. Once . . . less than two years ago, she had been too shy to go in, even with Anand beside her. Now she walked boldly along the path, dragging the kid, who was driven mad by the sight of the Mission lawn. There was not the usual crowd of sick people coming and going, and this surprised her. But she was not too concerned, for she had but one concern now.

She went bravely up to the door of the clinic, and rapped on it. She heard the knock echoing, but the door was not opened. She knocked again, louder this time, with the handle of the sickle. At last the door was opened and a man's querulous face, with two moons of eyeglasses, looked out.

"Clinic not open," he said in English. "Come tomorrow." She did not understand his English, but she put her hand against the door so he could not close it, as she could see he intended doing.

"I bring books," she said in her faltering English.

He took them unwillingly. "Who sent these?" he asked indifferently.

By sheer miracle she understood what he asked. She gazed up into his face beseechingly. Didn't he realize that it is impossible for a woman to speak her husband's name? Had he lived in India even for a month, without finding out that fact? Dared she risk the further anger of the gods by doing anything so inauspicious? She was afraid to take such a terrible chance. So she reached out to his hands and opened the books, hoping that something about their pages would make him recall to whom they had been loaned. She knew this was not the Doctor Sahib. This must be Doctor Steele, the stingy, narrow man Anand had told her about. What could she do?

"Memsahib Mom?" she said hesitantly.

"This is the one day she keeps for herself," Dr. Steele said crossly. "And you people would like to trample all over that if you have a chance. You can't see her now. You'll have to come back another day."

She could not understand what he was saying.

He pulled the door shut, and when Soni still clung to it, he motioned impatiently that she must remove her hand. Through the shut door, she called out to him in frantic Marathi, "Listen to me. My lord worked for you here at the clinic for a long time. He loved you people, and you loved him . . . and now he is very ill. He needs you to come and help him. Let me come in and see Memsahib Mom. She will know what to do."

The door opened just a crack, and the glass moons peered out. "I can't understand what you're saying," the doctor said. "I know you've some patient you want us to see. But you'll have to come back tomorrow. We simply have to have one day to ourselves. Go away now."

She shook her head desperately, letting the tears fall down her face. It seemed to her almost demoniacally humorous that neither of them could understand what the other said. She *knew* each must have some words within them which could be recognized by the other. If only he would take the time for them to find these words! But she saw he was denying her any help. The door closed again, very gently this time. The goat tugged at her furiously, seeing no reason why it should not feast on the rare grass. She let him pull her into a run, and when he stopped at the edge of the lawn to begin gobbling the grass, she dragged him away. She was crying without restraint now, all the worry of the two days breaking loose. She pulled at the goat with much more than her usual strength, and at last she got him out of the Mission compound and on to the road.

The two of them trotted along now, Soni seeing nothing to the left or the right. As she came nearer to the temple of Ayie Devi, she heard the pulsing of the two tom-toms of the men who were donating their services as an inducement for the purchase of the goat. They were sitting on each side of the little temple at a respectful distance, beating with their hands on the drums. They scowled at her, because it had taken her so long to arrive and they wanted to get back to their business.

She dragged the goat up the steps. It was bleating now, as if it suspected what was going to happen. She murmured her prayers to the goddess with difficulty, for the animal would not let her kneel quietly. She knew that the dreaded moment had come when she must kill the frisky little beast for the sacrifice. She was trembling with nausea and fear, and for a moment she thought she could not possibly fulfill the hideous necessity. The kid's eyes looked into hers, and she thought, Oh my poor little one . . . how could a goddess demand that you be killed? I am only a woman and yet I want nothing on earth to suffer. How could a goddess be more cruel than I? But she knew she must stop such blasphemous thinking, here in the temple.

She took the blade of the sickle firmly in her hand and thrust the point into the soft furry neck of the animal. Its large docile eyes crossed in amazement that such a thing could happen, and it opened its triangular mouth in an almost human scream. Every impulse in Soni was to drop the sickle and release the goat, and run away from the temple. But she knew she must not do this. She closed her eyes and drew the curved blade across the throat, and on her hand she felt the horrible warmth of blood. The kid braced its legs and tried to pull away, then suddenly it went limp and fell against Soni's knees.

She found herself violently ill, but clenched her teeth and put the sagging body where its blood would flow across the foot of the statue. Then she ran down the steps and across the road and leaned against a tree. It was only when she found that she had nothing to vomit, that she realized she had not eaten for two days.

She did not know how she could go back to the hut, for she had no strength and barely could pull one foot from behind the other. She was afraid to eat a piece of fruit offered by the vendors along the government road, for her stomach was churning with repugnance at what she had just done. Everywhere she looked, she saw the astonished eyes of the poor little goat, and she could not help rubbing her hand over and over with her sari, to clean it from the repulsive warmth that had flowed over it.

When she came within sight of the hut, she knew that her lord was still alive, for through the twilight she could see the silhouettes of all the family and strangers against the little fire which was burning in the dooryard. Rama was seated on the ground, still moaning and rocking back and forth in his double grief. Shushilla bai, the mother, sat stonily beside him, locked in her own anguish. Tara bai was carrying food from person to person, pressing it upon those who did not want it. Inside the little house, the guru was still praying beside the silent form on the charpai . . .

It was only when she sank down beside Anand's cot, that she realized there had been something strange in every face into which she had looked just now. *Nobody had met her eye.* What was it? Something more dreadful than the illness was lying in secret behind each face. She reached out her hand and touched Anand's arm. No, he was not dead, for the flesh was still burning with fever. What then? What were they trying to hide from her? Was something wrong with Shushilla, her precious child? She ran to the door of the hut, and looked about. Mira bai was walking up and down before the fire, cradling the baby in her arms, and even from here Soni could see her mother's lips moving in a prayer.

She turned back to the interior of the hut. The guru got to his feet, and came over to her, his face stern beneath the holy markings of clay with which it was inscribed.

"My child, the gods have asked me for a very painful gift, if your lord is to have his life."

"What gift?" she asked, scarcely moving her lips and not breathing for the strangling fear.

"The gods have been displeased with the wretched faithless wife of this man," he said as if he were talking to someone only remotely concerned in this situation. "She must pay a ransom for her guilt."

"What guilt lies on that wretched faithless wife?" Soni asked in a whisper.

"You know the guilt. It need not be named," the guru said. "So now the gods demand a living sacrifice."

For a moment she could not realize what the guru was saying. A living sacrifice? Had she not sacrificed the living goat? His terrified eyes were even now staring into her own so that she thought she must be losing her mind. But the guru's face was insisting upon the meaning of his terrible words.

"The girl-child . . . she must be given to the temple to become a temple bride."

"But . . . my lord loves her more than anything else on earth," she said.

"Then, for that very reason, the sacrifice may be accepted in exchange for his life," the guru said. Then he began scolding her because she had given this proud family only a girl-child. Each of Rama's other sons had begun their line with a fine boy . . . and she had disgraced Anand, who was his father's favorite. Surely she would be willing to atone for this by giving up the wretched little creature to a life spent serving the temple!

As she listened to the bitter words, her mind went back to the birth agony she had suffered. Actually, her joy in the child had been so great after she came to accept a daughter instead of a son that she never before had remembered the physical and mental pain. But now it sprang up from the forgotten depths, as excruciating and alive as when it was happening. It had all been for nothing . . . but a reproach and a guilt. And now the child itself, was to be given up and banished forever from their sight.

Soni knew that in a small village like Marvali this could not be happening, but she had heard that such things took place in larger towns. The babies were never seen again, because the priests immediately exchanged them with distant temples.

"You will take the child tonight . . . while breath still travels in and out of this poor body which the gods are torturing."

Dazedly she went over to the charpai and bent above the unconscious face. With her sari fringe she wiped the perspiration from it. For a long time she looked into the unconscious face, and as she looked she became strong. Nothing mattered except this man. Even her child . . . her beloved child . . . was less important than he. And if the gods had decided, there was no use fighting the gods. She whispered to him, "What am I but mud, unless you live to put life in me? Live, my darling, and you shall have seven sons as noble as you are. Sons from my womb, or from some other."

She dropped her head on his chest, in wordless grief. Then she rose quickly and went out of the hut. The fire was very bright in the darkness and every waiting face was turned toward her, to see what kind of woman she was. She went over to Mira bai and took the baby without a word.

"Oh, my child," Mira bai said. "They will not even let me come with you. You must go alone, with only the guru."

Soni nodded dully. Alone, or with a thousand people . . . what difference would it make?

The baby was wrapped in her pink shawl, sleeping. But as soon as her instinct told her she was in her mother's arms, she began nuzzling at her breast with blind hunger. As consolation to both of them, Soni gave the child her breast, and when she felt the little lips, all the strength of her body seemed to drain away and she thought she would swoon on the ground. But she knew she must hold herself upright, for the guru had come out of the hut and was walking toward her, tall and terrifying in his swirling yellow garments. In the light from the fire his clay-marked face was stern and hideous. Without glancing at Soni and the nursing child, he passed close to them and Soni fell into step, six paces behind him. At the foot of the hill, two tom-tom players were waiting to accompany them to the temple. Who had hired them? Govind, no doubt, for he was the head of the family.

The tom-toms marked their steps, slow and agonizing. At the edge of the town, a group of stragglers waited, for news that the living sacrifice was going to be made had spread as soon as the tom-toms were hired. The crowd walked silently behind the little procession, but some of the women wept and wailed. Such a fine family . . . and yet that did not protect it from the anger of the gods! That handsome son with all his show of books and education! And this wife . . . why, she had even dared teach some of the women to read, though every woman who had gone to her house in the afternoon now denied she had ever opened a book. It would be a lesson to the whole town, wouldn't it?

As the crowd neared the temple of Ayie Devi, the men had to drop out and watch from beside the road, for only women could approach this shrine devoted to their sorrows. As they came near, the guru left the group and went behind the banyan trees to his walled house some distance in the rear of the temple. He had had a long hard day, and he was ready to take his rest. Before daylight he would have to steal up the back steps and pick up the infant who would be lying on the lap of the Mother-god. But there was no need to disturb his slumber by having a noisy, wretched baby in his house all night.

The thought crossed his mind of the hyenas who sometimes come very close to villages during the monsoon season when it is not easy for them to find their food. But he discarded that picture immediately; the gods would have to take care of this gift which was being given to them. After all, he had done *his* part when he got the baby for them. He yawned sleepily, and hoped the old widow who took care of him had something good ready for his meal.

The drummers hid themselves behind the banyan trees, and the wailing crowd of women and children huddled at the foot of the steps. The figure of Ayie Devi was placed so any penitent could not be watched. They thought this a most inconsiderate arrangement. They stopped their wailing and listened carefully, in case Soni might make some outcry. But there was no sound; even the baby was quiet.

Inside the small enclosure, two coconut-shell lamps were burning, throwing long flickering distortions over the crude face of the goddess. The mutilated body of the goat had been removed, and Soni quickly looked away from the stains she herself had left here. She was grateful that the horrible little body was gone; Shushilla, baby though she was, would have been frightened, left with such a thing. When Soni had seen the goat, innocent and frisky in the bazaar, her first thought was that it would have made a lovely pet for her child. But now the memory of it was drenched in horror. Soni knelt before the statue, trying to find some comfort in the face. Every bit of her seemed to be reaching out, imploring the goddess for pity. Ever since the guru had told her that she must give up her child, she had been too stunned to realize fully what was happening, but now she was awake to the full catastrophe.

With an unritualistic word of apology to the goddess, she rose from her knees and went over to a dark corner of the little room, where she gave the baby her breast for the last time. The child looked up into her face and smiled and waved her plump little hands in joy. Soni gave her as much as she could drink from both breasts. Tomorrow they would ache because there was no child to relieve them. Tomorrow all of her would ache with longing for this small sweet one. But Anand would be getting well by tomorrow. . . .

She went back to the feet of Ayie Devi and said prayers, some in words as she had been taught, but many more in voiceless urgency. Shushilla, warm and comforted and filled with food, was fast falling asleep in her arms. Soni did not know how long she knelt there, but at last she realized she must leave. She would not weep, for that would take some grace from the gift. And tears from the eyes were too superficial for this sorrow; her body felt as if a million tears were flowing from every part of it.

She moved the baby so gently that the very rhythm of its breath was not disturbed. The crossed legs of the goddess made a huge lap like a cradle . . . but a cold stone cradle. She stood up, trembling, and looked for the last time at her sleeping child, so beautiful and beloved. Then she turned quickly and went down the steps from the shrine, her face covered with her sari. The women were still gathered beside the banyan trees. They let her walk down the long path alone, then they began following, like a multiplied shadow of sorrow.

It was so late now that the road back to Vardana was almost deserted. She ran along at the edge of the highway, swallowed up in the tree shadows, numb as ice. Then, gradually her mind seemed to be thawing to hope. Ayie Devi could not possibly do anything so cruel as to take both the child and the husband. If she had any mother in her at all, she could not do that . . . and she was the Great Mother. So this meant. . . .

She felt almost confident now; suddenly her legs seemed to have new strength in them, and she quickened her pace. But without warning a big form loomed up before her and stopped her, a great tall man with a dark face.

Oh darkness . . . fold your arms around me, she cried within herself. Let me be hidden from whatever is in this man.

"Woman," he said in a deep voice.

"No." Then she realized he was wearing the uniform of a home guard soldier.

"Woman . . . I saw you taking your child to the temple."

"I cannot talk about it, sepoy."

"Maybe I can help you, woman. I will go and get the child and take it to Memsahib Mom at the Mission. She cannot bear to see a baby in danger."

For a wild moment, hope spurted up in Soni. Then she saw this was only a temptation sent by the gods to undo her sacrifice. If she fell into this temptation, then the sacrifice would surely be in vain.

"Why do you bother me?" she cried angrily. "Who are you to undo the will of the gods? If they have asked for my child to be given to the temple, who are you to deny their will? I know who you are . . . an unholy Christian."

The dark face above her seemed to glow with kindness, and the deep voice said, "Dear woman, you cannot want your baby to be lost."

She put her hands over her face, but a sob escaped her and she shook her head helplessly. "Oh, why did you tell me? Why didn't you just do . . . whatever you could do without telling me?"

"That is what I should have done," he said. "Go home now to your husband . . . . Some time I will find you and tell you . . . ."

She took her hands down from her face and, still weeping, she shook her head in denial. But she saw that he was reading her eyes. She broke away from him, for fear she would commit the crime of hoping, and the vengeful gods would look down and see that hope.

She continued trotting through the darkness, keeping her mind fit to be scrutinized by Ayie Devi. Was he a mortal man, that sepoy? Was he not probably just a vision conjured up to test her loyalty? Well, she had passed the test. And Anand would live! Surely they could demand nothing more. And if they did ask for anything more, what would it be? His education, of couse, his love of learning, and that great hunger in him to bring the modern ways to his village. All right, then, Anand must give up that hunger. As soon as he was well enough she must tell him this vision she had along the road . . . she must make him understand and promise . . . .

She was almost home now, running breathlessly through the last little strip of footpath beside the river. Then up the slope. She could see the dooryard still peopled with family and strangers, waiting around the fire. Some of them were bundles on the ground. That meant that Anand was still alive. Of course he was alive; how could he be anything else after her great sacrifice?

She went silently past the fire. No one spoke to her; they averted their faces, almost in shame, because they could not bear to look at a woman who had given so much in sacrifice. Mira bai half rose where she was sitting on the ground, and then sank back. What could be said to such a woman as this? She was not a daughter tonight. She was something much greater than a daughter. Tonight the only mother big enough to speak to her was the Great Mother herself. Tomorrow, when human grief began to come back to her she would become a sorrowing child again. Then she would need a human mother's consolation.

Soni pushed aside the mat, and stood in the door of the hut a moment, listening. Only Rama was sitting beside his son, and Rama was dozing, his shaggy head sunk on his chest. She listened to the weary breathing of the old man, her ears alert to catch the fitful breathing of the man who was her very life. She could not hear that breathing. She swooped to the charpai and found it empty. Her heart stopped beating for a moment, for she knew that Rama had moved the body from the cot to the sacred ground, for only the ground is worthy to hold a dying Hindu. In the half-darkness, she saw the inert form, wrapped in its sutherungee, with the sacred light burning beside it. On her knees she bent her head to listen, and she could hear only her own frightened heart beating. He was not breathing . . . he was not breathing at all.

She fell across his body, her whole being crying out to share his death. If he was not alive, how could she live? Then she heard a terrible piercing wail, and for a moment did not realize it was coming from her own throat.

18

LIFE DISSOLVED AROUND HER THE WAY A cloud is torn to nothingness by a furious wind. One day her life was intact, filled to the brim with the small beauties and the large ones, with wonder and learning and love. And a week later there was nothingness. There was scarcely a trace where her life had been. The earth had totally forgotten that it ever held such a life on its bosom.

Anand's beloved body had been swiftly prepared for the burning. Soni herself had torn a strip from her sari and had tied the fingers together, and then had bound the toes . . . the last service she could ever offer to this master of her life. Crushed betel leaves had filled the mouth, to keep it sweet. After the body had been dressed in its purple satin marriage coat, it was wrapped in new white cloth from head to foot. Only the face was left uncovered, and this was to show that Anand had left a widow.

In an excess of grief, Rama tore off the pearl earring and gave it to Anand's body. Anand's ears had never been pierced, so Rama laid the pearl in the hollow of the dead boy's ear.

He hung over the body and let his tears fall on Anand's face. "My son, my son . . . you must take the pearl, for I am unworthy of it. It brought you back to the land . . . for my sake . . . but there I failed you."

Govind tugged at his father's arm, trying to lift him from

his groveling position. "Father, hush. You do not know what you are saying. Take the pearl back. This is unsuitable."

But Rama shook him off without even looking at him and went on talking to Anand, "My son . . . I shall explain it all to you when we meet in our next life, and you will forgive me. You will know then what happened."

Govind said to the uncomfortable men who had to witness this, "My father's mind is unbalanced by grief. You can understand that. This is his favorite son. His very favorite."

Gopal saw the pearl lying incongruously in the little cup of Anand's ear, and knew that in an hour it would be melted by flames. The little sphere which could have endured through centuries, would become nothing. And for this nothing, much had been sacrificed . . . honor and peace, and sweetness of mind. For this a back had been bent, and hair had been grayed, and nights that once had been a canopy of security over the earth had shrunk to being a tight skullcap that pinched the brain with petty planning.

He saw the pearl and knew he had looked his last upon it, and he said to himself, Let it go. It is worth nothing to anybody now. It will be only a shiny slime in the ashes.

As soon as the sun rose, the mourning procession had walked through the village, the women friends beating upon their chests and the little neighbor girls sobbing as it passed. Rama led the procession carrying an earthen vessel of burning embers. Behind the bamboo litter on which the body lay, all the men of the immediate family and of the kutumb followed.

After the procession had passed through the bazaar, it wound its way up to the burning ghats. As the direction changed, everyone took special care to see that no man's shadow fell upon the mortal clay. A pyre of wood had been prepared by caste friends, and upon this the body was placed. Rama poured scented oil and melted butter over the bier,

and placed a lighted ball of cow dung fuel on the body. Then
the old man walked three times around the pyre, praying,
while all the men stood back with uncovered heads. A lighted
torch was touched to the four corners of the bier, and in a
moment the whole was hidden in flames.

Soni and the other women had not been present at the
funeral. But during this time, Soni was supposed to destroy
her own married status as completely as Anand's body was
being destroyed. Her foot must be stripped of the marriage
ring worn so proudly, and all her other jewelry must be put
aside forever. Her colored saris must be given away, for never
again would she wear anything but plain white cotton.

The earth would have no meaning for her, because her
lord had departed from it; even the sky would be blank for
her, for now there would be no need to follow the moon and
stars to know in advance the days of feasting and fasting. Her
horoscope from here on would go unread, because the hand
of her master had forever closed for her the book of life. For
a widow there are no events, either good or bad.

The last thing she did was to hide the glass bangles of the
baby Shushilla in the wicker basket. Rama had brought sets
of two sizes for the child to grow into; the bangles would
never be worn now. They went into the basket without a
tear, for no tears were left to be shed.

Her own bangles she crushed on the stone wall around the
hut, grinding them to powder which the wind accepted.
Somewhere Anand's spirit would see that bright dust blowing,
and he would remember the beauty they had known together.

In the next few days Rama and Govind told her kindly that
she might always have a place in their family if she wished.
Since her poor father had no home of his own to which she
could return as a widow, she might have the privilege of
caring for Rama's family, cooking their food and running

their errands. If she so desired, she could live alone in the little birth house behind Rama's large dwelling. Govind and his family had decided they would move into Anand's hut, and enlarge it in a way suitable to their dignity.

The birth house was filled with the horror of memories for her, but she went obediently to it, carrying her wicker basket and her own lothi and the tulasi twigs. On the backside of Rama's wall, the animals lived in their stalls, and these were her near neigbhbors. Sometime, she thought, they might become her friends, but now she could not look at an animal without seeing the startled eyes of the goat and feeling his blood upon her hand.

The first night she was alone in the birth house, she had visitors. She was sitting on the doorstep, where the midwife used to sit and rock the child, when she saw two figures coming through the trees outside the wall of Rama's house, one tall and masculine, the other humbly running along behind as a female should.

"Woman," the voice said . . . the voice she never would forget.

"Sepoy!" she cried. "So you are a living man . . . and not just a vision sent to torment me."

He shook his head, not knowing what she meant, and turned to his wife who had come up beside him. "I have brought my own woman so that I might speak to you without harming your reputation."

"Of course," Soni said, nodding, and trying not to show the mad hope that had sprung up in her.

"But I have not brought you good news, woman," the soldier said.

"I do not expect good news," Soni said dully. "Who am I to have good news when my lord has left the earth?"

"I tried to rescue your baby," the sepoy said. "I ran back

to the Mission. I told Memsahib Mom that a baby had been left at the temple. The Memsahib said, 'It is not right for me to go to the temple and take the baby, even to save it. But if I found it here on my doorstep, I would take it in and care for it.' She looked at me to make sure I knew what she meant. So I ran to the temple, every step."

"And?"

"The baby was not there."

The wife of the sepoy, a primitive little creature, said, "I think perhaps a hyena got it. They are hungry this time of year. And my husband saw blood at the foot of Ayie Devi."

The sepoy turned on her and struck her. "Be quiet, woman," he said. "Your ignorant mouth is always chopping like a hatchet!"

Then he turned to Soni. "I do not believe a hyena got the baby. God would not let such a thing happen, for I was praying."

"God has let many terrible things happen," Soni said before she could stop her lips. "I, too, was praying for many days . . . yet *everything* happened."

The sepoy ignored what she had said, and continued as if he had not heard her. "I think the guru took the baby immediately to another temple in some distant city. That is what they do, you know."

She nodded, grateful for his tenderness, but not consoled by it. "My baby is gone. I gave her to the gods. I know she is gone," she said painstakingly. Her hand, of its own accord, went to her swollen breasts, and the sepoy's eyes kindled with pity, as if he, man though he was, could feel the pain in those forsaken, desolate breasts.

After a long moment he said gently, "God will show you what to do."

Soni shook her head violently so that her tears swung out

from her face, as the eggs had swung in the egg dance Anand had explained to her long ago. "No. The gods are finished with me."

"My child, you must not think that. There is but one God and He is Love. He will never let you go, when once you find Him. Go looking for Him."

But she only shook her head more vehemently, and the sepoy saw that this was not the moment to tell her about his own God. So he motioned to his squatty little woman, said goodbye to Soni and went back through the trees along the wall of Rama's house. Soni could see from the slow way he was walking that he was praying for her, and she thought angrily, There is no use to pray for me, so don't waste your time, sepoy. Then she covered her face with her hands and wept. For now, added to everything else that she had lost, she saw she had lost her faith in the gods.

Rama, to whom the passing of time had become as the blowing of smoke, was now insisting that Soni's hair be shaved as a mark of widowhood. Shushilla bai and the other women in the family feebly protested that this was no longer necessary in modern India. But they chose the wrong words to dissuade him, for Rama said determinedly,

"That talk of being modern! Have you not learned your tragic lesson? Must the gods take another child of ours to show they are displeased by all this following of the modern ways? It is for this very reason Soni must do as the old traditions say."

Tara bai said, "She is so young. I was nearly thirty, and we did not shave my head."

"It would have been better if we had," Rama grunted.

"My head was shaved," Hera bai said. "Rama is right. The gods are displeased enough with a widow, without flaunting her hair in their faces."

Rama said, "I will arrange for the barber to come. The astrologer will find the auspicious day for our family to observe the sorrowful rites of the widow." Then he added, "This will be the last time it will be necessary to consult Soni's horoscope."

Unexpectedly Gopal, who came to the house on an errand, tried to prevent the shaving. "It is no longer necessary," he said. "Our government has a new law which the House of the People is deciding about. Anand himself told me about it. It is called the Hindu Code Bill. Part of it concerns widows."

"This is not a law for governments to make. This was decreed by the gods," Rama said stubbornly.

Soni, who was serving the men of the family their midday meal, scarcely breathed, hearing this argument. Anand was here! His *meaning* was in this room, timidly advanced by her own father . . . and angrily fought by Rama. But Anand was here in essence!

Gopal was saying, "Your son did not believe in the cruelty our system forces upon widows. He had a wide and wonderful mind that stretched into the future for its ideas."

Rama was unexpectedly touched by these words, and his wrinkled old face was suddenly bent in sorrow.

Gopal said gently, "He would be grieved to have his wife deprived of all womanliness."

Soni heard the words as if Anand himself had said them. What that fine man had intended to do with his life . . . the freeing of her mind from darkness, the giving to India one more awakened and enlightened woman to serve and help . . . this would be lost with the rest that was gone, unless she arose from her abject desolation, and carried out his plans. It was a thought so revolutionary that for a moment she was stunned with fear.

But suddenly she saw it was an assignment given to her by her lord, so it must be carried out. The words of wifely devotion taught her long ago by Mira bai rang in her mind: *Her sole rule of life should be that her good works please him.*

Could a shaven-headed widow huddled in an empty birth house please a man who had the vision Anand had? Would his soul be satisfied when it saw her, drab and dreary, concerned only with cooking and serving food, while her mind slipped back into illiteracy? She knew what he had expected of her, for he had told her from the start. He wanted a soul to be born in her as passionately as she had wanted a son born from her body . . . .

After the meal she scoured the brass trays and the lothis, and if someone asked her a question she answered promptly. But she scarcely realized what she was doing, for already she had started on her great journey. The distance she traveled in that hour is the longest in human experience. It may take a decade, or a generation, or a century; yet sometimes it seems as if it is made in a single brave leap. It is the distance between being enslaved and becoming free. The trip cannot be given; it must be taken. It cannot be decreed by law; it must be grasped for oneself through a glimpse of higher law. The distance cannot be covered in a vehicle in which one lies supinely; it must be traveled step after step by gaunt volition.

Must she explain to Rama and ask his permission? No. One's own soul gives the permission. Perhaps that is the whole, important meaning.

She went back to the birth house and picked up the wicker basket. This was all she had, and she would carry it with her because sometime she would find a baby who needed glass bangles for its little arms, and they were waiting in this wicker basket . . . . Her work would be among people who needed what she had to give, which was love and the art of making happiness.

She put her white sari over her head and walked along outside the wall of Rama's house. Nobody noticed her as she went through the village lanes, for no one pays attention to a wraith-like widow going on somebody else's errand. Straight to the other side of Vardana she went, and across the footpath up to the government road. She knew the way well now, but she never walked along it without remembering the first time, with Anand. He had wanted to take her into the Mission then, but she was too timid to go inside the gates. How different everything might have been if she had not been too timid! Well, she was no longer afraid. This morning she might have said she was not afraid because she had nothing more she could lose. This afternoon she knew she was not afraid because she had much, much to gain.

The trees of the Mission compound were just ahead, and she saw the people straggling in and out of the opened gates. She turned in, and walked along the gravel path. A lifetime . . . a deathtime . . . not just for Anand but for her old self . . . had passed since she walked along this path a few days ago, dragging the poor little goat driven mad with delight at the sight of the grass.

She went through the door, and along the corridor, her heart beating excitedly. People were in every room. Then by intuition she recognized the person she was looking for, a round little gray-haired woman with large glasses on her nose. She was putting a bandage on a little boy's ear.

"Memsahib Mom?"

"Yes, my dear?"

"I come," she said.

The Memsahib turned around and looked at her. Naturally she did not know who Soni was, but her eyes behind the glasses became very tender.

"What do you want of me, vidhava?" she asked, using the word for widow, which is the term of respect.

She waited a long time while Soni struggled with English words to tell that she did not want anything *from* anyone, but that she had brought something she wanted to give. Then, hearing the English words were not obedient to the Indian girl, Memsahib Mom said them gently.

"Are you saying you want to join our other women who help us here?"

"Yes, yes. My English is not yet finished."

"Your English is better than my Marathi," Memsahib Mom said graciously. "When can you begin?"

"I am begun," Soni said seriously. "I bring myself and my basket. All."

The Memsahib finished the bandage, gave the little boy and his mother a comforting pat, took their eight annas for the treatment, then turned back to Soni bai.

"Now, wouldn't you like me to show you the Mission? First, I'll introduce you to our newest member . . . newest until you joined us. We've had her only a week. Have you guessed? She's a baby."

Soni carefully picked out the only word she could understand in the sentence, and smiled. "I can nurse baby," she said, motioning to her breasts.

"A woman brought her here. I suspect that she stole her from the temple. She came to our door after dark and handed her to Dr. Steele, who opened the gate, and before he could say anything, she ran away."

Soni, listening carefully, could find no word in this that gave her a clue to its meaning. But she smiled intelligently, as if she knew.

Memsahib Mom went on, "Funny thing, a soldier had come up earlier and begged me to go get the baby from the temple. Of course I couldn't do that . . . But anyway, she is safe with us now."

With all her might, Soni was trying to understand what Memsahib Mom was saying, but she could not follow the words. This woman talked too fast, much too fast. And there were little bubbles of delight in her voice that interfered with the words. But Soni didn't want to seem impolite and ignorant, so she kept smiling as if she understood. They walked along the corridor together.

"My husband teached me some English. I learn more from you," she said in her most polite treble.

The round pink face of the American woman smiled down at her understandingly, as if Memsahib Mom already loved what she perceived to be here.

"I learn from you, too, vidhava," she said softly.

Then she put out her hand and opened the door of a small sunny room. A baby was crying gently, as if she wanted her mother.